# THE LONELY PASSION
# OF JUDITH HEARNE

# The Lonely Passion of Judith Hearne

## BRIAN MOORE

ISIS
LARGE PRINT
MAINSTREAM SERIES
Oxford, England
Santa Barbara, California

The Jefferson-Madison
Regional Public Library
Charlottesville, Virginia

WITHDRAWN

LP
F
Moore

Copyright © Brian Moore. 1955
First published in Great Britain 1955 by
André Deutsch Ltd,
105 Great Russell Street, London WC1B 3LJ
First published in the U.S.A. by
Little, Brown & Company Inc.

Published in Large Print 1988 by
Clio Press, 55 St. Thomas' Street, Oxford OX1 1JG,
by arrangement with André Deutsch
and Little, Brown & Company Inc.

All rights reserved
British Library Cataloguing in Publication Data.

Moore, Brian, *1921-*
   [Judith Hearne]. The lonely passion of
   Judith Hearne.
   I. Title
   813'.54 [F]

ISBN 1-85089-273-3

Printed and bound by Redwood Burn Ltd.
Trowbridge, Wiltshire.

Cover designed by CGS Studios, Cheltenham

To Jacqueline

# CHAPTER
# ONE

The first thing Miss Judith Hearne unpacked in her new lodgings was the silver-framed photograph of her aunt. The place for her aunt, ever since the sad day of the funeral, was on the mantelpiece of whatever bed-sitting-room Miss Hearne happened to be living in. And as she put her up now, the photograph eyes were stern and questioning, sharing Miss Hearne's own misgivings about the condition of the bedsprings, the shabbiness of the furniture and the run-down part of Belfast in which the room was situated.

After she had arranged the photograph so that her dear aunt could look at her from the exact centre of the mantelpiece, Miss Hearne unwrapped the white tissue paper which covered the coloured oleograph of the Sacred Heart. His place was at the head of the bed. His fingers raised in benediction. His eyes kindly yet accusing. He was old and the painted halo around His head was beginning to show little cracks. He had looked down on Miss Hearne for a long time, almost half her lifetime.

The trouble about hanging the Sacred Heart, Miss Hearne discovered, was that there was no picture hook in the right place. She had bought some picture hooks but she had no hammer. So she laid the Sacred Heart down on the bed and went to the bay window to see how the room looked from there.

The street outside was a university bywater, once a good residential area, which had lately been reduced to the level of taking in paying guests. Miss Hearne stared at the houses opposite and thought of her aunt's day when there were only private families in this street, at least one maid in every house, and dinner was at night, not at noon. All gone now, all those people dead and all the houses partitioned off into flats, the bedrooms cut in two, kitchenettes jammed into linen closets, linoleum on the floors and "To Let" cards in the bay windows. Like this house, she thought. This bed-sitting-room must have been the master bedroom. Or even a drawing-room. And look at it now. She turned from the window to the photograph on the mantelpiece. All changed, she told it, all changed since your day. And I'm the one who has to put up with it.

But then she shook her head to chase the silly cobwebs from her mind. She walked across the room, inspecting the surface. The carpet wasn't bad at all, just a bit worn in the middle part, and a chair could be put there. The bed could be moved out an inch from the wall to hide that stain. And there on the bed was the Sacred Heart, lying face down, waiting to be put up in His proper place. Nothing for it, Miss Hearne said to herself, but to go down and ask the new landlady for the loan of a hammer.

Down she went, down the two flights of stairs to the kitchen, which was used as a sitting-room by Mrs Henry Rice. She knocked on the curtained door and Mrs Henry Rice drew the edge of the curtain aside to peek through the glass before she opened the door. Miss Hearne thought that a little rude, to say the least.

"Yes, Miss Hearne?"

Beyond the open door Miss Hearne saw a good fire in the grate and a set of china tea things on the table.

"I wondered if you had a hammer you might lend me. It's to put up a picture, you know. I'm terribly sorry to be troubling you like this."

"No trouble at all," Mrs Henry Rice said. "But I have a head like a sieve. I never can remember where I put things. I'll just have to think now. Listen, why don't you come in and sit down? Maybe you'd like a cup of tea. I just wet some tea this minute."

Well, that really was a nice gesture to start things off. Very nice indeed. "That's very kind of you," Miss Hearne said. "But I hate to put you out like this, really I do. I only wanted to put my picture up, you see."

But as she said this she advanced across the threshold. It was always interesting to see how other people lived and, goodness knows, a person had to have someone to talk to. Of course, some landladies could be friendly for their own ends. Like Mrs Harper when I was on Cromwell Road and she thought I was going to help her in that tobacconist business. Still, Mrs Henry Rice doesn't look that type. Such a big jolly person, and very nicely spoken.

The room was not in the best of taste, Miss Hearne saw at once. But cosy. Lots of little lace doilies on the tables and lamps with pretty pastel shades. There was a big enamel china dog on the mantelpiece and a set of crossed flags on the wall. Papal flags with silver paper letters underneath that said: EUCHARISTIC CONGRESS DUBLIN. That was in 1932, in the Phoenix Park, Miss Hearne remembered, and my second cousin, once removed, sang in the choir at High Mass. Nan D'Arcy, God rest her soul, a sudden end, pleurisy, the poor thing. John McCormack was the tenor. A thrilling voice. A Papal count.

"Sit up close to the fire now. It's perishing cold out," Mrs Henry Rice said. A Dublin voice, Miss Hearne thought. But not quite. She has a touch of the North in her accent.

Miss Hearne saw that there were two wing chairs pushed close to the fire. She went towards one of them and it turned around and a man was in it.

He was a horrid-looking fellow. Fat as a pig he was, and his face was the colour of cottage cheese. His collar was unbuttoned and his silk tie was spotted with egg stain. His stomach stuck out like a sagging pillow and his little thin legs fell away under it to end in torn felt slippers. He was all bristly blond jowls, tiny puffy hands and long blond curly hair, like some monstrous baby swelled to man size.

"This is Bernard, my only boy," said Mrs Henry Rice. "This is Miss Hearne, Bernie. Remember, I told you about her coming to stay with us?"

He stared at Miss Hearne with bloodshot eyes, rejecting her as all males had before him. Then he smiled, showing dirty yellow teeth.

"Come and sit by the fire, Miss Hearne," he said. "Take the other chair. Mama won't mind."

Rejected, Miss Hearne sat down, fiddled with her garnet rings, moved her thin legs together and peered for comfort at her long, pointed shoes with the little buttons on them, winking up at her like wise little friendly eyes. Little shoe eyes, always there.

"Sugar and cream?" Mrs Henry Rice asked, bending over the tea things.

"Two lumps, please. And just a *soupçon* of cream," Miss Hearne said, smiling her thanks.

"Cup of tea, Bernie?"

"No, thanks, Mama," the fat man said. His

5

voice was soft and compelling and it shocked Miss Hearne that this ugly pudding should possess it. It reminded her of the time she had seen Beniamino Gigli, the Italian tenor. A fat, perspiring man with a horrid face, wiping the perspiration away with a white handkerchief. And then, when he opened his mouth, you forgot everything and he became a wonderful angel, thrilling everyone in the theatre, from the front stalls to the gods. When Bernard spoke, you wanted to listen.

"Just a little cup, dear?"

"No, Mama."

"Miss Hearne." Mrs Henry Rice handed a teacup with the little silver teaspoon clattering in the saucer. Miss Hearne steadied the spoon and smiled her thanks.

"And have you lived long in Belfast, did you say?" Mrs Henry Rice said, poking the fire into a good blaze.

"O, since I was a child, yes," Miss Hearne said. "You see, my aunt lived here, although my parents lived in Ballymena."

"I see," said Mrs Henry Rice, who did not see. "And whereabouts did your aunt live? Was it on this side of the city?"

"O, yes," Miss Hearne said. "It was on the Lisburn Road. You see, my parents died when I was very young and my dear aunt, rest her soul, took me to live with her in Belfast."

"Well, we all have to move around," Mrs Henry Rice said. "I was born and raised myself in

Donegal, in a little place called Creeslough. And then, when I was only a bit of a girl, I was packed off to Dublin to attend a secretarial college. And lived there with an uncle of mine. And met my late husband there. And then, Mr Rice, that's my late husband, he was posted from Dublin to Belfast. And here I am. It just goes to show you, we all have to run from pillar to post, and you never know where you'll end up."

"Indeed," Miss Hearne said. "But it must have been interesting for you, living in Dublin for so many years."

"O, Dublin's a grand city, no doubt about it. I've never been what you might call fond of Belfast. Of course, it's not the same for you. You'd have lots of friends here. Is your poor aunt dead long?"

"A few years ago," Miss Hearne said guardedly.

"And do you have relatives here?" Mrs Henry Rice asked, offering a plate of Jacob's cream puff biscuits.

"Not *close* relatives," Miss Hearne said, fencing her way over familiar ground. They were all a bit nosey, landladies, it was to be expected, of course. They had to know what class of people they were getting, and a good thing too. You couldn't blame them.

"My aunt came from a very old Belfast family," she said. "They've nearly all died out now, but they have a very interesting history, my aunt's people. For instance, they're all buried out in

Nun's Bush. That's one of the oldest cemeteries in the country. Full up now. It's closed, you know."

"Well, that's interesting," Mrs Henry Rice said, uninterested. "Have a bikky, Bernie?"

"No thanks, Mama."

He yawned, patting the opened circle of his mouth with a puffy hand. Above the yawn his eyes, unblinking, watched Miss Hearne, bringing the hot blood to her face.

"I do believe I'll just throw off this cardigan, if you don't mind."

"I'll hold your cup," Mrs Henry Rice offered amiably. "This room does get a little hot with a good fire going. But Bernie feels the cold a lot, always has."

Who does he think he is, no manners, staring like that. Give him a stiff look myself. But no, no, he's still looking. Upsetting. Turn to something else. That book, beside him, upside down, it's *esrev*, verse, yes, English Century Seventeenth. Reading it, yes, he has a bookmark in it.

"I see you're interested in poetry, Mr Rice."

"O, Bernie's a poet. And always studying. He's at the university."

"I am not at the university, Mama," the fat man said. "I haven't been at Queen's for five years."

"Bernie's a little delicate, Miss Hearne. He had to stop his studies a while back. Anyway, I think the boys work too hard up there at Queen's. I always say it's better to take your time. A young fellow like Bernie has lots of time, no need to rush through life. Take your time and you'll live longer."

That fatty must be thirty, if he's a day, Miss Hearne told herself. Something about him. Not a toper, but something. O, the cross some mothers have to bear.

And the cross brought back the Sacred Heart, lying on the bed in the room upstairs, waiting for a hammer to nail Him up. Still, it was nice to sit here in front of a good warm fire with a cup of tea in your hand. And besides, Mrs Henry Rice and this horrid fatty would make an interesting tale to tell when she saw the O'Neills.

For it was important to have things to tell which interested your friends. And Miss Hearne had always been able to find interesting happenings where other people would find only dullness. It was, she often felt, a gift which was one of the great rewards of a solitary life. And a necessary gift. Because, when you were a single girl, you had to find interesting things to talk about. Other women always had their children and shopping and running a house to chat about. Besides which, their husbands often told them interesting stories. But a single girl was in a different position. People simply didn't want to hear how she managed things like accommodation and budgets. She had to find other subjects and other subjects were mostly other people. So people she knew, people she had heard of, people she saw in the street, people she had read about, they all had to be collected and gone through like a basket of sewing so that the most interesting bits about them could be picked out and fitted together to make conversation. And that was why even a queer fellow like this Bernard Rice was a blessing in his own way. He was so funny and horrible with his "Yes, Mama," and "No, Mama," and his long blond baby hair. He'd make a tale for the O'Neills at Sunday tea.

So Miss Hearne decided to let the Sacred Heart wait. She smiled, instead, at Bernard and asked him what he had been studying at the university.

"Arts," he said.

"And were you planning to teach? I mean, when your health . . ."

"I'm not planning anything," Bernard said quietly. "I'm writing poetry. And I'm living with my mother." He smiled at Mrs Henry Rice as he said it. Mrs Henry Rice nodded her head fondly.

"Bernard's not like some boys," she said. "Always wanting to leave their poor mothers and take up with some woman and get married far too young. No, Bernard likes his home, don't you Bernie?"

"Nobody else knows my ways as well as you, Mama," Bernard said softly. He turned to Miss Hearne. "She's really an angel, Mama is, especially when I don't feel well."

Miss Hearne couldn't think of anything to say. Something about him, so insincere. And staring at me like that, what's the matter with me, is my skirt up? No, of course not. She tugged her skirt snug about her calves and resolutely turned the conversation towards a common denominator.

"We're in Saint Finbar's here, I believe. That's Father Quigley's parish, isn't it?"

"Yes, he's the PP. Isn't he a caution?"

"O, is that so? I heard he was a wonderful man," Miss Hearne said. "Goodness knows, religion is a comfort, even in conversation. If we hadn't the priests to talk about, where would we be half the time?"

"He's very outspoken, I mean," Mrs Henry Rice corrected herself. "I'll tell you a story I heard only last week. And it's the gospel truth."

Mrs Henry Rice paused and looked sideways at Bernard. "Last week," she said, "Father Quigley was offered a new Communion rail for the church from a Mrs Brady that used to keep a bad house. And do you know what he told her?"

"What Mrs Brady would that be?" Miss Hearne said faintly, unsure that she had heard it right. A "bad house" did she say? It certainly sounded like it. Well, that sort of place shouldn't be mentioned, let alone mentioned in connection with the Church. You read about them in books, wicked houses, and who would think there were such places, right here in Belfast. She leaned forward, her black eyes nervous, her face open and eager.

"Well, as I said, she's the one that ran a bad house for men over on the Old Lodge Road," Mrs Rice said. "A terrible sort of woman. So, like all

11

those bad women, she began to get afraid when she knew her time was coming near, and she decided to go to confession and mend her ways. The house was closed up last year and she's been a daily communicant ever since. So, a couple of weeks ago — I heard it from one of the ladies in the altar society — she went to see Father Quigley and said she wanted to present a new Communion rail to Saint Finbar's. Wrought iron from Spain, all the finest work."

Mrs Henry Rice paused to watch Miss Hearne's reaction.

"Well, I never!" Miss Hearne said.

"And do you know what Father Quigley said to her? He just drew himself up, such a big powerful stern man, you know what he looks like, and he said, 'Look here, my good woman, let me ask you straight out, where did you get the money?'"

"Good heavens," Miss Hearne said, thrilling to every word. "And what did she say to that, the creature?"

"Well, that took her back, no denying. She just fretted and fussed and finally she said she made the money in her former business. Her *business*, if you please. So Father Quigley just looked down at her, with that stiff look of his, and said to her, he said: 'Woman,' he said, 'do you think I'll have the good people of this parish kneeling down on their bended knees to receive the Body and Blood of Jesus Christ with their elbows on the wages of sin and corruption?' That's the very thing he said."

"And right too," Miss Hearne commented. "That was putting her in her place. I should think so, indeed."

Bernard pulled the poker out of the coals and lit a cigarette against its reddened end. "Poor Mama," he said. "You always mix a story up. No, no, that wasn't the way of it at all. You've forgotten what Mrs Brady said, right back to him."

Mrs Henry Rice gave him a reproachful glance. "Never mind, Bernie. I did *not* forget. But I wouldn't lower myself to repeat the insolence of a one like that Mrs Brady."

"But that's the whole point," Bernard said, pushing the poker back among the coals. "Wait till I tell you her answer." And he leaned forward towards Miss Hearne, his white, fat face split in a smile of anti-clerical malice. His voice changed, mimicking the tones of the bad Mrs Brady.

"She said to him: 'Father, where do you think the money came from that Mary Magdalene used to anoint the feet of Our Blessed Lord? It didn't come from selling apples,' she said. And that's the real story about Father F.X. Quigley, if you want to know."

When he said this, Bernard laughed. His cheeks wobbled like white pudding.

"What a shocking disrespect for the priest," Miss Hearne said. Where did the ointment come from anyway? Sometimes it made you see that you should read your Douay and know it better in

**13**

order to be able to give the lie to rascals like this fat lump. But for the life of her she couldn't remember where Mary Magdalene had got the money. What matter, it was an out-and-out sin to quote Scripture to affront the priest. She put her teacup down.

"The devil can quote Scripture to suit his purpose," she said.

"Just so," Mrs Henry Rice agreed. "But what else could you expect from the likes of Mrs Brady? No decent woman would talk to her."

"Well — when I think of it — that hussy!" Miss Hearne said. "It's downright blasphemy, that's what it is, saying a thing like that in connection with Our Blessed Lord. O, my goodness, that reminds me. My picture. It's of the Sacred Heart and I always hang it up as soon as I get in a new place. I mustn't be keeping you. The hammer."

"The hammer. I forgot all about it," Mrs Henry Rice said. "Now, let me think. O, I know."

She stood up, opened the door and yelled into the hall.

"Mary! May-ree!"

A voice called back. "Ye-ess!"

"Get the hammer out of the top drawer in the dresser in the attic," Mrs Henry Rice bawled. She closed the door and turned back to Miss Hearne.

"Another cup of tea before you go?"

"O, no, really, it's been lovely. Just perfect, thank you very much."

"She's a new girl, you know," Mrs Henry Rice

said, nodding towards the door. "I got her from the nuns at the convent. A good strong country girl. But they need a lot of breaking in, if you know what I mean."

Miss Hearne, completely at home with this particular conversation, having heard it in all its combinations from her dear aunt and from her friends, said that if you got a good one it was all right, but sometimes you had a lot of trouble with them.

"You have to be after them all the time," Mrs Henry Rice said, moving into the familiar groove of such talk. "You know, it's a wonder the nuns don't do more with them before they send them out to take a place. Badly trained, or not trained at all, is about the height of it."

"Even when these girls are trained, they're not used to the city," Miss Hearne said. "I know the trouble friends of mine have had with convent-trained girls, taking up with soldiers and other riff-raff. Indeed, I often think the nuns are too strict. The girls behave like children as soon as . . ."

But she did not finish because at that moment there was a knock on the door and Mary came in. She was a tall, healthy girl with black Irish hair, blue eyes and firm breasts pushing against the white apron of her maid's uniform. Miss Hearne looked at her and thought she would do very nicely indeed. If you were civil to these girls, they often did little odd jobs that needed doing.

So she smiled at Mary and was introduced by Mrs Henry Rice. The hammer was given into her hands and she fumbled with it, saying thank you, and that she would return it as soon as she had finished hanging her picture. Mrs Henry Rice said there was no hurry and to let them know if she needed anything else, and then Miss Hearne went back up the two flights of stairs to her room.

She found a picture hook and began to nail the Sacred Heart over the head of the bed. And then, thinking back on the people downstairs, it occurred to her that while Bernard Rice was interesting in a horrible sort of way, he was also creepy-crawly and the sort of person a woman would have to look out for. He looked nosey and she felt sure he was the sort of slyboots who would love prying into other people's affairs. And saying the worst thing he could about what he found. Instinctively, she looked at her trunks and saw that they were locked. Just keep them that way, she told herself. I wouldn't put it past him to creep in here some day when I'm out. Still, his mother is certainly friendly, if a little soft where her darling boy is concerned. And the fire and the tea were nice and warming.

She stood back and surveyed the Sacred Heart. Prayers, she must say later. Meanwhile, she drew the curtains and lit the gas stove. With the electric light on and the gas stove spluttering, warming the white bones of its mantles into a rosy red, the new bed-sitting-room became much more cheerful.

Miss Hearne felt quite satisfied after her cup of tea and biscuit, so, after unpacking some more of her things, she laid her flannel nightgown on the bed and turned the covers down. It had all gone very well really, and the cab driver had looked quite happy with the shilling she gave him for carrying the trunks upstairs. It should have been more, but he hadn't said anything nasty. And that was the main thing. She was moved in, she had chatted with the landlady and as a bonus, she had a couple of interesting stories to tell. The one about Father Quigley was not for mixed company, but it was certainly interesting. She decided to discard Bernard's ending. It just wasn't suitable and spoiled the whole point. And then there was Mrs Henry Rice and Bernard himself. They'd be something to talk about. Maybe some of the young O'Neills knew Bernard if he had been at Queen's.

Miss Hearne unpacked the little travelling clock which had come all the way from Paris as a gift to her dear aunt. It was only seven, too early to go to bed. But she was tired and tomorrow was Friday, with nothing to do but unpack. Besides, if she went to sleep soon, she wouldn't need any supper.

She put the clock on the bed-table and switched on the little bed lamp. Then she undressed and knelt to say her prayers. Afterwards, she lay between the covers in the strange bed, watching the shadows of the new room. When the reddened mantles of the stove had cooled to whiteness and the chill of the night made goose-pimples on her forearms outside the covers, she looked over at her dear aunt and then turned her head to look up at the Sacred Heart. She said good night to them both, then switched off the bed light and lay, snuggled in, with only her nose and eyes out of the covers, remembering that both of them were there in the darkness. They make all the difference, Miss Hearne thought, no matter what aunt was like at the end. When they're with me, watching over me, a new place becomes home.

# CHAPTER
# TWO

Her eyes, opening, saw the ceiling, the frozen light of what day? Sight, preceding comprehension, mercifully recorded familiar objects in the strangeness of the whole. Led the blind mind to memory; to this awakening.

She sat up, her hair falling around her shoulders, feeling a gelid draught through the flannel stuff of her nightgown. Her thighs and calves, warmed in the moist snuggle of sheets, were still lax, weary, asleep. The gilded face of her little travelling clock said ten past seven. She lay back, pulling the yellow blankets up to her chin and looked at the room.

A chair, broadbeamed, straight-backed, sat in the alcove by the bay window, an old pensioner staring out at the street. Near the bed, a dressing-table, made familiar by her bottle of cologne, her combs and brushes and her little round box of rouge. Across the worn carpet was a wardrobe of brown varnished wood with a long panel mirror set in its door. She looked in the mirror and saw the end of her bed, the small commotion of her feet ruffling the smooth tucked blankets. The wardrobe was ornamented with whorls and loops and on either side of the door mirror was a circle of light-coloured wood. The circles seemed to her like eyes, mournful wooden eyes on either side of the reflecting mirror nose. She looked away from those eyes to the white marble mantelpiece, cracked down one support, with its brass fender of Arabic design. Her Aunt D'Arcy said good day in silver and sepia-toned arrogance from the exact centre of this arrangement, while beside the gas fire a sagging, green-covered armchair waited its human burden. The carpet below the mantelpiece was worn to brown fibre threads. She hurried on, passing over the small wash-basin, the bed-table with its green lamp, to reach the reassurance of her two big trunks, blacktopped, brassbound, ready to travel.

She twisted around and unhooked the heavy wool dressing-gown from the bedpost. Put it on her shoulders and slid her feet out of bed into blue, fleecy slippers. Cold, a cold room. She went quickly to the gas fire and turned it on, hearing its startled plop as the match poked it into life. She spread her underthings to warm; then fled back across the worn carpet to bed. Fifteen minutes, she said, it will take fifteen minutes to heat the place at all.

There was no hurry. Friday, a dull day, a day

20

with nothing at all do to. Although it would be interesting at breakfast to see what sort of food Mrs Henry Rice gave and who the others were. She lay abed twenty minutes, then washed in cold water and went shivering to the mean heat of the stove. She slipped on her underthings under the concealing envelope of her nightgown, a habit picked up at the Sacred Heart convent in Armagh and retained, although keeping warm had long supplanted the original motive of modesty, which occasioned the fumblings, the exertions and the slowness of the manoeuvre. When she finally pulled the nightgown over her head, she was fully dressed, except for the dress itself. It was time for her morning hair-brushing exercise. She set great store by it: it kept one's hair dark, she said, and if you did not wash the hair, ever, it kept its sheen and colour. Her hair, visible proof, was dark brown with a fine thickness and smooth lustre.

So each morning it was her custom to sit conscientiously at the mirror, her head bent to one side, tugging the brush along the thick rope of her hair, counting the strokes, thinking of nothing except the act of doing the exercise, her head jerking slightly with each long, strong stroke of the brush.

But this morning, hair brushing actually had to be hurried because it would never do to be late one's first morning in a new place. Especially when there were other boarders to meet. She had said three, Mrs Henry Rice, were they men or women? Maybe, most likely, men, and what if one was charming?

Her angular face smiled softly at its glassy image. Her gaze, deceiving, transforming her to her imaginings, changed the contour of her sallow-skinned face, skilfully refashioning her long pointed nose on which a small chilly tear had gathered. Her dark eyes, eyes which skittered constantly in imagined fright, became wide, soft, luminous. Her frame, plain as a cheap clothes-rack, filled now with soft curves, developing a delicate line to the bosom.

She watched the glass, a plain woman, changing all to the delightful illusion of beauty. There was still time: for her ugliness was destined to bloom late, hidden first by the unformed gawkiness of youth, budding to plainness in young womanhood and now flowering to slow maturity in her early forties, it still awaited the subtle garishness which only decay could bring to fruitation: a garishness which, when arrived at, would preclude all efforts at the mirror game.

So she played. Woman, she saw her womanish glass image. Pulled her thick hair sideways, framing her imagined face with tresses. Gipsy, she thought fondly, like a gipsy girl on a chocolate box.

But the little clock chittering through the seconds said eight-fifteen and O, what silly thoughts she was having. Gipsy indeed! She rose, sweeping her hair up, the hairpins in her mouth coming out one by one and up, up to disappear in her crowning glory. There (pat) much better. A little more (pat) so. Good. Now, what to wear? A touch of crimson, my special *cachet*. But which? Reds are so fickle. Still, red is my colour. Vermilion. Yes. The black dress with the vermilion touch at collar and cuffs. Besides, it hasn't been crushed by the moving.

She opened the wardrobe, breaking the unity of its imagined face. Her dressing-gown fell like a dismantled tent at her feet as she shrugged her angular body into the tight waist seams of the dress. Then, her garnets and the small ruby on her right hand. She rummaged in the jewel box, deciding that the pink and white cameo would be a little too much. But she wore her watch, the little gold wristlet watch that Aunt D'Arcy had given her on her twenty-first birthday. It didn't really work well any more. The movement was wearing out. But it was a good watch, and very becoming. And goodness knows, she thought, first impressions are often last impressions, as old Herr Rauh used to say.

Then back to the dressing-table to tidy the strands of hair which her dress had ruffled. A teeny touch of rouge, well rubbed in, a dab of powder and a good sharp biting of her lips to make the colour come out. There, much better. She smiled fondly at her fondly smiling image, her nervous dark eyes searching the searching glass. Satisfied, she nodded to the nodding, satisfied face. Yes. On to breakfast.

The dining-room of Mrs Henry Rice's Camden Street residence was furnished with pieces bought by her late husband's father. A solid mahogany sideboard bulged from one wall, blossoming fruit bowls and empty whiskey decanters on its marble top. The table, a large oval of the same wood, islanded itself in the centre of the room, making passage difficult on either side. Around the table eight tall chairs rode like ships at anchor. Daylight fought its way down to the room past grey buildings and black backyards, filtering through faded gauze curtains which half hid two narrow windows. Over the sideboard this light discerned a gilt-framed oil painting in which a hunter raised his gun to fire at the misty outline of a stag. Beside the door, like an old blind dog, a grandfather clock wagged away the hours.

Around the table the guests sat in semi-gloom, silent except for the tiny crash of teacups and the tearing of hard toast. Cups and saucers moved up and down the table like items on an assembly belt, entering the little fortress where, ringed around by teapot, hot water jugs, tea cosies, milk jug, sugar bowl, plates, cutlery and a little bell, Mrs Henry Rice dispensed stimulants. Matutinal in a flowered house-coat, her hair sticking out from her head like a forkful of wet hay, she smiled a welcome to Miss Hearne and gestured her to a seat at the opposite end of the room.

"This is Miss Hearne, our new boarder, everybody. I'll do the rounds so that you can all get to know her. Now, first, this is Miss Friel. Miss Friel. Miss Hearne."

Miss Friel bit on her toast and laid the crust reluctantly on her plate. She looked to Miss Hearne and nodded. Light blue dress, grey lisle stockings, short clipped whitish hair, like a fox terrier. A Pioneer Total Abstinence Pin rode her shelving bosom. Hard chapped hands and a red roughness about the wrists. There was a book in front of her, propped up against the jampot.

"Mr Lenehan."

Mr Lenehan rose, his head turned sideways, his thin mouth curving into a sickled smile. His clothes were clerical black and a battery of cheap fountain pens raised their silver and gold nozzles like a row of decorations across his chest. His collar was white, waxy, uncomfortable, imprisoning a dark green tie, loosely knotted around a brass collar stud.

"Vary pleased to meet you, I'm sure," Mr Lenehan intoned.

Miss Hearne nodded, smiled, her eyes going on to the next, the most interesting.

"And this is my brother James. Mr Madden. Miss Hearne."

He was a big man. He alone had risen when she entered. He held his linen napkin like a waiter, waiting to seat her. She looked at his well-fed, rough-red face. His smile showed white false teeth. He was neat, but loudly dressed. A yellow

25

tie with white golf balls on it, a suit of some brown silky stuff like shantung. Her brother, Mrs Henry Rice had said, but surely he was an American. Who else but an American would wear that big bluestone ring on his finger?

"Glad to know you, Miss Hearne."

I guessed right. An American for sure, by the sound of him. She smiled, waited for his male movement, the turning away, the rejection. But he winked at her with a merry blue eye and bending down, he drew her chair out from the table. He did not turn away.

They sat down, formally. Mrs Henry Rice asked her preference in matters of sugar and milk. The assembly line was set in motion and from the American's blue-ringed hand a cup of tea was given into Miss Hearne's possession. She said her thanks. Mrs Henry Rice smacked the little bell. Jing-jing-jing it cried.

Mary, young and flustered, put her face around the edge of the door.

"Yes'm."

"Did you bring Mr Bernard up his tray?"

"Yes'm."

"Well, bring some hot toast then, for Miss Hearne. And see if the *Irish News* is here."

Miss Hearne stirred genteelly. Miss Friel turned a page in her book and noisily bit off another mouthful of toast. Mr Lenehan took out a silver watch, consulted it, snapped the case shut. He slurped his tea and wiped his mouth with a napkin.

"I'm late," he told the company. Nobody said anything. Miss Hearne, trying to be polite, looked at him in inquiry. He saw his audience. "Time and tide wait for no man, alas. Isn't that a fact, Miss Hearne?"

"Indeed it is, Mr Lenehan."

"Well, very nice to have met you," Mr Lenehan said, pushing his chair back from the table. He looked at the others. "So long, all."

The American waved his hand. Miss Friel did not look up. Mrs Henry Rice nodded absentmindedly.

"So long," Lenehan said again. And hurried out on his match thin legs. Good riddance, Miss Hearne thought, to bad rubbish. Why did I dislike him so much? O, well, maybe he's not so bad after all. Old before his time. And something about him. Unpleasant.

She looked at the other. Mr Madden. And saw that he was looking at her. Embarrassed, she turned to Mrs Henry Rice.

"I see a family resemblance. You and your brother. Yes, there's a family resemblance, all right."

"James spent most of his life in the United States," Mrs Henry Rice told Miss Hearne. "Some see the likeness between us, but it escapes me. Still, I suppose it's always that way with brothers and sisters."

Mr Madden seemed pleased to be included in

the conversation. "May's younger than me," he offered.

"But the likeness is there," Miss Hearne said. "O, it's there all right. Are you just over for a holiday, Mr Madden?"

Mr Madden carefully buttered a slice of toast and spread it thick with jam. "Lived thirty years in the States," he said. "New York City. I came back here four months ago."

"O! To stay?"

He did not answer. He ate toast. Quickly, she hurried over her *gaffe*, feeling her face grow hot at his silent snub. "I've always wanted to visit America," she said.

He did not look up. She hurried on: "I'm sure you must find Belfast dull, after New York. My goodness, after all that excitement. It's so up-to-date and everything. New York, I mean."

Mr Madden arrested his teacup in mid-air, put it back on his saucer. "You can say that again. Greatest city in the world." His eyes focused, found her and she smiled as though they had mutually agreed on something which had escaped the others. Her awkwardness was forgotten. For once, she had found the key.

"What part of Ireland you come from?" he said.

"O, I'm from Ballymena originally. But I've spent most of my time here in Belfast."

"That so?" He produced a package of cigarettes. "Mind if I smoke?"

"O, no. I don't smoke myself but smoking

never bothers me."

"That's good." He laughed without laughter, watching Miss Hearne.

He wants to talk, she thought, he's lonely. And she returned his look. Then she helped him, made it easy for him to tell what he wanted to tell: America.

"O, Belfast's not like New York, I suppose. You must get lots of snow and sunshine there."

"All kinds of weather. I've seen it go up to a hundred and ten in the shade, in summer. And in winter, down to ten below zero. I've seen it so hot you'd have to change your shirt twice in one morning." He stopped, vaguely conscious of indelicacy. But she put him at ease.

"Well, there must be an awful lot of laundry to do then. It must be exhausting. In summer, I mean."

"We got air conditioning, and central heating in winter. They never heard of that over here."

Miss Friel closed her book with a snap and stared at the grandfather clock. She got up and went out without a goodbye. Mrs Henry Rice, informative, drooped her huge bosom over the table like a bag of washing. "She's a school-teacher," she said. "Public elementary."

"O?"

Mary came in with toast and the *Irish News*. Miss Hearne took toast, noticed that there were four slices, no sign of an egg, or anything.

"Butter?" Mr Madden offered butter and she

29

saw that he was admiring the little gold wristlet watch on her wrist. She was glad she'd worn it. She looked at Mrs Henry Rice but Mrs Henry Rice had opened the *Irish news* and was reading births, marriages and deaths.

"And how do you find Ireland, Mr Madden, now that you've come home?"

"Been a lot of changes." He stared at the teacup. "It's different."

"So you prefer New York then?"Mr Madden inhaled. Cigarette smoke spewed from his large nostrils. "New York's a rat race." he said.

She didn't know what to answer. Really, what could he mean, a rat race? They certainly had queer expressions, these Yankees.

Mrs Henry Rice put the paper down. "You'll excuse me now, Miss Hearne, but I must go up and say good morning to Bernard. Just ring for Mary if you want more tea."

As Mrs Henry Rice moved towards the door, Miss Hearne's nervousness increased. She had been forward, no two ways about it, asking all those questions, leading him on. And now she was to be left alone with him. Alone. The dining-room with its cold morning light, its heavy furniture, its dirty teacups and plates, became quiet as a church. Alone with this lonely stranger, she waited for his fumbled excuses, his departure. For now that the others had gone, it would be as it had always been. He would see her shyness, her stiffness. And it would frighten him, he would remember that he was alone with her. He would listen politely to whatever inanity she would manage to get out and then he would see the hysteria in her eyes, the hateful hot flush in her cheeks. And he would go as all men had gone before him.

And as she waited, with her hands pressed hard against the edge of the table, she felt the blushes start, the hateful redness and fire creep up her neck. She set her features in a stiff, silly smile and scuffed her feet under the table. She turned to him, still smiling, and a mechanical silly voice leaped out of her mouth, shocking her with the forward thing it said:

"O, you must tell me more about America, Mr Madden. I'd love to go there."

"Well," he said. "I could talk all day and never finish. What did you have in mind?"

In mind. Something, something had to be said.

"Well, is it true that the men over there put their wives on a pedestal, so to speak?"

He laughed, a big heavy laugh. He didn't seem at all put out by her blushes, by her silly voice.

"Yes, that's correct, more's the pity. That's what's wrong with the system, if you want to know. Guys beating their brains out to keep their wives in mink. It's the women's fault. No good. You should see some of the girls that walk on Broadway or Fifth. All dressed up with a dollar sign for a heart. Walking cash registers. Me, I wouldn't have nothing to do with them."

Wouldn't have nothing, well he certainly wasn't very well educated, whatever else he was. So he didn't get married. "O, that's not like Ireland, Mr Madden. Why, the men are gods here, I honestly do believe."

"And right too. Head of the house. That's the teaching of the Church. What the man says goes. Now, in the States, the women want it both ways. They do not work and they want to be boss as well. And dumb, well, you wouldn't believe how dumb some of those dames are."

He was so big, so male as he said it that she felt the blushes start up again. His big hand thumped the table.

"Well," she said. "Irishmen certainly wouldn't stand for that, would they?"

"Every man's a sucker for a good shape. I know. In my business, you see some funny things."

Dangerous waters. Discussing women's figures, well, who but an American would have the vulgarity? Change the subject. "And what is your business, Mr Madden?"

"Hotel Business. I was in the hotel business right on Times Square. You've heard of Times Square?"

"O, yes, of course. I've seen it on the newsreels. When the war was over and it showed all the people cheering. And all those huge advertisements. O, it must be an exciting place to live."

He smiled: "Times Square. Watch the world go

by. The things I've seen in fifteen years on Broadway. It's an education. Why, I couldn't even begin to . . ."

"Well, don't begin then," Mrs Henry Rice said. She stood at the opened door, monumental, stern. "I'm sorry, Miss Hearne, but I must let Mary tidy up. Jim would sit here all day boring the life out of you with his talk about New York."

"O, but it isn't boring, Mrs Rice. On the contrary, I think it's most exciting."

Mr Madden stood up, indignant. He pointed at Miss Hearne. "This lady is interested in what goes on in the world. Not like you and Bernie."

Mrs Rice did not seem to hear. "There's such a lot of work to be done. You know what maids are like, Miss Hearne. You have to be after them all the time. That's why I like to have the dining-room done by ten."

"Of course."

Mr Madden went to the door. "Glad to have met you, Miss Hearne. We must have another talk real soon."

"Yes, indeed we must." Said with her gayest smile to show him she liked him.

Then Mrs Henry Rice offered her the *Irish News* to read and she took it and went upstairs to her room to finish unpacking. No need to hurry. Going over her linens, her packages of letters, and her collection of picture postcards, laying each thing away carefully in tissue paper, all of it could take a long time if you did it methodically. A long

33

time.

But when the big trunks were opened and their trays were laid on the bed, Miss Hearne knelt in silence on the floor, abstracted, her hands idle, her mind filled with what had happened that morning. He had been so glad to talk to her. And he had looked so big and stern and manly, hammering his fist on the table while he laid down the law to her. A big handsome man with that strange American voice.

He came into the room, late at night, tired after a day at work in his hotel. He took off his jacket and hung it up. He put his dressing-gown on and sat down in his armchair and she went to him prettily, sat on his knee while he told her how things had gone that day. And he kissed her. Or, enraged about some silly thing she had done, he struck out with his great fist and sent her reeling, the brute. But, contrite afterwards, he sank to his knees and begged forgiveness.

Judy Hearne, she said, you've got to stop right this minute. Imagine romancing about every man that comes along.

Her busy hands flew, unpacking the linen sheets, putting them away in the dresser drawer. But she paused in the centre of the room. He noticed me. He was attracted. The first in ages. Well, that's only because I've been keeping myself to myself too much. Go out and meet new people and you'll see, she told her mirror face. And the face in the mirror told it back to her, agreeing.

Why did he come home to Ireland? A visit maybe, to see his family. But he doesn't seem on very good terms with his sister. He'll go back to New York, of course, back to his hotel. Mr and Mrs James Madden, of New York, sailed from Southampton yesterday in the *Queen Mary*. Mr Madden is a prominent New York hotelier and his bride is the former Judith Hearne, only daughter of the late Mr and Mrs Charles B. Hearne, of Ballymena. The honeymoon? Niagara Falls, isn't that the place Americans go? Or perhaps Paris, before we sail.

But the mirror face grew stern and cross. You hardly know him, it said. And he's common, really he is, with that ring and that bright flashy tie. O, no he's not, she said. Don't be provincial. Americans dress differently, that's all.

A church bell tolled far away and she prayed. The library book would be due Wednesday, wasn't it? Do you know, I'm awfully uninformed about America, when I come to think of it. Outside, the grey morning light held, the rain still threatened. I could go down to the Carnegie library and read up on it. Especially New York. And then tomorrow at breakfast, I'd have questions to ask.

Maybe, she said, hurrying towards the wardrobe to pick out her red raincoat, maybe he'll be in the hall and I'll meet him and we might walk downtown together. I must hurry because if he's going out, it should be soon.

35

But the hall was a dark, damp place with no sign of anyone in it. Mary had cleared the dining-room, restoring the chairs to their original anchorage around the table. The curtained door to Mrs Henry Rice's kitchen was shut and the house was silent, a house in mid-morning when all the world is out at work.

She went out, dejected, and walked along Camden Street with her head full of black thoughts. Why had she bothered to come out at all? The library and looking up America was only nonsense, when all was said and done. Besides going out only made you peckish and it was such a temptation to have a regular restaurant lunch. Well, you won't. You'll fast, that's what you'll do.

At the library on Royal Avenue the man wasn't helpful. But she made him climb the ladder twice to get her three books, one a picture book of New York and two books on America in general. She carried them to one of the slanting reading tables and sat down, slipping her neutral coloured glasses from her bag. Then amid the old men and students in the muted noises induced by "Silence" signs, she read about America, Land of the Free, the New Colossus. All very heavy going, economic tables and business articles. She turned to the picture book and there was a picture of Times Square, and (gracious!) the hotels were immense, five times as big as the Grand Central, the Royal Avenue, or even the Gresham, in Dublin. O, he couldn't own one of those. And what was his job?

There were so many jobs in a hotel. Maybe an assistant manager. Surely in the administration somewhere. Otherwise, he would have said a cook, or a waiter, or whatever. O, certainly nothing like that.

She read and read because she could feel the little crab of hunger nipping away at her insides. She tried to forget him, the expensive little rascal, but he just nipped harder. Finally, when the clock on the wall said three, she decided that just this once she'd have to give in to him, despite her resolution. She gave the books back and went to a milk bar at Castle Junction and treated herself to a glass of milk and a raspberry tart. Afterwards, she looked at the shop windows for a while. But they hadn't changed since last week, so this was dull sport.

As she was looking in the window at Robb's, a little boy came running out, dragging his school satchel, his grey wool stockings down about his heels.

Tommy Mullen! She hurried over to him, forcing him to stop. His mother was a friend of the Breens, before the Breens moved to Dublin. Tommy had taken piano lessons last year. She saw the keyboard, his rather dirty hands, his wandering inattention, his fits of sulks and rages. No talent. His mother had stopped the lessons.

"Well, if it isn't little Tommy Mullen. And how are we getting along?"

"Lo, Miss Hearne," he said, turning his coldcheeked little face away from her kiss.

"Well, and how's my boy? My, we're getting big. Too big to kiss, I suppose. I'm sure we've forgotten all our piano lessons now."

He looked indignant. "No, I've got a new teacher. A man. Mr Harrington is his name."

"O, is that so?" she said bleakly. "Well, isn't that nice. I hope you are practising hard, eh, Tommy?"

"Yes, Miss Hearne." He looked around, inattentive. "There's the bus," he yelled. "Bye, bye." And ran off in the direction of the Albert Memorial.

A man. Another teacher. She walked down Cornmarket slowly, feeling the shaking start inside of her. No wonder his mother was so cool, nodding from the other side of the street when I saw her. Well, it wasn't because I charged too much, goodness knows. Could I have said anything that time I stayed for tea? No, of course not. I never said he had no talent. O, anyway.

Still, one less pupil, that's what it amounts to. Or two less. Because she didn't want Tommy to keep on but she said she'd get in touch with me about the little girl. She won't now. Harrington, who's he? Well, the nerve of some people. After all the time I slaved away with that boy. After all the extra half-hours without any additional charge. I don't know what's happened to my lucky star these past months. What's happened to me, anyway? You'd think I had the plague, or some-

38

thing. That's four pupils gone in the last six months. Only little Meg Brannon now and goodness knows how long that will last. As much ear for music as a heathen chinee.

The clock in Cornmarket said four. She walked down Ann Street with its jumble of cheap shops, its old shawled women and its loud crying fruit vendors. I wonder will the Technical School take me on for the embroidery class next term? Mr Heron said he hoped he would be able. But nobody does embroidery any more, that's the truth of it. They have to have enough to make a class. And you can't sell it. Ruin your eyes at piece rates.

She came out near the docks and turned hastily back towards the centre of the city. The docks were no place for a woman to be wandering about, in among all those rough pubs and the Salvation Army. At Castle Junction the clock said half-past four. Go home. She walked back towards Camden Street. It began to drizzle but she was thinking about money, so she paid it no heed.

Her Aunt D'Arcy had never discussed money. A lady does not discuss her private affairs, she used to say. And the D'Arcys never had to look where their next penny was coming from. There had been the house on the Lisburn Road. She had thought that it would fetch quite a bit. And then her aunt had said that Judy wouldn't have to worry, there would be plenty until the right man came along and even if he didn't. That was a long

39

time ago, she said that. Ten years. More, thirteen, if I'm to be honest about it, Miss Hearne thought. First, there was the mortgage on the house. And then the money we owed Dan Breen. And the annuity she left me, it was small then and nobody in the whole length and breadth of Ireland could live on a hundred pounds a year nowadays.

O, I should have kept up my shorthand and typing, no matter what. The piano lessons, yes, I tried to make a go of it. And fair's fair, I was doing quite well until Mrs Strain spread that story about Edie and me all over town. You might know, being a Protestant, she wouldn't have one ounce of Christian charity in her. Bad enough for me, but poor Edie, lying up there in that home, couldn't raise a hand to help herself. I should go and see her. But the last time, all thoses bars on the windows and the old women in dressing-gowns. Depressing. Mrs Strain, what did she know, anyway, going off half cocked like that? Amanda, her little girl's name. What a silly name.

No charity, isn't it the truth? People have none. And the Technical School, you'd think they could keep the embroidery class going just for old times sake. After all, there might be a revival of interest. Still, two girls dropped out last term, that leaves only four, not enough unless they can find new students.

She stopped at Bradbury Place. The rain was quite heavy now. She went into a shop and bought a quarter-pound of Kraft cheese and a bag of thick white biscuits. I have enough cocoa, she said, two cups. An apple, I must buy, to get the goodness of some fruit.

It was half-past five when she walked up Camden Street, wet with the rain in her shoes and her hair tossed by the blustery rainy wind. She let herself in as quietly as possible, hoping Mrs Henry Rice would think she had come home later, after having dinner out somewhere. She took her shoes off as she went up the creaky stairs.

The bed-sitting room was cold and musty. She lit the gas fire and the lamps and drew the grey curtains across the bay window. Her wet raincoat she put over a chair with a part of the *Irish News* underneath to catch the drops. Then she took off her wet stockings and hung her dress up. In her old wool dressing-gown she felt warmer, more comfortable. She put her rings away in the jewel box and set a little kettle of water on the gas ring. It boiled quickly and she found only enough cocoa for one cup.

The rain began to patter again on the windows, growing heavier, soft persistent Irish rain coming up Belfast Lough, caught in the shadow of Cave Hill. It settled on the city, a night blanket of wetness. Miss Hearne ate her biscuits, cheese and apple, found her spectacles and opened a library book by Mazo de la Roche. She toasted her bare toes at the gas fire and leaned back in the armchair, waiting like a prisoner for the long night hours.

# CHAPTER
# THREE

Shoes shined, clean white shirt, tie knotted in a neat windsor, suit pressed, top o' the morning, James Patrick Madden went into breakfast. His good humour fled when he saw them. Didn't even look up, except the new one. Miss Hearne. She said good morning. He gave her his old doorman smile, a sort of half-wink in it.

"And how are you today?"

"O, I'm very well, thanks."

Not a sound out of the rest. May, with her face in the paper. And that Miss Friel, she thinks I'm a lush, or something. Lenehan, a know-nothing that thinks he knows everything.

His sister poured tea. Tea, Mr Madden considered a beverage for women in Schraffts. A good cup of coffee now, that would hit the spot.

"O, Mr Madden!" (She was all worked up about something.) "I happened to be in the library yesterday and I was looking at a picture book about New York. It reminded me of our conversation. About it being such a wonderful city, I mean."

He smiled at her. Friendly, she is. And educated. Those rings and that gold wrist-watch. They're real. A pity she looks like that.

"That's nice," he said. "Quite a town, eh? You see the Brooklyn Bridge?"

"O, yes indeed.

Pleased, Mr Madden smiled again. In the four months he had been back in Ireland, he had found very few Irish people who showed any interest in the States. Most of them seemed to resent comparisons. An intelligent woman like Miss Hearne was a pleasure to talk to.

"And the George Washington," he said. "That's quite a bridge. We got a lot of good bridges in New York. There's the Triborough . . ."

"There's a whole lot of bridges in Ireland too, but we're not for ever talking about them." Lenehan interjected sourly.

Who asked him? "Bridges! You call them bridges? Listen, Lenehan, I'm talking about real bridges. Big bridges."

"Ahh, give over," Lenehan said. "Sure, that's all you Yanks ever think of. Blowing about how big and grand everything is in the States. What would be the point of building a big bridge over the Lagan, or the Liffey? Answer me that now. And if it's bridges you want, we were building bridges in Ireland before America was ever thought of."

Why isn't he at work, instead of sticking his nose in where he's not wanted? But he remembered that it was Saturday and Lenehan had all the time in the world on Saturdays. No good talking, he concluded sadly. He'll just ball it up. Better I speak to her later, when we're alone. Maybe ask her out, or something.

"Good morning all," a soft voice said and they all looked at the door. Bernard, his dressing-gown trailing, his plump body in red silk pyjamas. Mrs Henry Rice smiled fondly at her boy.

"Come and sit down, Bernie. Have a cup of tea."

"I rang my bell twice and not a sound out of that girl," Bernard said. "I suppose she was out all night gallivanting with some soldier or other. I'm starved, lying up there, waiting for her."

"Maybe some bacon and egg?" Mrs Henry Rice said coaxingly.

Miss Friel, Mr Lenehan, Miss Hearne and Mr Madden looked up, anger plain as hunger in their faces.

"Bernie's very delicate," said Mrs Rice to no one in particular. "The doctor says he has to eat a lot to keep his strength up."

Bernard sat down and seemed to think about food. Then, gleefully watching the boarders, he gave his order. "Two eggs, Mama, four rashers of bacon. And Mary might fry some bread to go with it."

Mrs Henry Rice, submissive, jingled the little

44

bell. Mary came to the door and was given her orders. The boarders exchanged glances, united in their hatred. Miss Friel, with the air of a woman storming the barricades, picked up a piece of toast, buttered it, then re-buttered it so that the wedge of butter was almost as thick as the toast itself. There, she seemed to say. If it's a fight you want, I just dare you to say a word.

Mrs Henry Rice ignored the butter waste. Her eyes were on her darling as he sipped his tea.

"Well now," Bernard said pleasantly. "What were we talking about when I interrupted? The wonders of America, was it?"

Mr Madden bit angrily into a hard piece of toast. Ham and eggs for him. Nothing for me, her brother.

Miss Hearne, watching him, saw that he was angry. And no wonder. Really, it was a bit thick, feeding up that fat good-for-nothing while the boarders, not to mention her own brother, went without. Still, it was better to pass these things over. Bad temper, bad blood, as Aunt D'Arcy used to say.

"Yes, we were talking about America." Miss Hearne told Bernard. "About how wonderful it must be."

"And what's wrong with Ireland?" Mr Lenehan wanted to know.

"O, I suppose when all's said and done, there's no place like Ireland," Miss Hearne agreed. "I know. Most of my friends have travelled on the

45

Continent and you should hear some of the things they say. Backward, why you wouldn't believe how backward the Italians are, for instance."

Mr Madden coughed. "Pardon me, Miss Hearne, but there's nothing backward about the States. Why, the States is a hundred years ahead of Europe in most things. And ahead of Ireland too. Why, Ireland is backward, backward as hell." He stopped in confusion. "If you know what I mean." he finished lamely.

"America sells refrigerators for culture." Bernard said. "They come to Europe when they need ideas."

"Culture! What do you mean, culture? Why, we've got the finest museums in the world, right in New York City. Grand opera at the Met, a dozen plays on Broadway, the finest movies in the world. Anything you want, New York's got it."

"Now, James — " Mrs Henry Rice said. "No need to shout."

Mr Madden smiled an angry smile. "What have you got here in the way of entertainment?" he asked Bernard. "A few movies — *British* movies. And a few old 'B' pictures. No clubs, and couple of plays that wouldn't last a night anywhere else. What have you got, eh."

"That's not the point," Bernard said. "I'm not talking about Belfast."

"And what are you talking about then? What do you know, a kid of your age that never was further than Dublin?"

Bernard grinned at Lenehan. "The atom bomb, Mr Lenehan. That's the American contribution to Western civilization. Am I right?"

"Damn right," Lenehan said. "And they didn't even discover that. Sure, it was the Europeans who worked out their sums for them. They got the theory right and then they let the Yanks build it."

"And who else could of built it?" Mr Madden shouted.

"Who else had to build it?" Bernard said. "Sure, they'd never have beaten the Japs without it. And now they want to ruin Europe while they try it out on the Russians. Culture, he says."

"And doesn't somebody have to stand up to the Russians?" Miss Hearne said indignantly. "Godless atheists, that's what they are. They're worse than Hitler, far worse."

"No worse than the Protestants and Freemasons that are running this city," Mrs Henry Rice cried. "Hitler was no worse than the British."

Mr Madden brought his fist down hard on the table, upsetting his teacup. "Okay! Okay! Tell me the Russkies are nice guys. But don't ask us to help you when the commies come running up this street, yelling, 'Throw out your women!'"

The very thought of it gave Miss Hearne the shudders. "Quite right, Mr Madden. The Pope himself has denounced them. It's a holy crusade is needed, and America will be in the van."

"In what van?" Mr Madden wanted to know. "America will be out front, that's what." He glared at Bernard, who had started to giggle. "We didn't ask to get in any of Europe's wars, did we? We didn't ask to come over and win them for you. But brother, you hollered loud enough for us to come running when the chips were down."

"You're in Ireland, remember that, Uncle James," Bernard said in his soft compelling voice. "Ireland stays neutral in anybody else's troubles. So don't belabour me about intervention. What are you anyway, an American or an Irishman? When you came home from the States, you hadn't a good word to say for the place. But let anyone else say a word against it and you're up like a tiger."

"That's what I'd like to know," Lenehan said, cocking his birdy head sideways. "That's just what I'd like to know. If it was so blooming terrific in America, why did you ever come home? And why is all the Yanks flocking over here every summer and telling us how wonderful Ireland is?"

Mr Madden gasped like a big fish landed on a dock. But he said nothing. Miss Friel, who had read steadily throughout the discussion, closed her book and stood up. "I suppose that clock is right?"

"Right by the wireless. I set it just when the pips struck eight." Mrs Henry Rice said.

"Well, I must run then," Miss Friel announced to the company.

The others appeared not to notice her departure. Bernard received his ample breakfast from the maid and settled in to eat it. Mr Lenehan slurped his tea, watching Mr Madden over the rim of his cup. Mr Madden surveyed the scene then stood up. He nodded pointedly at Miss Hearne. "So long now," he said.

"O, are you off, then?" she smiled up at him to show she was on his side.

"Well, I guess I've got more to do than sit here listening to a couple of Irish minute men."

Lenehan put down his teacup with a clatter. "Is it me you're referring to? And what's a minute man, if I might ask?"

"Bunch of guys around New York hand out leaflets. Irish-American patriots, they call themselves. Screwballs."

Lenehan pecked his head forward like a rooster in attack. "What do you mean, Irish?" he said thickly. "Are you implying that . . . ?"

Mr Madden chuckled. "We get all kinds of screwballs in New York. Now, take these guys, they're just like the people in Belfast. No matter what the argument is, they always drag Ireland in. Always handing out leaflets against the British. Why nobody in New York, or anywhere else, gives a good ghaddam — pardon me, ladies — what happens to the Six Counties."

"Is that a fact?" Lenehan shouted. "Well, the British give a damn, for one. And . . ."

"There's the whole wide world to worry about. So why bother about Ireland?" Mr Madden said. "The Irish, I'll tell you the trouble with the Irish.

They're hicks."

"Look who's talking. You were a hick once yourself."

"Hicks," Mr Madden repeated, smiling happily. "They think everybody is interested in their troubles. Why, nobody cares, nobody. A little island you could drop inside of Texas and never see, who cares? Why, the rest of the world never heard of it."

"Is that a fact?" Lenehan shouted. "And you call yourself an Irishman. An Orangeman, more likely. Well, I'll have you know, my fine Yank, that there's more famous men ever came out of Ireland than ever came out of America. And I'll have you know that there's plenty of better Irishmen in the States than you, thanks be to God. And furthermore. . ."

Mr Madden's drink-red face was beaming now. "Yeah?" he said. "That's what you think." And he turned his back on the shouting clerk. He walked slowly out of the room dragging his left leg a little.

Out in the hall he burst out laughing. I got him. That slow burn he was getting up when I told him about the minute men. Both of them, never saw anything but their own backyard. Miss Hearne saw my point. An educated woman.

He climbed the stairs to his room. Bernard, the fat slob — couldn't insult him. That — ah, forget it. Forget it. Don't let him get you down. His fedora went down over his right eye. From the wardrobe he picked his fall coat, imported mohair, light tan, the coat he bought to come home in. So's I'd look good. And who cares? In this town nobody'd know the difference. He slammed the front door as he went out.

But walking into the city, his anger disappeared like bubbles from water turned off the boil. Instead, the heavy depression of idleness set in. Walking alone, he remembered New York, remembered that at ten-thirty in the morning New York would be humming with the business of making millions, making reputations, making all the buildings, all the merchandise, all the shows, all the wisecracks possible. While he walked in a dull city where men made money the way char-women wash floors, dully, alone, at a slow methodical pace. In Belfast Lough the shipyards were filled with the clang and hammer of construction but no sound was heard in the streets. At the docks ships unloaded and loaded cargoes, but they were small ships, hidden from sight behind small sheds. In Smithfield market, vendors lounged at their stalls and buyers picked aimlessly at faded merchandise. In the city's shops housewives counted pennies against purchase. In the city's banks, no great IBM machines clattered. Instead, clerkly men wrote small sums in long black ledgers.

Mid-morning. James Patrick Madden walked into town, favouring his bad leg, home, back home in a land where all dreams were calculable and only the football pools offered outrageous

51

fortune. A returned Yank who hadn't made his pile, a forgotten face in the great field of Times Square, and Irishman, self-exiled from the damp hills and barren rocky places of his native Donegal. No lucky break, now or ever. Nothing to do.

Before the accident he had worked twenty-nine years in New York and at no time had more than three hundred dollars to his name. On the credit side, he had educated his motherless daughter, sent her to a convent, seen that she never wanted. On the credit side, America had always found him jobs: subway cleaner, ticket taker in a stadium, counter help in a cafeteria, janitor, hall porter, club bouncer, and, last and best, hotel doorman. A good job, with good tips.

There had been other comforts. Drink to warm and cheer, the odd fast buck, joyfully spent, the blowhard talk, passed hopefully among the boys. Companionship in a land of lonely joiners. And being Irish you could wear it like a badge in New York City. Religion, a comfort for the next world, not this. And good to know you were on the winning team.

And then there was the dream. The dream of all Donegal men when they first came across the water. The dream that some say the pile will be made, the little piece of land back home will be bought and the last years spent there in peace and comfort. A dream soon forgotten by most. Making good means buying goods. Goods attach, they master dreams and change them. The piece of land in County Donegal becomes a two-tone convertible. The little farm that Uncle Sean might let go changes to a little place in Queen's. Making your pile means making your peace with the great new land. But the dream still has its uses. And its addicts. It serves for the others, for the men under the el on a December night, for the hundreds of thousands of Irish who never had a gimmick, a good connection, a hundred dollar bill, or a piece of a business. For them, for Madden, the dream was there for warming over with beer or bourbon. The little place went Hollywood in the mind. The fields grew green, the cottage was always milk-white, the technicoloured corn was for ever stooked, ready for harvest.

The harvest never came. But it had come for him, for James Patrick Madden, a lucky sonofabitch. It had come out of nowhere on a City bus, making a quick getaway in traffic against a changing light. It had come with sudden pain, then vomit and oblivion in a careening, screaming ambulance headed through all lights for Bellevue. It had come fast in an out-of-court settlement. Ten thousand dollars in his fist and a chance to make the homecoming dream come true.

And so, James Patrick Madden, home, reached the centre of the city and stood there undecided. Behind him, Donegall Place and the formal pomposity of City Hall; before him, Royal Avenue, Fifth Avenue of the city, a jumble of large buildings, small to his eyes. The centre, where he stood, Castle Junction, to him a streetcar re-routing stop, an insignificance, an insult to senses attuned to immensity.

He boarded an Antrim Road bus, escaping his disappointment, and sat up top on the double-deck, thinking of Fifth, of the parades, of the clear brilliant fall weather, the hot reek of summer, the crisp delightful nip of winter. But saw the grimy half-tones of this ugly town, saw the inevitable rain obscure the window-pane, felt the steamy sodden warmth rise from the clothes of his fellow passengers

His destination was Bellevue, a municipal park under the shadow of Cave Hill. The park, formal, unlovely, its amusements a mere glimmer of Palisades or Coney Island, had already disappointed him. But he liked the long ride and the view of the lough. From the observation point you could see ships sail out to the Irish sea, watch the soft hills melt under approaching rainclouds. For Madden, it was as though, standing there, he stood at the gateway to all the things he had left behind, all the things he had ever done. It was a link with his other world.

But that morning the link was broken. The rain wept itself into a lashing rage and the lawns, the cafés, the approaches to the park were deserted. He got off the bus, huddled under a shelter, and, after fifteen minutes, caught the next bus back. It was twelve-thirty when he reached Royal Avenue again. Time for a bite of lunch.

He had set himself an allowance of a pound a day, plenty, if he watched the drink. But when the bus deposited him at Castle Junction, he turned towards a public house and went in the door of the saloon bar, stiff-legged and eager. The drink had always been a trouble. And now, with so many long days to fill and with the unsurety of his plans, it was the only thing that brightened his homecoming.

Behind the bar John Grogan bid him good day. Mr Madden ordered a Bass Number One and a ham sandwich. John Grogan served it, wiped his hands on a white towel and went down to the end of the bar to check his stock. Mr Madden bit into the sandwich, eased his fedora to the back of his head, and thought of a trip to Dublin. He ate the rest of the sandwich and dismissed the trip as too expensive. Besides, who did he know in Dublin, and what would he do there? With this prospect disappearing, he reviewed, rejected, turned painful corners, came back to old faded dreams, touched them lightly, abandoned them.

He was alone in the bar excepting two men who sat in a booth at the back, talking business over pints of Guinness. Alone, and he couldn't help thinking.

On the credit side there was the fact that a pound a day was less than three dollars and three dollars would not be enough in New York City. Cheaper to live in Ireland. And May hadn't asked him for any rent yet. And Ireland was where you wanted to be, he told himself bitterly. Anyway from that Hunky bastard with his snide cracks and his bigshot ways.

That Hunky. Steve Broda, real estate salesman, Newark, New Jersey; owner of a cream Buick convertible with white-wall tyres; owner of a twenty-five-thousand-dollar ranch style bungalow home; husband of Sheila Madden, only child of James Patrick Madden, of the Bronx. Sheila, long of leg, blonde of hair and one hundred per cent America. Not a sign of the Irish in her. Sheila, a tiny squalling red-face when the nurse gave her into her father's arms, November 1922, two weeks after Annie died.

Steve and Sheila, second generation, hating their forebears. Old Man Broda, with his funny talk. He was on to them though. He saw it before I did. That sonofabitch, laying her before they were married, a nice thing for a convent girl. And me, Mr Madden remembered, me he called a dumb Irish mick. Ashamed of me, him that couldn't keep his trousers zipped until he took her to the priest. And he made her as bad. Ashamed of me, me that brought her up, that educated her, that never left himself a nickel as long as she needed it. A doorman, he said I should have done better — ahh — have a drink.

"Another Bass."

The time of the accident. Me laid off, it was only natural she'd ask me to come and live with them. But he didn't want that, the Hunky, too good for me he was. And then when the compensation came through, you'd think he got it for me, you'd think I was spending his money, instead of my own. Whyn't you go back to Ireland, Dad? He put her up to saying that. You've always wanted to, Dad. Steve will help, I'm sure he will. He'll help, all right. Anything to get rid of me.

Hell, I got dough. I can get on a boat and go anywhere. Sailing up the Battery. Statue of Liberty. Hello. I'd park my bags and hightail it over to Mooney's, under the el. See their faces when I walk in. Back from the ould sod. And how was it, Jimmy boy? How was it? Back from the old sod. And you can keep it, brother. Argument. That'd make an argument. Culkin crying in his beer about Croke Park in 1911. I'd give it to him. Horseshit, I'd say. You never had it so good, Dan. We never knew when we were well off.

The door of the saloon banged open and a man came in, green pork-pie hat, trench coat, white chamois gloves. His shoes were old brogues, beautifully shined. His moustache was straw-coloured, his nose was long and his eyes were large and watering. He looked uncommonly like an ageing parrot.

"Goddammit, it's cold!" he called out. "John, set me up a glass of port, like a good man. First today. And how's our American friend today? What's the word from New York?"

"I'm fine and dandy, Major, fine and dandy,"

Mr Madden said, giving his old doorman smile, his big tip wink. "But that rain's a helluva note. Wouldn't you say that's a helluva note?"

The major peeled his gloves off and sat down on a high stool beside Madden. His hands were delicate, yellowed by tobacco, and permanently shaking. He drew the glass of port towards him carefully and lifted it fast to toss back in his throat.

"Godblessus and saveus, but that warms all the way," he said. "Now, John, I'll trouble you for a piece of that meat pie and another glass of this excellent port."

John Grogan put a slice of pie on a plate, put a knife and fork beside it, poured another glass of port. Then he wiped his hands on a towel and stood with his buttocks resting against the back of the bar. He folded his arms, a quiet man, a watchful man.

Major Gerald Mahaffy-Hyde ate the pie, every last crumb of it. He drank half of his second glass of port. Then he saw John Grogan waiting, a quiet, watchful man. He took a ten-shilling note from his handsome wallet and paid. The wallet contained only ten shillings. He put the wallet away, slid the change into his trousers pocket and turned to Mr Madden.

"You know," he said reflectively, "there's no country in the world where the cost of living is going up the way it is here. And it's these damn socialist influences over in Britain. That's what did the damage. Never mind whether our fellows are in, or those labour cranks, the result is the same. The harm's been done. Soak the rich and all that. And dammit a man like myself, retired on a pension he's the victim, do you see? These damn socialists have no use for us. They're out to ruin us, that's their game."

Mr Madden cradled his Bass. "Socialistic, eh? Back home in the States we had that trouble."

"Most interesting," the major said, nodding his parrot head. "Of course, you fellows over there didn't stand any nonsense. Quite right too. Harm's been done here. Sometimes it makes me wonder whether a fellow wouldn't be better to find himself some island to retire to. Like the West Indies. Cheap, lots of servants, sunshine and damn good rum."

A bare-breasted native girl shyly dropped her sarong. Tuan Madden patted her smooth rump, raised a rum punch to his lips. "M'mm, something in that, Major. I never thought of it that way. Not like Ireland, cold and rain all the time. You know, a guy could go out there, set up a little business, something the natives don't have, maybe a curio shop for the tourists. A little capital, you could have yourself a time."

"Get away from it all," the major said with relish. "Let them have their century of the common man in Ireland if they want it. People like myself, people who helped to keep the country running when these socialist fellows were hanging around the street corners of Britain, we're the ones they're out to get."

Apolitical, Mr Madden dismissed all this. "Get yourself set up, maybe a little store, get some local help to work for you, sort of supervise, eh?"

"O, I've been out in those waters," Major Mahaffy-Hyde said, looking speculatively at his empty port glass. "Jamaica, Bermuda, Haiti, Cuba. Some wonderful spots. I remember in Haiti, it's a nigger republic, you know, some of the white men there lived like kings. Great whacking big houses, villas, mansions, a dozen servants. Pretty little mulattoes. Hot-blooded little things, the tropics, the sun does it. Fondle a few round bottoms!"

"Great big white mansions," Mr Madden chortled. "Brother!" His eyes saw past the oak panelled bar to a distant shore.

"Niggers run the place," the major said. "But there's no race hatred. Everybody speaks French."

Mr Madden saw Harlem, remembered an ugly incident on Lennox Avenue. Razors. "Ugh! I don't like jigs. New York's full of them."

The major looked longingly at the empty glass in his hand. "This is different, old man. Some beautiful little brown wenches in these places. Get yourself a maid and all the damn comforts of home for about three pounds a month." He tried a gambit. "Care for another?"

"Dark meat, eh?" Mr Madden chuckled. "No, no, this one's on me — John — two more."

"Why, there are red-headed natives all over those islands," the major said. "In Jamaica, blacks name of Murphy. The Irish planted their seed there all right. Olden days, pirates, deserters. Some wonderful stories. And their descendants. Imagine having a brown nubile little Murphy on your knee." His parrot lips curved wickedly. "We Irish conquered by peaceful penetration," he chuckled.

Mr Madden slapped him on the back. "I bet you did your bit yourself, Major, when you were with the British Army, eh, Major?"

"By God, I did, James. By God, I did!"

John Grogan quietly placed a glass of port and a bottle of Bass on the bar. He wiped his hands on a towel and went back to his books. Major Mahaffy-Hyde sighted the port glass, grasped it in his shaking, delicate hand and leaned back, a good mercenary, giving value in talk. Encouraging Madden to dream, helping him towards drunkenness, towards the open confessional of drinking talk.

"By God, I think you're right, James. A fellow like you, an American, he'd known a lot of tricks. Why, you fellows are natural salesmen. Dammit, if Americans could sell refrigerators to the bloody Eskimos, they could sell anything to those niggers. Yes James, I can see you taking your ease in your own villa with a couple of comely bedwarmers by your side."

"You got a point, Major. You got a point. Now, take the business end. Take soft drinks. Now, if I

61

could get a concession . . ."

Shortly after four, John Grogan ceded his place at the bar to Kevin O'Kane. Before leaving, he respectfully approached Mr Madden and asked him if he would mind settling up now. Mr Madden stopped talking. Major Mahaffy-Hyde excused himself and went to the toilet. Mr Madden paid the reckoning. Major Mahaffy-Hyde returned to find Mr Madden sitting with the dejected air of a man who knows he is half drunk and has been caught for all the rounds. The major felt in his pocket and threw some silver on the bar.

"One for the road, now," he said. "My treat. Let's drink to the new king of the islands."

"Mine's a double," Mr Madden said roughly. Sonofabitch never paid for a drink. Yankees walking free drink concession, that's how he figures me.

He remembered Creeslough. How often he'd thought of it in the years when he rode the subway trains, when he stared across Times Square on rainy afternoons. How he had seen it in memory, transformed, a vision of peace and a slow peaceful way of living. And the reality, when he went back. The long bleak street and the warm cosiness of Lafferty's pub. Free pints of porter, boys. Madden, did you say your name was? Well, is that a fact? A son of old Dinty Madden, of the Glen. Well, do you tell me now? Well, thank you very much, I *will* have another, Mr Madden. And what is it like in the States these days? Do you tell me so? All of them, country boys and men with their tongues hanging out, waiting for him to buy another. Spilling his guts out to them, talking about the old days and them, Donegal men, listening to the Yank, waiting for him to stand another round. And when he stopped buying, they began to talk about corn and crops, and pigs and the fair day. All a million miles away from what he knew. He had no place there.

And now, in Belfast, the same game. Your own fault, Mr Madden told Mr Madden drunk. After this one, get the hell out.

The double whiskey was served. He drank it in anger. Then got unsteadily off his stool and said good afternoon to the barman.

"I'll walk along with you, James," the major said, putting on his white chamois gloves.

"I got a date."

"Oh-hoh! A lady fair?"

"Yeah." Trapped by the falsehood, he elaborated. "A Miss Hearne. A business proposition. We might go in a deal together. I got something lined up."

"Well, that's interesting. I didn't know you were going to set up shop here."

"Ahh, I got a couple of deals cooking," Mr Madden said hurriedly, shutting off the talk. "Be seeing you."

He went unsteadily to the door, pushed it open, met the wet face of the afternoon. Rain. What a country!

He walked out into Royal Avenue, crowded now with people going home from work. His fedora rode the back of his head, his drinker's face was wet with rain drizzle. Can't go home like this. Loaded.

A honking post office van honked at him and the driver roared a local insult: "The tap of yer head's chocolate!"

"Get the hell outa my way," Mr Madden roared, stumbling in the gutter beside the van.

A black uniformed policeman took his elbow. "Get back on the pavement. The light's against you."

Mr Madden was sobered by the sight of the arm that held his arm. "Okay."

Watch it, he counselled his drunken self. Watch it. You're loaded, he could take you in.

He nodded to the policeman and the policeman let go his arm. He walked crookedly, watched by the policeman. A movie. Sleep it off. He saw a movie house. Paid, went inside, sprawled out in a back row and slept. Snored. Somebody complained. An usher's flashlight found the face, woke him up.

He watched the movie for a while, slept again and opened his eyes when the lights went on at the change of programme. His watch said nine. He went out, ate in a cheap café and walked back to Camden Street. Another wasted day. The hell with it.

Sober now, he opened the front door quietly

and looked down the hall to see if the light was on in his sister's ground floor nest. All was dark. Painstakingly (only by an argument if she smelled it off me again) he went up the stairs, past Miss Friel's door, past Miss Hearne's and turned towards the flight that led to the third floor and his room.

There was a noise up there, a whispering. He waited again. May? With Bernie maybe. No. He tested each step when he moved again. The light in Bernard's room was out. Lenehan's door was ajar and the noise of Lenehan's snores could be heard in the landing. Mr Madden went past this door to his own and turned the handle.

Behind him, he heard a loud sudden giggle. He swung around, open-mouthed, in the rage of a man caught in a foolish action.

"O, no," he heard. "No, no."

A woman's voice, soft, worried, sensual. It came from the half-flight of stairs that led to the attic. Jesus, it's the maid. I wonder what . . .?

He went up. The light was on under her door. Giggles, a creak of bedsprings, a whispering. He waited, an old hotel doorman, waited.

"O, Bernie, Bernie don't."

Mr Madden wrenched the door open.

"What's goin" on here?"

Mary, transformed by nudity, sat on the edge of the narrow broken-down bed. She wore only coarse black lisle stockings and a pair of faded blue knickers.

And Bernard. Mother naked. Mr Madden came inside and closed the door. So that's it. And her only a kid. But what a kid. What a build.

Bernard found his red silk dressing-gown, dragged it around him like a wrestler preparing to leave the ring.

"Want something?"

Mr Madden's face bled red with anger. "What do you mean, want something? What the hell do you think this is, a whore-house? A kid of her age, I should . . ."

"Go back to your room," Bernard said venomously. "At once. It's none of your business."

"None of my business?" Madden watched as the girl pulled a blanket off the bed, wrapping it around the white nakedness of her body. Only a kid, but . . .

Christ, what'm I thinking? (Briefly, the picture of Sheila and that Hunky swam before his eyes. It's guys like him that — and young girls like her) "What the hell you mean, my business? Whose business is it? What would your mother say, eh? What's your mother goin' to say?"

Mary began to weep, black curls tumbling over her face.

"Never mind my mother. What are you, a Peeping Tom, or something?"

With an effort Madden took his eyes off the girl. "So it's me is in the wrong, eh? Well, we'll see about that. What about you? What about her? What would her father say, dirty little hoor, a nice thing for a Catholic home."

Righteous indignation filled him, flooding his brain with the near-ecstasy of power. The day's futile drinking, the loneliness, the frustrations, all swam away and left this glorious rage in their stead. No respect. Sheila, listen to your father! Laughing at me — taking her pants down behind my back, that Hunky. And her. As bad. Listen to your father! I'll show . . . I'm your father! Old brawler, old underdog authoritarian, he moved towards the terrified girl. "And you — get your clothes on. Tramp, hoor in a decent house."

His fingers tore the blanket away from her body. Master of the room, he smacked, open-handed, leaving red marks on her thighs.

"Dirty little hoor!" He grabbed her, fondled her in rage, sprawled her across the bed.

"O, mister, please, mister. Don't, mister."

"Leave her alone!"

"Dirty little hoor!" Standing over her, he flailed her buttocks. Sheila, the woodshed, should of paddled you sooner. I'll teach you, teach you.

"Leave her alone! LEAVE HER ALONE!"

Bewildered, he allowed Bernard to pull him away. He keeled over on his crippled foot, his breathing harsh and painful. Weak, giddy, he watched ever widening circles explode before his eyes.

It cleared. He saw Bernard's face. "Come on," he said. "Get back to your room."

"You too."

"Okay."

They went out together, leaving the girl whimpering on the bed. Stood in the darkness of the corridor in the exhaustion that follows passion.

"I should tell May. I should tell your mother. A kid like that, you could be arrested. I could fix *you*, all right."

"Fix who? You went mad in there. Stark mad. You'd have raped her if . . ."

"I'd of what?"

Bernard put a pudgy finger to his lips. "Shh! Keep your voice down. You'll waken the whole house. I could make it sound bad against you too. And Mary would back me up. It would be two against one, remember that."

"You're crazy . . ." But what happened? Wearily, Madden tried to remember. Saw her. Only a kid. Like Sheila. I paddled her. Lost my head. That's all. That's ALL.

"You screwed her, not me," he said angrily. "Don't forget that."

"All right. But you pulled the blanket off her."

Did I? What's the matter with me? What a shit I am. Lost my head. The drink, my trouble. But him, he's as bad. Worse. Did it sober. "All right, forget it," he said. "Let's go to bed."

In uneasy alliance they descended the stairs.

# CHAPTER
# FOUR

Sunday was the great day of the week. To begin with, there was Mass, early Mass with Holy Communion, or a late Mass where you were likely to see a lot of people. The special thing about Sunday Mass was that for once everyone was doing the same thing. Age, income, station in life, it made no difference: you all went to Mass, said the same prayers and listened to the same sermons. Miss Hearne put loneliness aside on a Sunday morning.

And on Sunday afternoons there was the visit to the O'Neills, the big event of the week. It began with a long tram ride to their house which gave you plenty of time to rehearse the things you could tell them, interesting things that would make them smile and be glad you had come. And then there was the house itself, big and full of children, all shapes and sizes, and to think you had known even the big ones since they were at high. It was as though you were a sort of unofficial aunt.

Almost.

On her first Sunday morning in Camden Street, Miss Hearne decided to go to eleven o'clock Mass. After all, Saint Finbar's was now her new parish and it would be nice to see the other parishioners. She would wear her very best. Besides, some of the boarders might be going to eleven. Mr Madden, perhaps.

But when Mr Madden came down to breakfast, she saw that he looked ill, or (because she knew the dreadful signs of it) as if he had been drinking. Still, he said good morning to her very pleasantly. Although it was embarrassing the way he said it. Because all the others were there and Mr Madden did not speak to any of them.

Bernard said good morning to his uncle, unusually polite, Miss Hearne thought. But Mr Madden gave Bernard a very odd glance. As for Mr Lenehan, you could see he was still angry about what Mr Madden had said yesterday.

But thank heavens Mrs Henry Rice carried the conversation with a complaint about how, when she came home from eight o'clock Mass, she found that Mary had run off to nine o'clock and left her with the breakfast to make.

"And with kippers to fry," Mrs Henry Rice said, passing a kippered herring and a slice of fried bread along to Miss Hearne. "It wouldn't be any other morning she'd take it into her head to go to early Mass. No, she has to do it on Sunday and me left here with the biggest breakfast of the week."

Miss Hearne agreed that you couldn't be after the maids nowadays, they had it far too much their own way.

Miss Friel closed her book. "It's a good thing the girl is attentive to her religious duties. It's when they start missing Mass and Holy Communion that you should be worried. That's when they're up half the night with boys."

"No fear of Mary getting mixed up with boys," Mrs Henry Rice said. "Sure, she's only a child, just out of school."

"This is a nice piece of kipper," Mr Madden said. "Nice to have a change. I mean, instead of toast and tea."

Nobody could say anything to that, agree or disagree, without insulting Mrs Henry Rice to her face. So nobody said anything. The meal continued in silence, Mr Madden being the first to stop eating. He wiped his lips like an actor finishing a stage meal and put his napkin down in great satisfaction.

"Do you have the time, by any chance, Miss Hearne?"

She blushed. Of course the little wristlet watch was not working, only there for show, and she hadn't the faintest.

"O, I'm sorry, but my watch must have stopped. I forgot to wind it."

"I think the clock's right," Bernard said. "It's twenty to eleven."

Miss Hearne put down her napkin. "Goodness,

I must hurry. I'll miss the eleven o'clock if I don't get a move on."

"I'm going to eleven o'clock Mass myself." Mr Madden said. "Mind if I walk along with you?"

"O, not at all. I'll be very glad of the company."

Mrs Henry Rice looked at Bernard.. "Are you going to eleven, Bernie?"

"I'll go to twelve," Bernard said, and the way he said it, Miss Hearne knew he had no intention of going at all. No wonder he talked like an atheist.

She and Mr Madden went upstairs together to get their coats and hats. They met in the hall a few minutes later and he opened the front door for her, offering his arm as they went down the steps. She did not take it. It seemed just a little bit forward, the way he did it.

She was thinking of things to say as they went down Camden Street. Then she saw his dragging walk and all words left her. *He has a bad leg, why did I never notice it? His walk, dragging his left leg, and that shoe is specially built. OmyGod, he's a cripple!*

At the corner of the street they came face to face with the reddish Gothic facade of Queen's University. He looked up at it.

"That Bernie. A college education, well they certainly didn't teach him much."

"He *is* a little queer," she said tentatively.

"Queer? He's no queer, believe me. He's just a no good mama's boy, never did a day's work in his life. Don't let that poetry stuff fool you. That's

72

just a gimmick, so's he can say he's working. No, he's got a cinch. Why should he work when May keeps him?"

He looked sideways at Miss Hearne. "You been to college? You seem like an educated woman."

"No, I'm afraid the Sacred Heart convent in Armagh is as far as I went," Miss Hearne said pridefully, because, after all, the Sacred Heart convent was the best in Ireland. The best families sent their girls there. Would he know that, being an American? "It's considered the best convent though," she added.

"I never went to college. Had to get out and hustle for myself. I made out too, did fine."

I wonder if he's rich? Out walking on a Sunday morning with a strange man, what would Aunt D'Arcy have said? Still, he looks quite prosperous and respectable. That limp, you would hardly notice it. After all, I never noticed it before. All Americans have money, they say. I wonder what he did in the hotel, would it be rude to ask him."

"And did you go into the hotel business right away, when you arrived in American?"

"No."

They walked in silence for a while. "Always had my own car," Mr Madden told the wind. "Always had my own car, even in the depression."

She didn't know quite what to reply to this, but something had to be said. "People earn a lot of money in America, don't they?"

"Some people. But it's a young man's country.

They got no use for you when they figure you're over the hill. Y'see, I always had it in mind to come back to Ireland when I was older. Maybe marry again and settle down."

Miss Hearne felt something turn over in her breast. "And did your poor wife pass on long ago?"

"The year we went over. She's dead going on thirty years. It was the crossing that killed her, the boats were different in those days. Had the baby about a week after we landed. Sheila, my girl."

"O, so you have a family then."

"Well, just the one. She's married now. I was living with her and the husband before I come home. I figured I was in the way, lying up around the house after my accident. This leg, y'see. So I told them I'm going back to Ireland, kids, I said. Back home."

He's lonely, thinking of his old age like that. But how odd that he would discuss his private affairs without really knowing her at all. It was like something in a story, people meeting, struck by a common *rapport*, a spart of kinship or love. Although that was silly and she was being daydreamy again.

"I'm sure your daughter must miss you, all the same."

"Some chance. Kids nowadays don't care."

They crossed the street as the light flashed green. He took her arm as they stepped off the pavement. She did not reject his aid.

"O, children of the present generation are awfully thoughtless. Even here in Ireland. Friends of mine, the O'Neills . . ."

"Same thing here," he interrupted. "Come back to settle down and you can't even get respect from the likes of Bernie."

"So you're planning to stay here?"

"Maybe. I got a couple of deals cooking. I might go to the West Indies, I hear there's a lot of possibilities there. Depends. Or I might go into business in Dublin. If I had a partner."

I wonder if he's old? Over fifty certainly. Maybe younger. But big, well-preserved, a man full of life and vigour. Did he retire, I wonder, or was it the accident to his leg? They don't retire early in the hotel trade, remember Mr Bunting that was the manager of the Arcady hotel in Dublin,, seventy if he was a day.

"Did you have a lot of running about to you in your job? In hotel work, I mean? It must have been a terrible strain."

"No, it was okay." He did not elaborate. He did not speak again until they reached the church and then only to ask if she preferred to sit up at the front. They made the Sign of the Cross together and his fingers brushed against hers in the Holy Water font. Then they walked up the aisle and he stood aside to let her pass into the pew before him. The seat he had chosen was directly under the pulpit. Before he knelt down, Mr Madden took a clean white handkerchief out of his trousers

75

pocket and spread it on the dusty board to protect the knees of his trousers. He found his large brown rosary, wrapped it around his knuckles, and placed himself in an attitude of prayer.

But he did not pray. He thought: I wonder would she tell it in confession? When May said she ran off to early Mass this morning, maybe it was to tell the priest on both of us, he could phone back to the house and raise hell, a child, May said, Christ, some child, I should have left her alone, none of my business. Pulled the blanket off her, he said. Ah, the priest couldn't do a thing like that, secrets of the confessional. And she's a scared kid, little roundheels, couldn't have much religion, just ran out because she was scared to face me at breakfast. Ah, don't worry, you're okay, here in church with Miss Hearne, a fine woman, a lady, a pleasure to talk to her it is. But if she knew about me, Miss Hearne, if she knew about last night — ahh, I'm no good, drinking like that, pulling at that kid, but she was old enough though, what a build. Christ — I mean, Blessed Jesus Christ — why did I think that right in the church, an impure and filthy thought right in God's house. O my God I am heartily sorry that I have offended Thee and because Thou are so good, I will not sin again. Not a mortal sin, no, I never, only tried to break it up, teach her a lesson, didn't do a thing. Act of contrition, that's absolution, couldn't go to confession today anyway. Sunday, no confessions heard, if I die tonight, be in a state of grace. Say a rosary now, show my good intentions. Forget all that dirty thoughts stuff.

This was religion. Religion was begging God's pardon on a morning like this one when the drink had made your mouth dry and the thing that happened last night with the serving girl was painful to think about. It was making your Easter duty once a year, going to Mass on Sunday morning. Religion was insurance. It meant you got security afterwards. It meant you could always turn over a new leaf. Just as long as you got an act of perfect contrition said before your last end, you'd be all set. Mr Madden rarely thought of Purgatory, of penance. Confession and resultant absolution were the pillars of his faith. He found it comforting to start out as often as possible with a clean slate, a new and promising future.

Miss Hearne, seeing him begin to pray, took out her Missal and set a little marker at the Gospel of the day. She was not, she sometimes chided herself, a particularly religious person. She had never been able to take much interest in the Children of Mary, the Foreign Missions, the decoration of altars or any of the other good causes in which married and single ladies devote themselves to God and His Blessed Mother. No, she had followed her Aunt D'Arcy's lead in that. Church affairs, her aunt once said, tend to put one in contact with all sorts of people whom one would prefer not to know socially. Prayer and a rigorous attention to one's religious duties will contribute far more towards one's personal salvation than the bickering that goes on about church bazaars. Miss Hearne had her lifelong devotion to the Sacred Heart. He was her guide and comforter. And her terrible judge. She had a special saint, to whom she addressed her novenas: Anne, mother of Mary. She used to have a special confessor, old Father Farrelly, Rest in Peace. She had never missed Sunday Mass in her life, except from real illness. She had made the Nine Fridays every year for as long as she could remember. She went to evening devotions regularly and never a day since her First Communion had she missed saying her prayers.

Religion was there: it was not something you thought about, and if, occasionally, you had a small doubt about something in the way church affairs were carried on, or something that seemed wrong or silly, well, that was the devil at work and God's ways were not our ways. You could pray for guidance. She had always prayed for guidance, for help, for her good intentions. Her prayers would be answered. God is good.

As she knelt there, beginning her prayers, the organ ground out a faltering start and the choir started up discordantly in the gallery. Then the voices caught up with the music, lifted above it and the priest appeared, shuffling across in front of the altar, peering over the covered chalice so that he would not trip on the carpet. Two small alter boys scuttled after him, settling themselves on the altar steps with the ease and nonchalance of little boot-blacks on the steps of some great temple.

The Mass began. The choir sat down noisily in the gallery as the priest mumbled the opening prayers. Miss Hearne looked at him, the celebrant of the Mass, Father Quigley, he must be. She kept her eyes on him until he turned, a tall man with the hollow cheeks and white face of an inquisitor. His hair was still strong and black but it had made its own tonsure, leaving a little saucer of white baldness at the back. His hands, she noticed, were long, with long spatulate fingers, gesturing spiritual hands.

Then the organ groaned again and the choir stood up and sang. The crowd of worshippers immediately set off a tictac burst of coughing which rose in one part of the church, moved on, died, then started up afresh in an entirely different place. The latecomers jostled, whispered and shuffled at the back of the church, and the singing of the choir was all but drowned in the resultant noise and confusion.

But Miss Hearne knelt upright, her heart singing a *Te Deum*, a full chant which admitted no distraction. For here she was in church, after all these years, with a good man kneeling beside her, not the youngest or the handsomest surely, but a man who had not forgotten her in the moment of meeting, a man who had kept his faith and said his beads and had not been turned away from God's love by bitterness or evil or any sinful temptation.

She gave thanks then to the Sacred Heart that He had sent her the trials and tribulations of her last lodgings that she might move to Camden Street and meet Mr Madden and walk with him to Mass and from him hear the secret things of his life. And she went up unto the altar of her Lord, her Lord who rejoiced in her youth. She sang His praises and she asked her soul why it was sad and why did it trouble her. I believe in God, said the Missal, and she believed and praised Him again for He was her salvation and her light.

"*Confiteor Deo Omnipotenti!*" cried the priest and she confessed to Almighty God, to the Blessed Mary, ever Virgin, Blessed Michael the Archangel, Blessed John the Baptist, the Blessed Apostles Peter and Paul and to all the saints and to you, Father, that she had grievously sinned in thought, word and deed. It was her fault, her fault, her most grievous fault. Thus, the *Kyrie* and *Gloria* passed in alternate praise and blame as the priest moved towards the first Gospel. The congregation groaned and shuffled to its feet and the Gospel was read. Then in the noise of the people kneeling again, the priest rushed ahead to the Offertory and turned around to become not the living speech of the Missal but Father Francis Xavier Quigley, tall, ascetic, hollow white, pointing an accusing finger at his parishioners.

80

"Quiet!" he shouted. "And let me tell those people who just came in at the back of the Church that they're late for Mass, that they've not fulfilled their obligation and that they should be ashamed of themselves. They'd better leave now because they'll have to come back to twelve o'clock Mass to fulfil their duty."

Then whirled, with a swinging lurch of vestments, back to the altar. The congregation practised silence. But Mr Madden turned his head towards Miss Hearne and winked. No laughing matter, Miss Hearne thought. Father Quigley seemed like a terribly stern man.

The priest offered the chalice and she read her Missal, thinking of Father Quigley and of this tall man from across the water who knelt beside her. Both big men, both stern men, both men who were not afraid of anything. She shut her Missal and offered up a special prayer to the Sacred Heart, asking Him if this could be the answer to all her novenas and good intentions: if this man who knelt beside her might not be the one the Sacred Heart had chosen Himself to help her in her moments of pain and suffering, to uphold her and help her uphold the right, to comfort her and act as a good influence in her struggle with her special weakness. And at the sacred moment of the Consecration, she touched her breast three times and asked the Sacred Heart for a sign, a sign that would reveal to her whether He in His infinite patience and mercy had answered her prayers.

81

Before the last Gospel the congregation sat up on the seats and Father Quigley picked up the book of announcements and made his way across in front of the altar. A tiny altar boy ran ahead to open the gate and the parish priest went slowly across the aisle to the pulpit, leafing through the lists of the dead. As he mounted the pulpit steps, he was hidden from the congregation and the whispering started again. But then he emerged at the top like a watchman and the heads lifted, the sounds died to silence. At the back of the church, the ushers, moving quietly from long practice, passed the brass collection plates among their number.

Father Quigley laid the announcement book on the edge of the pulpit and sighted the clock underneath the organ loft. It began to rain outside and the stained glass window grew dark, darkening the whole church as though it were evening and the sun had sunk out of sight. In this gloom, this sombre preliminary lighting, the priest's white and gold vestments shone brightly out of the murk above his congregation. He lifted his long white hand and made the Sign of the Cross. Then he began:

"I had in mind to say a few words about the Gospel of today, which you have all read, or at least the good people have read, the ones that bring their Missals and prayer-books to Mass of a Sunday morning and try to follow the Holy Sacrifice. But I'm not going to talk about the

Gospel, because this Gospel doesn't deal with the subject which has to be settled in this Church today, before this kind of hooliganism goes any further."

He paused, stared hollow-cheeked at the crowded gallery. Then pointed a long spatulate finger at the people sitting above.

"You know what I mean, you people up there," he shouted in hard flat Ulster tones. "You that's jiggling your feet and rubbing the back of your heads along the fresh paint that was put on the walls. I mean the disrespect to the Holy Tabernacle and the Blessed Body of Our Lord here in it. I mean coming in late for Holy Mass. I mean inattention, young boys giggling with young girls, I mean running out at the Last Gospel before the Mass is over, I mean dirtying up the seats with big bloothers of boots, I mean the shocking attitude of people in this parish that won't give half an hour to God of a Sunday morning but that can give the whole week to the devil without the slightest discomfort. I mean the young people, and a few of the older ones too, some of them that should know better but don't because ignorance and cheekiness is something that they pride in and the House of God is just a place they want to get in and out of as fast as possible and without any more respect for it than if it was a picture house, aye, not half as much, for you can see those same people of a Saturday night, or any night they have a couple of shillings in their pockets, you can see them lining

83

up two deep outside a picture house. But I'll ask you one thing now, and I want you to examine your conscience and tell me if it isn't true. Have you seen the young men of this parish queuing up to get into a sodality meeting? Or have you ever seen the girls and women of this parish lining up to get into the Children of Mary devotions? You have not, and I'll tell any man he's a liar if he says he has. Because I haven't and I'm not at cinemas or dog tracks or dance halls during the week, I'm here, that's where I am, here in the Church, with a few good souls listening to me and the benches empty, the sodalities, just a few good men stuck in the front benches and the House of God empty, aye, empty.

"But the dog tracks aren't empty, are they now? Celtic Park or Dunmore Park on the nights the dogs run, they're not empty. Oh-ho no! No, no, the trams are full of young men and old men, and the buses too, and those that don't have the price of the tram after the races are over are thick as flies on the pavement. And the taxis are kept running full blast too. Aye, there are dogs in those taxis, dogs sitting up like human beings while human beings walk. And there are men in those taxis too. Men with bags of money on their knees and book-makers' boards stuck on top of the taxis on the luggage racks. Aye, dogs ride home in taxis while Irishmen of this parish walk home without a penny piece in their pockets after giving it all away without a murmur. But let me ask for the money tomorrow for a new coat of paint for those walls that the young people of this parish seem to take a delight in dirtying up, and see the story I get. O Father, times has been very hard. Ah, yes, very hard. But not too hard to give that week's wages to the dogs. No, never that hard. And not too hard for the young bits of girls nowadays to have plenty of money for powder and paint and silk stockings and chewing gum and cigarettes and all kinds of clothes which you wouldn't see on a certain kind of women in the old days. And not too hard to slap down a couple of shillings any night in the week to go into the cinema and look at a lot of people who're a moral disgrace to the whole wide world gallivanting half naked in glorious technicolour. Oh, no, there's always plenty of money for that."

He paused, breathing heavily. Looking up at him, Miss Herne saw his nostrils flare like a horse that has run a race. Such a powerful speaker, she thought, so very direct. Not the old style of priest at all, doesn't mince words, does he? But the young people, well, I think he's right, goodness knows, those young girls I saw at . . .

"Plenty of money!" Father Quigley roared. "Plenty of money! Plenty of time! Time and money. But they don't have it for their church! They don't even have an hour of a Sunday to get down on their bended knees before our Blessed Lord and ask for forgiveness for the rotten things they did during the week. They've got time for sin, time for naked dancing girls in the cinema, time to get drunk, time fo fill the publicans' pockets and drink the pubs dry, time to run half-way across the town and stand in the rain watching a bunch of dogs race around a track, time to go to see the football matches, time to spend hours making up their football pools, time to spend in beauty parlours, time to go to foreign dances instead of *ceilidhes*, time to dance the tango and the foxtrot and the jitterbugging, time to read trashy books and indecent magazines, time to do any blessed thing you could care to mention. Except one.

"They — don't — have — time — for — God."

He leaned forward, grabbing the edge of the pulpit as though he were going to jump over it.

"Well," he said quietly. "I just want to tell those people one thing. One thing. If you don't have time for God, *God will have no time for you.*

"And speaking of time, your time will come before the judgment seat of Heaven. Don't you worry about that. And then it won't matter a brass farthing whether you were a dandy at the football pools, whether you know every film star by name from Charlie Chaplin to Donald Duck, whether you can reel off the name of every dog that ever won a race at Dunmore or Celtic Park.

"*There'll be no time for that. No time at all.*

"No, good people, there'll be no time for all that. But there'll be time enough to find out how you attended to your religious duties, there'll be time enough to make a reckoning of how many hours you spent on your bended knees praying to our Blessed Lord for forgiveness of your sins."

He paused and looked through the gloom at the clock. Miss Hearne, fixed with attention, heard a faint, unmistakable sound beside her. Mr Madden was asleep. O, the mortification of it. She nudged him, trying to make it seem accidental, and he opened one eye, then closed it.

"Aye, there'll be a change of temper then," Father Quigley roared above her. "And those young people standing here in this church, standing there like a bunch of hooligans at the back, waiting their chance to run out at the Last Gospel, what will God say to them on that terrible day? What will He say? Will it be, 'Come ye blessed of My Father, inherit the kingdom prepared for you?' Will it be that now? Do you think it's likely? Or will it be, 'Depart from Me, ye cursed, into everlasting fire that was prepared for the devil and his angels?' Will it be that now? Will it be that?"

"Not if *I* can help it, it won't. Not in *this* parish. Beginning next Sunday, I'm going to order the ushers to close the doors at the Offertory and not open them until Mass is over. If anybody is sick or has some good reason, he or she will be let out. Otherwise, not. Because Mass is the whole Mass and not a football match with people running in and out of the church as if it was a cinema."

He paused and stared at the congregation. Then

he made the Sign of the Cross.

"In the name of the Father and of the Son and of the Holy Ghost, amen. Your prayers are requested for the souls of the following who died last week or whose anniversaries occur about this time: John Cullen, Thomas McCabe, Ellen Higgins, Hugh Gormley, Patrick Kennedy, Mary . . ."

As Father Quigley droned through the list of names, the collectors silently took up their stations, brass plates in hand. Assistant collectors licked their pencils and folded their notebooks open. Miss Hearne saw Mr Madden take half a crown from his pocket. She felt in her purse, found the sixpence she had put aside for this moment.

After mumbled prayers for the dead, the collection speedily went to work, moving down the aisles with practised ease. The priest stood at once side of the altar, immobile, with his back to the congregation, until a little bell discreetly signalled the completion of the collection. Then he began in rapid Latin and the Mass moved towards a close.

"*Ite Missa Est,*" Father Quigley cried loudly, and the congregation collected prayer-books, slipped on gloves, nudged purses and umbrellas in preparation for the closing prayers. Outside, the rainclouds scudded past like big ships sailing out of harbour. A morning sunlight filled the church. A heavenly sunlight, Miss Hearne thought, as it blinded and bathed her with its shining light. It faded then and she bent her head to her pew and gave thanks. Was it the light of God? Was it the answer to her prayers, was it the Sacred Heart giving her a sign, now that the sacred mystery of the Mass was over, and there was time to answer the prayers of individuals? It had shone down on her, on him, blessing them with its light. O Lord, she prayed, let it be, make it be, give him strength to see Your way, let me be my guide, let him help me conquer my weakness, my wickedness.

She prayed, feeling pure, exalted, but closer to fear than exultation as the Mass ended and her prayers and exhortations dwindled before the reality of the people filing down the aisle into the world outside and the contradictions and unsureties of the streets. It was as though she had said her say, used all her arguments before a great and all-powerful judge and now the defence rested, the arguments were over and the decision would be announced in a dead anti-climax by some unknown secular juryman in the street, away from the House of God and the surety of prayer and good intention.

And, as they left the church together, she thought of the pure chance of it all, how it had happened so suddenly, after nothing at all had happened for so many years: how it was pure chance that he had happened to ask her to walk to Mass with him and that they had talked together in private, so to speak. For if he had asked her to walk with him to anywhere else but Mass, she would have had to refuse him on so short an acquaintance.

They stood together on the street corner and surveyed the dead Ulster Sunday. The shops were shut, the city had set its dour Presbyterian face in an attitude of Sabbath righteousness. There was no place to go, nothing to do.

"What did you think of the sermon?" she said.

"It was okay, I guess. But what's wrong with the movies? I don't get it."

"O, Father Quigley's quite a strict man, I hear. But a very honest speaker. You feel the sincerity leaping out of him, even though he's not the most cultured man when it comes to giving a sermon. But he's got a great presence, hasn't he?"

"He looks sick to me. I knew a priest in New York like that. He had TB."

"Most of the American priests are of Irish origin, aren't they?"

"Around New York, maybe. There's all kinds."

"The faith is very strong in America, isn't it?"

"Not like here. But we have some good priests. I knew Father Duffy. Used to see him often."

"O?" She looked puzzled.

"Father Duffy. Padre of the Sixty-Ninth in World War One. They put up a statue of him, right in Times Square. I used to look at it and think about him. I never figured why, but it used to remind me of Ireland, that statue." He smiled. "I used to say we both worked Times Square, Father Duffy and me. But he's been there longer.

The statue, I mean."

She watched him as he walked on, saw his face smile, saw it turn cold and serious. What could he be thinking of? He seemed to be trying to remember something, perhaps an engagement, perhaps an excuse to leave her. For eventually, they all made some excuse. But when they reached the end of the street, he turned and took off his broad-brimmed hat.

"I guess you've got a lot of things to do," he said. "You going back to the house?"

"O, yes. But I go to see my friends, the O'Neills, every Sunday afternoon. He's a professor at the university, you know. A very clever man. I used to know him when we were children. And now he's married with a lovely family of his own."

Why did I say that, she thought, why? But it was her old fault, the old boasts, the shields against pity, against being forced to say that nobody wanted to see you that particular day. The old mistake. Now he would go away.

"That so?" His face showed disappointment.

She tried to undo it: to let him know that life was not all gay friends.

"It's so nice to have someone to visit occasionally when one lives alone."

It was a forward thing to say, but she had to come out with it some time: besides, it was the truth, though nobody liked to admit being lonely. How many times before had she turned men away by her habit of boasting, of pretending that she had a good time all the time and needed no one. Looking at him, no longer young, with his rough-red face and his built-up shoe, she knew that he would be easily turned away, that he had not stayed so long alone without something of herself in him. And maybe, although it was a thing you could hardly bear to think about, like death or your last judgment, maybe he would be the last one ever and he would walk away now and it would only be a question of waiting for it all to end and hoping for better things in the next world. But that was silly, it was never too late. And so she waited, pretending not to see him lift his hand to say good bye, waited for something, for some little chance to keep him.

"Not much to do in this town, that's a fact," he said. He scuffed his feet on the edge of the gutter. "I find the time long too. Not like New York." Then, as if he had suddenly thought of it: "Do you like the movies?"

"You mean the pictures? O, yes."

"Doing anything tomorrow night?"

It was so vulgar, the way he put it, just like an invitation to a serving girl. But I mustn't think like that any more, she told herself. Nobody cares about manners nowadays. Times have changed, you know they have.

"Well, no," she said, smiling. "I don't believe I am."

"Okay, let's take in a show then. About seven,

would that be all right?"

"Lovely. And thank you very much."

"Fine." He raised his big hat. "I got a date uptown," he said. "So long now."

He hurried off across the street as though he were afraid she would change her mind and tell him so.

It was, she realized, the way she herself left others, after a successful theft of their time, after a promise, so terribly wanted, a promise that she could come again.

# CHAPTER
# FIVE

The fire was banked high and glowing in the handsome grate, the flowered chintz furniture covers had been freshly washed, and the silver, the brass, the mahogany, were polished and gleaming. Copies of the *Observer*, the *Sunday Times* and the *Sunday Independent* lay on the sofa and there were cigarettes in two silver boxes. The warm, well-used feel of the drawing-room, and the relaxed air of its occupants made the driving rain on the window-panes an additional comfort as though emphasizing that nothing in this dull provincial city could rival the pleasure of home on a rainy Sunday afternoon.

Shaun O'Neill lifted his head from a book and glanced at the ornate, painted clock on the mantel-piece.

"Five minutes," he said. "Or maybe ten. Let's say ten minutes at most before the advent of the Great Bore."

His mother shook her head: "How often do I

have to tell you not to talk like that? You'll be old soon enough yourself and glad of somebody to chat with."

Una, his sister, rolled her magazine into a baton and struck at him. He ducked, catching her wrist, and they began to wrestle.

"Now, stop that, you'll break something." Mrs O'Neill said.

Una freed herself and stood up with her back to the fire, a tall dark girl, wearing a smart grey wool dress.

"What's a word for danger in eight letters?" Professor O'Neill asked. He sat in his favourite armchair to the right of the fire with a newspaper crossword puzzle on his lap, a big man with a harsh, handsome face, a shiny bald head and a tortoiseshell-rimmed monocle set staring in his right eye. The monocle, attached to his coat lapel by a black silk ribbon which hooked over one of his large pointed ears, gave him a look of Mephistopheles in modern dress. He ignored the children's horseplay. His voice and manner were mild.

"Jeopardy," Kevin said, without looking up from his copy of *Picture Post*. He moved his small rump in its short trousers, rubbing his woollen-socked ankles together. "Is that it?" he asked his father.

"Doesn't go. At least, it doesn't fit with some of the across words.

"Where's Kathleen?" Mrs O'Neill looked

around the room, a small plump woman with grey hair and large brown eyes which missed nothing in her particular circle. "I thought Kathy was here. Is she studying, does anyone know?"

"Can I have one of those sweets, Mam?" Shaun asked, pointing to a box of chocolates on top of a bookcase.

"You cannot. You've just eaten enough lunch for two."

"Yes, but I'm going out. I told Rory Lacey that I'd go over some physics with him."

"O, so we're going out now, are we? I thought you said you were staying in. You didn't do a single stroke of work all week-end and now everything has to be done when I want you to spend a little time with poor Judy Hearne."

"Talk of the devil," Una said. "Is that the doorbell?"

They all looked up, listening.

"It's only me!" Shaun cried, in a high-pitched feminine voice. Una and Kevin echoed it.

"It's only me! It's only me!"

Professor O'Neill stood up hurriedly, gathering the *Sunday Times*, his pipe, matches and tobacco pouch. "I'll be in my study if you want me."

Shaun bounced up from the sofa, big boned, adolescent. "I'll come with you, Daddy."

"You'll stay here, sir," Professor O'Neill said. "Stay for half an hour at least, to help your mother." He looked at his son and raised his hand against an unspoken protest. "Now, that's enough. No nonsense."

The O'Neills' maid was coming upstairs as the professor left the drawing-room. "It's Miss Hearne, sir."

"Well, just wait until I get into the study, Ellen. Then show her up to the drawing-room."

Below, in the darkness of the hall, Miss Hearne was taking off her wet raincoat. She handed it to Ellen when the maid returned.

"Thank you, Ellen. Just hang this somewhere. I'll find my own way up."

She climbed the stairs slowly, giving young Kevin time to escape to the chilly solitude of the attic and his chemistry set. Just like his father, she thought, seeing his small legs scuttle around the curve of the bannisters, two flights above her. Always running off to work on something or other. Dear Owen, the child takes after him.

The drawing-room door was ajar. I wonder how many of them are in? Una and Shaun, and perhaps little Kathleen. And Moira herself, half asleep already. She knocked lightly on the drawing-room door.

"It's only me!" she called.

There was a sound of movement inside and then Moira O'Neill came forward, her arms outstretched in welcome. "Judy dear. And how are you?"

Behind her, standing by the sofa giggling about something, were Shaun and Una, brother and sister, with their mother's gay dark eyes. Miss

Hearne smiled at them; her little nephew and niece, she liked to think.

"Hello, Miss Hearne." Shaun said.

Una burst into another peal of laughter.

"Una!" Mrs O'Neill took Miss Hearne's arm. "I don't know that's the matter with them, Judy. They've been laughing themselves sick all afternoon."

"O, the young in heart," Miss Hearne said, smiling. She went towards the fire — such a lovely room, warm and pleasant — and sat down in the chair vacated by Professor O'Neill.

"My goodness, I was almost drenched coming over her. What a day! And how are you, Una dear? What's the news with you?"

"Same as ever, Miss Hearne. Exams, exams." Una sat down on the sofa and looked out the window. "I wonder will it clear up?"

Mrs O'Neill returned to her chair beside the fire and picked up a bundle of knitting. "And what's the news with you, Judy?"

"Well, you know I've moved into my new digs."

"O, yes, of course. And what are they like?"

She forgot it, she forgot it completely. As if I would forget something as important as moving, if it was her who was doing it! "Well Moira, it's over in Camden Street. I told you about it last week."

"Camden Street. I know it," Una said. "Near the university."

"It used to be one of the best parts of the city. I

remember my dear aunt used to visit a family there — well, let me think what the name was. Wait — it will come in a minute. Anyway, it was a very good neighbourhood in the old days."

She saw Shaun smile when she mentioned her dear aunt. The younger generation are so cynical, she thought. Not well brought up, what Mr Madden said was quite right. Mr Madden, I wonder should I mention him?

"This place is run by a woman called Rice. A Mrs Henry Rice, a widow. Did you ever hear tell of her?"

Moira O'Neill paused momentarily in her knitting. "No, I don't think so."

"Neither did I. Anyway, she has the funniest son you ever saw. Bernard, his name is, and he's the oddest-looking creature alive."

Una snapped her fingers. "Wait a minute. Bernard Rice. Has he long blond hair, in sort of ringlets? A fat fellow?"

"The very man." Miss Hearne cried. "I'm sure it's the same one." And as she leaned forward to tell more, Una turned to Shaun and said:

"He used to be at Queen's, before my time."

"That's right, Queen's, he said so himself," Miss Hearne agreed eagerly.

"Wait till I tell you," Una said to her brother. "He's the original mammy's boy. His mother used to haunt the lecture halls, waiting to give him a feed, a sandwich or a thermos of hot soup. She used to plague him. He was supposed to be very bright, though. Honours English, I think."

"And what's the long hair in honour of?" Shaun said.

"She wouldn't let him cut it. She calls him, 'My baby'. Isn't that right, Miss Hearne?"

"Well, Miss Hearne said. "You seem to know a lot more about him than I do."

"Sure, he was famous around Queen's. Baby Rice, they called him. He was a big poet and talker. He was behind that crowd that got out the poetry magazine. You remember, Shaun, the mimeographed one."

"I never heard of him," Shaun said. "It's a wonder I didn't, seeing he was such a famous card."

His sister patted him playfully on the head. "You're too young."

"O, it seems like yesterday that I remember you both as babies in your little woolly suits," Miss Hearne cried, trying to catch some of that brotherly and sisterly warmth. "I remember Shaun saying to your mother here, and the two of you standing there and he said: 'I don't like Miss Hearne wiv'at hat!' "

But they turned glowering faces at her, rejecting the often heard story. Children don't like to be reminded of their baby days. O, I know that. Why did I put my foot in it?

Shaun got up off the rug and looked at the clock. "Holy smoke! It's past three. I told Rory Lacey I'd be over at his house at three."

His mother looked at him, her eyes cold to the falsehood. "It's still raining," she said. "You could phone him up and tell him you can't come."

"It's not far, Mam. I can take a tram. I should be back before five."

"You'll have to excuse me too, Miss Hearne, but I've got to do some studying," Una said. "The exam is in less than a month."

"Of course, Una dear. I don't even dare to think about the work you have to do nowadays. It's not like our time, is it, Moira? Why, when I was at the Sacred Heart in Armagh we never had such a thing as an examination from one end of the year to another. Of course, girls didn't learn Latin in those days. We seem to have managed to do without it."

"Not many people can afford to educate their girls to be ladies of leisure nowadays," Una said shortly.

"O, I know that. Nobody knows it better. I often wish I'd been given a more practical training myself. Still, I don't see what help Latin is to a girl who's preparing for life."

When she said this, Una and Shaun giggled and she remembered — if only I could remember it sooner — that she had said it often before. I mustn't repeat the same things, she though, I simply must try not to.

"Well, I won't keep you from your lessons, Una dear," she said. "And good bye, Shaun. Cover yourself up well if you go out. It's awfully cold, besides being wet."

Two good byes and they were gone, running out together, badly brought up children. And she was alone in the big bright room, with Moira O'Neill already nodding in the chair opposite. I wonder should I mention about meeting Mr Madden? No, better not. Moira O'Neill is the last one to tell about meeting a man who might be thought a little common. Remember how she never said a word, years ago, when everyone thought *she* was common.

And, as she watched Moira O'Neill, Miss Hearne's mind moved in a familiar spiral from present to past, made a journey which had become increasingly frequent since her dear aunt died. It was so much easier to go back now; going forward was so frightening.

In that journey she saw Moira as she had first seen her: young, charming, common, an upstart who had come from nowhere to claim the prize. A scheming hussy they called her then, an unknown girl born on a farm in Fermanagh and educated by her uncle, a parish priest in some small place. A student in one of Owen O'Neill's classes and he twice her age at the time. But she had carried him off, a well-connected man, a professsor and the son of a well-known lawyer with money on his mother's side. Miss Hearne remembered her Aunt D'Arcy's comment at the time: that Moira was no more in love with Owen than with the man in the moon; that she had tricked and guiled and provoked him into marriage. She remembered too, Owen's mother, old Mrs O'Neill, a stiff old lady if ever there was one and the way she had snubbed Moira when she heard of the engagement. And I hadn't a good word to say for her myself, Miss Hearne thought, remembering all the gossip that ran against the new bride. It wasn't kind of me. But I'll give her her due, Moira, she put up with a lot of cold looks at the time. Those Thursday At Homes and all his relatives nodding their heads. She just sailed through them, and you never knew what she was thinking. And you'd never know now. She's deep. But she's the type to remember. So I'd better hold my tongue about Mr Madden. She'd find the commonness in him, quick enough, seeing she had it in herself.

She pulled her chair closer to the fire and put on her extra cardigan. She always felt too hot or too cold and she carried an extra cardigan, just in case. Moira went on knitting and asked about the new digs, and how they were. And Miss Hearne told about Mrs Henry Rice and how poor the breakfasts were, only tea and toast, but kippers on Sunday. And about Mr Lenehan and Miss Friel. And that there was an American there too. A Mr Madden.

She stopped then and looked at Moira, waiting for a question. But Moira's head was going jump, jump, and her chin was resting on her bosom. Dozing again!

Miss Hearne watched Moira until there was a

103

snore. Then she picked up a paper and read it for a while. But there was nothing much interesting in the *Observer*. All book reviews, and dispatched from foreign countries and long political articles. Dull, dull, but she read it, for soon tea would come.

It came at four. Ellen knocked on the door and wheeled the tea wagon in, the cups on the top shelf, the cakes and biscuits on the second and the sherry, jams and cheese on the bottom.

"O, my goodness, I was dozing again," Moira O'Neill said, waking up. "Put it over there, Ellen, and go and ask the master if he wants some tea. Excuse me, Judy dear, I must have been asleep for ages. You should have wakened me."

"No, no, you must be tired with all those children around you," Miss Hearne said politely. "I thought you deserved forty winks. I was just reading the *Observer*. Such an interesting paper."

"Ellen — call Miss Kathleen and Miss Una. Those poor girls are at their books night and day," Moira said, smiling at Miss Hearne.

"But they'll be a credit to you, I'm sure. They've got their father's brains."

Professor Owen O'Neill, monocle gleaming against the flames of the fire, came in, thrusting his curved pipe in his pocket.

"Hello, Judy."

"Hello, Owen, still working away?"

And Kathleen, ugly little Kathy, Miss Hearne's favourite, came sidling into the room, coming up to shake hands properly, her freckled face set in a smile. Miss Hearne remembered the days with her dear aunt. O, she reminds me of me.

Una came too, the handsome one, joking with her father about some book he had recommended. They're all such great readers, Miss Hearne thought, it's a pity they don't like the same books as I do.

Then the sherry, golden, the colour of warmth, and a biscuit to nibble with it. The first sip was delicious, steadying, making you want a big swallow. But it had to last.

The others took tea. Cakes and cheeses were passed around and in the confusion of movement and talk, Miss Hearne lifted her glass stealthily and let the golden liquid flow down her throat, feeling the shudder of pleasure as it went down, warming her all the way. Then she accepted cake and began to eat. Ladylike, but she ate a lot. Sunday tea at the O'Neills meant that you didn't have to bother with supper. And with the good breakfast she had eaten that morning, it was a day with no money spent. Maybe a glass of milk though, before she went to bed.

"Another sherry?"

"Well, really, I shouldn't. But it's so good."

She drank a second glass quickly and young Una lifted the decanter. "Let me fill your glass up, Miss Hearne."

"No, thank you, I couldn't really. Two is my absolute limit."

There! She'd done it again, saying something she always said. She saw the small cruel smile on Una's face — like the day I came into the room and she and Shaun were saying over and over, imitating me, "Your mother will bear me out on that, won't you?" Over and over and it's what I always say — well, I won't say two is my absolute limit ever again. Anyway, a child like her, what does she know about life? Or life's problems.

Miss Hearne stared mistily at the empty sherry glass. Or this, the temptation she puts in my way. What does she know about about people, a young girl of her age? Mr Madden. James Madden, of New York. Mr and Mrs James Madden, of Belfast and New York. The former Judith Hearne, only daughter of — O, I must stop that at once.

And Miss Hearne smiled, an inward smile which lit her black nervous eyes. She pulled off her extra cardigan. "My goodness, it's warm now," she said, looking at ugly little Kathleen. "Isn't it, Kathy dear?"

After the tea things had been cleared away, Professor O'Neill and his daughters again retired to their rooms and books. Moira O'Neill began to look around her as though she had lost something and was trying to think where she had put it. She wants to get the dinner on, Miss Hearne decided, it's time to go. Although it would have been so nice to stay in the warmth, in the brightness of the room, among the family. Yet the children still say "Miss Hearne." Funny, you'd think they could say "Judy" when they know I like it. Judy. Like the old days on the Lisburn Road. Little Judy.

She felt the tears come into her eyes. That's the sherry affecting me. O, I mustn't be sloppy. Look at something — quick.

She looked at her long pointed shoes. It was always comforting to look at them when tears threatened. The little buttons on them, winking up at her like wise little friendly eyes. Little shoe eyes, always there.

Later, as she stood in the hall, putting on her raincoat, Moira opened the door and announced that the rain had stopped. And then, at the end of the avenue, hurrying, came Shaun, his hair sticking up like a fuzz of wet feathers on his head. He looked surprised to see her standing on the steps, as though she were waiting for him.

"Well, Shaun, what luck," his mother said. "Just in time to see Miss Hearne to her bus stop."

"O, please don't bother. I'm perfectly all right."

"Not at all," he said politely. "Just wait a second till I leave these books in the hall. I'll be with you in a jiffy."

They set off together, she bizarre and faltering in her crimson raincoat and her waxen flowered red hat; he embarrassed and uneasy, trying to find a subject of conversation. At the end of the avenue they stood under the harsh orange glare of the street light, urging the coming of the bus with hopeful remarks.

"Is that one?"

"No."

"I thought it was."

"I did too."

"They never come when you want them, do they?"

"Maybe that's one now?"

"No."

They made little half-turns, turning back towards each other, nervous awkward, hoping for it to end. This is the way with men, she thought, always like this. They don't seem to want to be alone with me, it's as if they're trying to get away. O, I know he's only a boy and I remember him as a baby I knit little woollen bootess for, but he's a man, a man like all the others. And he wants to get rid of me, to run off and do whatever men do when there aren't women around to hold them down. All like this, afraid to pair with me. Except James Madden? No, he wasn't. Just a little bit at the end of Mass, maybe, shuffling his feet. But then he asked me to go out. *He asked me out.* He wanted to say, he was afraid *I'd* run away. James Madden, a man's man. She looked at Shaun's young unfinished face. A boy, a baby boy.

Then the bus came rushing over the top of the road, a double-decker, a huge box on wheels, running down over the grey belt of wet road with the little driver sitting up straight against the glass in its flat face. It stopped, squishing its huge tyres and Shaun stepped off the pavement and held her arm as she went up beside the ticket-punching conductor. And she turned to say, as always:

"Thank you very much, Shaun dear. And be sure to thank your dear mother for me."

And the bell jangled, the driver started. The bus whirled off, to the last stop, the lonely room, the lonely night.

# CHAPTER
# SIX

## LENEHAN

Ah, but you want to see the codology that's goin'
on these days in my digs, yon big streel of a Yank
I told you about and that ould blether of a Miss
Hearne, the new one that just moved in, I tell you,
never seen the like of it, one ould fraud suckin' up
to the other and the pair of them canoodling, it
would turn your stomach. No, nothing like that,
the pair of them's past it and I don't think the
Yankee Doodle has that in mind at all. And as for
her, she never had it nor never will, if you ask me.
No, the geg of it is, as I was tellin' you, it's the one
ould fraud matched up against the other. She's a
real Castle Catholic type, very refained, the grand
lady with her rings and bangles and her la-di-da.
And this ould Yank, he wouldn't look me in the
face after the tellin' off I give him, a fine Catholic,
a bloody Orangeman at heart he is, but anyway, he
thinks she has a bit of cash put away, you can see

it the way he's suckin' up to her and she the same of him. And the best joke of it is, it's my bet and I'd lay a bottle of Jameson on it, neither one of them has a five-pound note to their name. He took her out to the pictures the other night and yesterday, when I was coming out of Mullen's after wetting my thirst, who should I see but the pair of them, strollin' along like young love. I folleyed them just for the crack of it, and you shoulda heard him givin' off steam about the glories of the States, you'd think he was John D Rockefeller, and her right back at him, as good as she got, about the wonderful times she had with her dear auntie. What age is she? I tell you that one will never see the fair side of forty again. But do you see the get of it, this boozy ould Yank, bloody ould lying flag-thumper talkin' a lot of balls about the Yew-nited States and this ould bag of a single woman, playing the Malone Road lady, and the two of them coddin' each other on until the day when they find out that neither one of them has a silver tanner to their name. D'you see the geg of it? Irish and Catholic, I tell you the most of the Catholics in this town are bloody little West Britons and, if they're not that, the pictures has turned them into comic cuts imitations of Yanks. And these two could well be the model, couple of ould farts, with their chat every morning about America, what the hell did America ever do for us, I'd like to know?

# MISS FRIEL

Mind you, Meta dear, I'm not one to complain, but if you knew the trouble I have sleeping in those digs of mine, it's a wonder I can keep my eyes open at all in class, the noisiest crowd of boarders I ever was in with and worse besides. I'm in terror of my life half the time when I go up those stairs at night. That American I told you about. A drunkard! Only last week I met him on the stairs when I was going up to bed, half seas over, he was, it was enough to put the heart across you. A big vulgar ill-spoken brute and the smell of whiskey off him would have killed a cat. It was as much as I could do to get past him on the stairs, he'd give you the shivers. Fifty? He's nearer sixty, but he doesn't let that stop him. There's a woman there in the digs, a decent enough soul, although, God knows, a temptation to no man, and you should see the way that drunken brute butters up to her, he'd butter up any woman who'd let him. *I* don't even let him speak to me, I keep my distance. But this poor woman is flattered by his attention, it's enough to make you sick, she's mad if she goes out with a man that drinks like that, how could you trust him? And foul language at the table, I had to complain about it, but what can you expect, it runs hand in hand with drink. When I think that most publicans here are Catholics, it makes me see red. I tell you, Meta, if you want to see what's wrong with Ireland, you'll just watch the people that come out of public houses. And take that Brenda Kelly that teaches over in Saint Aloysius, she and Patricia Herlihy came out of the training college at the same time, and Pat told me on her word of honour that Brenda Kelly drinks a couple of cocktails every single night in the week. Well, I ask you. If it's the likes of that we get to teach our children, can you wonder that they're emigrating and losing the Faith?

## MARY MCCLOSKEY

She could be doin' a line with the Yank, as Bernie says, but I never seen any signs of it. Bernie says the uncle takes her to the pictures and he took her to tea at the Plaza Hotel the other night, would be the first good feed she ever had if the bits of cheese and the cups of cocoa that I seen in her room are anny guide. It might be the dear feed though, she'd better mind her step with that ould Yankee slabber, I could tell her a thing or two, the time he come into my room that night when Bernie was there and grabbed at me, I know what was on his mind and it wasn't anny good, couldn't keep his hands to himself. I know what he's after, he has a bad eye on him, I seen him lookin' at me since then and that morning I was washing down the stairs with my dress up above my knees and him standin' below me on the landing, lookin' up. Never opened his mouth, just walked away, he could have stood there ten minutes if I hadn't seen him first. Ach, if it wasn't for the nuns and the letter the mistress would write my da, I'd look for another place, Bernie or no Bernie. Oney Bernie says he's going to marry me, sure I'm too young to be married, he knows that, that's why he says it. But Eily Monaghan got married at home at fifteen, that was because the fella done somethin'. All fellas is the same, they don't care about you, they just want satisfaction, an' it's a mortal sin I couldn't tell the priest, O what'm I goin' to do, maybe he'll marry me, it would be all right then, I could tell an' get absolution. Maybe he will, them pomes he wrote me, he's reely a lovely talker. But not good-hearted, that time he gave me the five pounds to buy the dress and coat, tellin' me to say my mother sent it, there's somethin' sneaky about him, couldn't look you straight in the eye, that's the height of it, all city people is the same, two-faced, he's feared of havin' a chile, always askin' when are you due? Annyway, all the better he's careful, he's a good date, you can eat all the pastries you like when you're out with him and he's a lovely dancer. Fat an' all, he's a lovely dancer.

## MRS HENRY RICE

I tell you, Bernie, it *is* my business, what my own brother does. Hasn't he been here nearly four months and never paid a penny of rent, not even a five-pound note to buy something for myself, and

114

him rolling in it, ten thousand pounds he has, if he has a penny. I tell you he has more money than he lets on, the least he might do is think of his sister, his nearest and dearest relative on this side of the ocean and not some old spinster woman that probably has plenty, a lady of leisure, if you please. Taking her out to the pictures and to dinner, if you please. If you think of all the dinners he's eaten here and never asked me if I had a mouth on me. No, that's not the point. I will not get rid of him, he's my own brother and besides, who would he leave his money to, he's getting on too, his health isn't good. His daughter? O, she's rolling in it, no fear of him leaving it to her, that husband of hers he hates. No, I'm going to put my foot down soon, see if I don't. I'm going to let her know that the bold Jimmy isn't the fine gentleman he pretends to be. Sure, how do I know what he takes her out for, if it isn't because she's the only person would listen to him and his eternal chat about new York? It's not the looks of her, he's not blind, maybe he thinks she has money too. Well, God knows. I can disabuse him of that idea. Either that or she's a miser, you should have seen her face when we were discussing the board and room and never eats a decent meal, just snacks that wouldn't keep a bird alive. O, when I think of it, all the prayers I've said and the novenas I've offered up that Jim would remember us over in America, since he got that money, and he was happy here, he wouldn't have forgotten us like this if she

115

hadn't run after him.

## BERNARD

Destroyed my thinking, he has, the bastard, that sinister look he's got, the informer type, a natural conspirator slinking around the house like a secret policeman. How could anyone possibly do any creative thinking in circumstances like these? And if he wants what it would seem logical for him to want — O blazes, why should I have to waste my time with this sort of sordid little intrigue when the work is suffering. I haven't done a tap for weeks. Everything was so peaceful until he showed up and aroused mama's cupidinous instincts. Cupidinous? Is that a word, no. Cupidity. Libidinous. Libidity. Ruthlessness. Get rid of him. Marry him off to his spinster if that's what he wants. But does he? Or is it money he's after, more likely, I'd think. But get rid of him — ruining my life her, the sod, and even Mary, the simple pleasures of the poor, I can't enjoy any more unless I'm sure he's out. Sadistic bastard. Ahh — never mind. Messire Machiavelli, I read, Niccolo's fine Italian hand. How'd it go? *When an evil has sprung up within a state the more certain remedy by far is to temporize with it: for almost invariably he who attempts to crush it — will what, yes — will rather increase its force and accelerate the harm apprehended from it.* And its present application. *Show him honour, regardless* of consequence. The evil will die out, Niccolo says, or its worst results will be deferred. The old British rule that, divide and conquer, a refinement of it. Niccolo's fine Italian hand. My fine Irish hand. Messire Riccio. Bernardus, it would be.

# CHAPTER
# SEVEN

Mammoth Mister Victor Mature, sweat streaming down his FACE, met and held the lion, bigger now as the close-up showed its MAMMOTH JAWS, its MAMMOTH FANGS. Fading to the small (double?) vanquishing the lion, and then, Victor Mature, life-size again, a handsome Samson, ready to meet his Delilah.

"Ooooh!" sighed the one and ninepennies. The screen, technicoloured bright, sent new wonders into the darkness. Samson Mature put forth his hand, took the jawbone of an ass and slew a thousand extras. Courts, princely men, the pomp of the Philistines, blonde woman Semadar (Angela Lansbury, she's lovely) and dark Delilah in two-piece silver sarong (Hedy Lamarr, she's lovely). A scentless splendour, a flat magnificence, the Bible in American nasals.

Miss Hearne, her glasses slipped furtively on her nose under the cover of darkness, saw Samson Madden stride in to the halls, dazzling all with the proud flex of his mighty biceps, the white flash of his smile. Saw Delilah, the woman who would destroy him, a beauty, irresistible. Blinded, chained to the wheel, Samson toiled, robbed of his virility, his great power, by her woman's whim. Then, ah, for all women have a soft spot, she, the temptress, is stricken by her deed. Raging, he seizes her, breaks the chains that bind him, goes forth to avenge himself on his enemies. He loves her still, he will always love her. And she went up unto the Temple of Dagon, her heart filled with love and longing. Through jeering hordes she leads him to the great columns, playing his secret game. He implores her, Delilah Judith, to leave for her own safety. She speaks to him of eternal love, but does not leave. She watches from the shadows, welcoming death. And Samson spoke with Madden's voice, unfolding the final stupendous spectacle.

Beside her Mr Madden ate jujubes and thought of California. Bible stuff was okay but there was too much talk in it. That lion though, that was something. He tried to remember a story someone had told him about Victor Mature. Lived in a tent while he was breaking into the movies. Stuck at it, only way to get anywhere. I'm going to ask her tonight. I got it all right in my mind now. After the movie. But now — wait! Samson is getting his stuff back. Those chains, tore like paper. And look at that! Thousands of extras. Blinded, led by a woman, Samson walked towards the pillars. The

Philistine mob jeered.

Blind, Miss Hearne thought, blind without a friend. How terrible. But she is there, his love, his guide.

Then, the big scene. Madden's experienced eye knew that this was it. It's colossal, hundreds of feet up. Strain, strain, he pushes the pillars. Look! Down. DOWN. Ker-ump! Millions of bucks it must have cost.

And then the ending. All's for the best, all's well. Colour, close-up, LIPS, FACES. And then the end, The End, coming right out at you, THE END. And the lights go on, everybody blinks.

She slipped her glasses in her purse and turned to him, smiling at Samson, seeing his red face, his bright tie. The lights dimmed again.

The news then, men diving, jumping, horses racing, planes zooming, cars roaring around corners, dividing into sections with all doing all at once. The house applauding, louder and louder. Miss Hearne and Mr Madden sat with their hands in their laps. No handclaps for her, a foreign queen. Let them give back the Six Counties and then we'll clap. Irish people, a disgrace, applauding like that. But Protestants, what can you expect, Scots Protestants, Black-hearted all.

After the news a cat and mouse comic. Smart-alec mouse escapes. She wonders why Mr Madden laughs. Comics are for children. Next Week We Proudly Present:

"Care for a coffee?" he said. "Let's go before

the queue gets in."

Upstairs in the mirrored chrome of the cinema restaurant, a waitress handed them menu cards, waited slackly for their order.

"Just coffee," Miss Hearne said.

He nodded. "Coffee. Two." And he looked around the big, half-empty room. "Up-to-date. Reminds me of home."

It was the fourth time he had taken her out and she knew by now that this sort of remark was a signal that he wanted to talk about America. There had been an evening at the pictures, two weeks ago, the first time. Both of them nervous, and he had eased it by talking of his daughter and the schools in New York. Then, during the walk in the Botnical Gardens, he told her of his exile's dream to settle down in Donegal. And the night he took her to dinner, he spoke of America, its wealth, its hugeness, its superiority to Ireland in all things material. It was all new talk and she had enjoyed listening. And now, a week later, faced with the prospect of sitting alone with her, he was trying to bring it around to America again. She would have preferred that he talk of himself, of her, of the future. But, nervous of him, she obliged.

"Are all the restaurants like this, then? Big places with modern stuff on the walls?"

"That and better." He seemed delighted with the question. He watched as the coffee was served, poured some, tasted it and held the cup up. "See

121

this? There's the trouble right there. This coffee stinks."

"Yes, I suppose it's better in the States. Of course, the people here are tea drinkers."

"Listen." He leaned forward. "I'm going to tell you something. You see this coffee? It's no good. Okay. Ever eat a hamburger here, or a hot dog? Sure you did. What they call a hamburger. But that's not a real hamburger, with mustard and relish. Real franks, you don't see them either, and the places that serve them — terrible! Y'know, in New York, on the corner of any street you can get a good hamburger, a good quick lunch. Like at Nedicks. Ever try to get a quick lunch in this town? You can't do it, can you?"

"I suppose not. But the people here don't eat hamburgers."

He smiled and put his big hand on her sleeve. Then he began to talk, his voice urgent, nasal, the voice of the salesman. As he spoke, she heard America, eager America, where men talk business as others talk love.

"Right Judy. You're absolutely right. Irishmen don't eat hamburgers, but who does? Americans do. Now, this is how I see it. Every year there's thousands of Americans come over to Ireland. Tourists. And they all go to Dublin and when they're in Dublin, they all walk on O'Connell Street. They want to see the sights. And to see the sights, they need time. They get homesick for some good American food, a quick lunch same as

122

they get at home. Now, that's where we come in, you and me, Judy. We can give them what they want."

But she heard nothing except Judy, Judy. Where did he find out her name was Judy and say it, Judy, like that, as if he had always known her? If he would say it again. Judy.

"That's my idea," he said. "And it's a moneymaker. What Dublin needs is a good American eating-place, right in the centre of town."

"A restaurant? But you'd need a lot of money."

"I have money. All I need's a partner, a person who believes in the future of this thing, same as me. I need a partner with equal capital. If I get that, I can't lose."

"It would be a cheap restaurant, wouldn't it? That's not a very nice job, running a place like that." (Samson in chains, Madden in a cheap coffee shop. No, no, he must be persuaded against it.)

He shook his head. "Wait a minute, Judy, you got the wrong idea. I'm not going to do it myself, I hire a chef and counter help. I just supervise. Think of the tourist business I'd get. And the publicity, word of mouth, people going back to the States, they say, 'Hey, I found a real American coffee shop right in the middle of Dublin.' Get it?"

"Well, it sounds like an awfully good idea.

**123**

Especially if you acted as manager."

"Suppose, just suppose, I came to you with a proposition like that. With the costs all worked out. What would you say?"

"Well — it's not for me to say. I mean, I'm not a business man. But I should think if I were, I'd probably say yes."

He looked at her. "You're not convinced. Then suppose I told you that I'll match any capital you put into it. What would you say then?"

"Well, I'm sure that would be convincing. Any business man would know you were sincere, in that case."

"Would *you* say yes?"

"O, I think I would. Yes, I'm sure you'll find a partner when the time comes. It's a very good idea."

"Great!" He leaned forward again and ran his big hand down her back. "You're a smart woman," he said. "You and me understand each other."

"Oh, Mr Madden!" Her face scarlet as her dress, she hastily pulled away.

"Jim. My friends call me Jim." He laughed. "Don't be so formal. I like you, Judy, you've got a good head on you."

"Well, thank you." She felt her hands shaking. "Thank you — Jim. Well, it's getting late. Shall we leave?"

But he seemed not to hear. "You know, a man has to have something to work for. Like a home and kids. That's what I miss now, my kid."

She nodded, his boldness forgotten, a look of pained tenderness on her plain narrow face. "Yes."

"Judy, I came home, I'll tell you straight out, because my kid doesn't need me any more. I could have gone on working, but what was the use? What was the use? Now, if I got this business going in Dublin, me and a good partner, I'd have reason to stay here. I'd be busy, see? That's what counts. Keep busy."

"Yes," she said. If it would keep him here, a restaurant, why not? "Yes, I'm sure you will, Jim. You'll get a partner. You won't have any trouble. I know. And I think it's an awfully good idea."

"Okay." He signalled the waitress. "I'll look into it, Judy. I'll check the costs and give you a full report. Okay?"

He paid the bill, over-tipped the girl, she noticed.

"Ready?" he said, and they went out through the brightly lit lobbby, past the waiting queues, out into the night wind which rushed like a thief along the streets. She looked up at the technical school where bright windows glared insomniac in the darkness. Mr Heron and the embroidery class. No need to worry about *that* any more. He did not speak and she, filled with a strange happiness, felt no need that he should. And so, they walked slowly down Wellington Place and reached the designated centre of the city, the staring white ugliness of City Hall.

There, under the great dome of the building, ringed around by forgotten memorials, bordered by the garrison neatness of a Garden of Remembrance, everything that was Belfast came into focus. The newsvendors calling out the great events of the world in flat, uninterested Ulster voices; the drab facades of the buildings grouped around the Square, proclaiming the virtues of trade, hard dealing and Presbyterian righteousness. The order, the neatness, the floodlit cenotaph, a white respectabe phallus planted in sinking Irish bog. The Protestant dearth of gaiety, the Protestant surfeit of order, the dour Ulster burghers walking proudly among these monuments to their mediocrity.

Box-like double-decker buses nosed into the Square, picking up patient queues of people, whirling them off quietly to the outer edges of the city. Like trained soldiers, Mr Madden and Miss Hearne marched to a queue and took their places behind a scuffed, furtive man who trailed a dejected greyhound on a leash. The greyhound nosed Miss Hearne's skirt, then turned away, moving his tiny padded feet in discomfort at the cold.

Standing there in the designated centre of the city, Miss Hearne waited, not to go home on the bus, but to go off, off to something better, something that might lead to something wonderful. She stood waiting for a word, waiting for him to tell that he needed her, that he wanted her.

He did not speak and yes, she knew, who knew better? It was hard to be forward, hard to find the words. She smiled: no matter, he would ask her soon. He was lonely, he had said he was lonely and he wanted her to share his life. It had been said, she felt, although it had not been put into words. That would come later.

And then the bus came rushing up and he helped her aboard. The conductor jangled the bell and they were off, off to the last stop, the pleasant memories of the evening, the night filled with hopes and plans.

But as he opened the door of the house in Camden Street, her pleasant thoughts were stopped by a light which flashed bright in the hall. Mrs Henry Rice stood in her curtained doorway, her hand on the switch, her sleeves rolled up, leaving her great white arms bare.

"Well, hello," she cried. "Did you enjoy the pictures?"

Mr Madden mumbled an affirmative. Miss Hearne smiled politely.

"Well, come on inside," Mrs Henry Rice said. "I've just finished washing Bernie's hair and I'm going to make a cup of tea."

Miss Hearne would have preferred to go directly to her room. But Mr Madden waited, leaving the decision up to her. And since Mrs Henry Rice was his sister, it didn't seem right to refuse. They took off their raincoats and went in.

Night gave a special flavour to Mrs Henry Rice's nest. The coloured lampshades glowed orange, blue and green and flames yawned noisily up the chimney. Already a state of nightly undress was evident. A pillow had been laid on a sofa and a blanket was folded beside it. In the centre of the room, kneeling on a rug, was Bernard, stripped to his bulging middle, his head immersed in a towel. A big enamel basin of soapy water stood beside him on the floor.

"Wait, now, Bernie boy," Mrs Henry Rice said. She sat down on an armchair beside Bernard and towelled his hidden features and hair. Miss Hearne, her dark eyes fluttering with embarrassment, looked steadfastly at a stag in a forest in a frame on the wall.

The naked mound of Bernard's back rose up and the towel was lifted. Mrs Henry Rice shook out the blanket and wrapped it around him as he squatted on his hunkers and beamed at the guests.

"Mama thought you would like a cup of tea, after being out in the cold," he said to Mr Madden. "But I told her you wouldn't. I know you'd rather have coffee."

"Thanks." Mr Madden said. "We had coffee downtown."

"Did you go to the pictures, Uncle James? What picture did you see?"

"Bend over, baby. Let your hair dry at the fire."

"O, we saw *Samson and Delilah*, an American

film," Miss Hearne said. "Very good too."

"That's nice. Did you like it, Uncle James?"

Mr Madden seemed amused by Bernard's politeness. He laughed. "You wouldn't like it. It's made in America. And you don't like anything from America, do you, Bernie?"

"That's not true," Bernard said, but his face got red as he bent towards the fire.

The sight of his naked back had a most unpleasant effect on Miss Hearne, but she just couldn't seem to keep her eyes off it. So when a singing kettle whistled in the scullery, she started up to ask if there was something she could do.

"If you'd just wet the tea, there's a dear, while I tidy up this mess," Mrs Henry Rice said. "The tea is in the canister beside the teapot and the cups are all set out in here."

Miss Hearne fled into the outer darkness of the scullery. The idea, she said to herself, a big grown man, half naked like that in the middle of the room, I didn't know where to look.

She found the tea, poured, measured, and filled the pot. Then, wrapping a pot-holder around it, she went to the scullery door and knocked for permission to come back into the nest, saying to herself she hoped that fatty would have his shirt on by now.

But they did not hear her. The sound of angry, quarrelsome voices rose from the room.

"It *is* my business, Jim. You'd think it was your house, not mine, the way you talk."

And the sound of Bernard's voice, shushing. Then Mr Madden: "What I do's *my* business, May. If I want to take somebody out, that's no skin off your teeth. I'm sick of this. I'm going to bed."

What could *that* be? She heard a door slam. She came timidly out of the scullery. "It's only me," she called. "Tea's ready."

"Yes, dear. Come on in," Mrs Henry Rice said.

Bernard had not put on his shirt. He sat wrapped loosely in the blanket. And Mr Madden had gone.

"Yes, he went to bed," Bernard said, watching her with amusement. "He didn't want any tea. He said to say good night."

"O?"

"And who was in the picture?" Mrs Henry Rice asked, taking the teapot out of her hands and putting it on a little hob beside the fire.

"Victor Mature, I think his name is," Miss Hearne said. He might at least have waited until she came back.

"I like him, Victor Mature. A fine big man. Now, come here, Bernie, and let me feel if your hair is dry. The tea will be wet in a minute."

Bernard let the blanket fall completely, revealing obese, almost feminine breasts. "Uncle James likes the movies. He goes three or four times a week."

"Well, Jim hasn't much to do with himself these days," Mrs Henry Rice commented. "It's a

**130**

terrible thing for an active man to stop work like that. I think he'd have been far better off to have stayed in the States and not come back here where there's nothing for him."

Nice loyalty between a brother and sister, Miss Hearne decided. Discussing him in that disparaging way in front of a stranger. For, after all, I am a stranger. To her, at least.

"Well," she said. "I understand Mr Madden is considering going into business over here."

"Business?" Mrs Henry Rice said. "It's the first I heard of it."

But Bernard said: "Well, he might at that. There's lots of things he could do."

"What, for instance?" Mrs Henry Rice wanted to know.

"Well, he has some money, Mama. He could start a small business."

"Is it the pub, you mean? And wouldn't he be his own best customer, if he did? You know, Miss Hearne, he'd be far better off, Jim, if he was to put his money into a house. A guest house, for instance. I've told him many a time I might run it for him. Ah, poor Jim, never had a head for business."

"O, is that so?" Miss Hearne said, with an edge to her voice. "I should have thought quite differently. Indeed, he impresses me as having a very good financial sense, your brother."

"Jim, is it? Opening the doors of taxis, that's more in his line."

"What's that?" Miss Hearne said, and her heart gave a jump.

"O, excuse me," Mrs Henry Rice said. "I shouldn't be boring you with family troubles. It's just that Jim annoys me, really he does, the way he wastes his time."

"Now, mother," Bernard whispered. "Miss Hearne wouldn't be interested."

"O, but indeed, I am," Miss Hearne assured him, and felt she could have bitten her tongue out as she said it. "What did you mean, opening the doors of taxis?"

"I meant he — "

"Now, mother, " Bernard spoke hurriedly. "Uncle James wasn't always a commissionaire. He had lots of jobs over there. And he did very well considering everything. Had his own car and gave his daughter a good education. It's not every man can say as much."

"A lot of good that does me," Mrs Henry Rice said. "I don't see much of it. Never as much as offered me a day's rent all the time he's here."

"Mother!" Bernard looked upset, more credit to him, Miss Hearne thought. But what was that, opening the doors of taxis? A commissionaire, did he say? A doorman? Oh, no!

"I'm sorry," Mrs Henry Rice said. "I suppose Jim has his good points after all. But I must say he doesn't spread himself, not on his family, anyway. Only on outsiders."

"Are you referring to me?" Miss Hearne said,

her dark shifting eyes suddenly lit with anger.

"Of course not,"

"O, yes you are. Did you ask me in here to insult me, I'd like to know?"

"Now, now, don't get all excited," Mrs Henry Rice said, holding out fat white arms in supplication. "I didn't mean anything of the sort. In fact, it never even occurred to me. Outsiders, no, I mean some of those fellows he spends his time with, buying them drinks, the bunch of good-for-nothings. Like that Major Mahaffy-Hyde that he's taken up with, a worthless streel of a fellow and not even a Catholic."

"I see. Well now, if you'll excuse me, Mrs Rice, I'm going to bed."

"Won't you have a cup of tea? it's ready now and I'd be mortified if you took offence where none was intended. Really I would."

"That's quite all right," Miss Hearne said, standing up. "We'll just say nothing more about it. Good night."

She gave the door a tiny bit of a slam when she went out. The immortal cheek of some people! You'd think I'd asked him to take me out and spend money on me. O, the nerve of her. The vulgar lump, with her precious Bernie sitting up there half naked and him a grown man. O, I'll give her notice, really I will. The cheek of her!

But the anger had brought on that awful shaking so that she could hardly get her key out of her bag to open the door of the bed-sitting-room.

133

A commissionaire, Bernard had said. A doorman.

As she fumbled with the key, a female voice whispered from the stairs above:

"Is that you, Bernie?"

Miss Hearne looked up and there was Mary, the maid, tearful and nervous, standing at the head of the stairs. Bernie, indeed, the child was pretty familiar with him, wasn't she?

"Mary, I wonder if you would help me with this lock? I can't see it in the dark here."

"O, yes, 'm'." And Mary came down, took the key and opened the door. She drew Miss Hearne's curtains, lit the gas stove and asked if there was anything else.

"No, no, good night. And thank you," Miss Hearne said closing the door on her. Funny, her being up and waiting for Bernard like that. But goodness knows, she had troubles enough of her own without worrying about servant girls.

She sat down on the bed to unpin her hat. Her eyes went to the mantelpiece and there was her dear aunt, looking down at her, stern, reminding her of her behaviour.

A nice thing, Judy, her aunt said. I don't know what's come over you. You'll be no better than a serving girl yourself if you get mixed up with that man. A doorman, Imagine! Common as dirt. And that awful sister of his, vulgar woman, insulting you to your face.

"She didn't," Miss Hearne told the picture. "She didn't insult me. And how do you know if she's telling the truth? He might not have been a doorman anyway. That might just have been talk. He's nice and he's polite. He *is*."

She looked away from her aunt's accusing stare, remembering that her aunt was hard to please, and a little selfish too, if the truth were known. You wanted me all to yourself, she told the picture. Just as long as I was there to read you Sir Walter Scott every evening and make your Bengers' Milk at bedtime, you didn't care what happened. You never let me meet anyone and you tried to put everyone off me. And Manus McKeown, the only young man who did come calling, do you remember what you said about him? O, yes, he wasn't good enough because his people owned a pub and sold drink after hours and had been prosecuted for it. And Manus that afterwards bought one of the biggest golf hotels in the country with the money he came into. O, he wasn't good enough for you, nobody's good enough for you, nobody ever was and nobody ever will be. And it's all your fault that I am where I am today, being insulted by some fat old landlady and living in furnished rooms.

She got up then and went to the mantlepiece. She turned the photograph towards the wall. Then she looked at the black *passe-partout* back of the photograph. There, she said, I'll do what I want without your interfering.

Judy, he had called her. Judy, and tonight he had said that he needed someone to do things for.

135

Tonight he had come as close as anything to telling her he wanted her for his wife. Only it had been on such a short notice. If they had known each other longer he would surely have spoken. Judy, the way he said it, with his American drawl. Judy.

But then before her, making the shaking start in her hands, came the faces of Bernard and his mother. Bernard, with his fat white tummy, his face uneasy, trying to talk nicely about his uncle, and his mother, sitting on her chair like a huge cream puff, her manner contemptuous, insinuating things about her own brother. "All he was fit for was opening the doors of taxis." James Madden, dressed up in the ridiculous uniform of the doorman at the cinema, bowing as he helped a lady and gentleman in evening clothes into a long black limousine. James Madden in revolving doors, with half a dozen suitcases tucked under his arms, James Madden saluting, as a taxi full of guests drew up outside the great hotel. A doorman, a lackey, a servant. Common, common as mud.

Contrite, she looked at the mantelpiece, at the photograph turned to the wall. You're right, she told her dear aunt, right, you could never introduce him to a man like Owen O'Neill. Or to Dan Breen, who had his own firm of solicitors and was a Master of the Hunt once. No, he might do all right for America but he wouldn't do for her. I'll just have to drop him, or drop out of things if I ever get mixed up with him. But drop out of what things? she said, nobody cares any more. And Dan Breen, since he moved to Dublin, never a word out of him or his family. Not a line. And that little Una O'Neill making mock of me every Sunday. Who cares what I do any more? Drop out of what, indeed? James Madden may be common, but he's a man, a good Catholic and he has enough money to live decently now with all those common jobs behind him.

Yes, and what's wrong with that? she asked the hidden face behind the photograph. What in the world is wrong marrying a decent man like that? And if he went to America who would know the difference what he is? One man's the same as another over there, rags to riches, the whole lot of them. There's not a single thing wrong with James Madden that a good woman couldn't change. And he's no fool, he can be taught to change his ways.

She lay back on the bed and the tears were in her eyes and her whole body was shaking. She mustn't think of it, because if she started wanting it, she'd have to have it and feel awful afterwards and be sick for days. No, no, she told herself, and looked up to the Sacred Heart for strength. He looked down, wise and stern and kindly, His fingers raised in Warning. No, He said, you must not do it. It would be a mortal sin.

"O, You're right, You're right, I mustn't," she said aloud, burying her face in the bedclothes, crushing and twisting up her best rose pastel dress. "No, no, and besides, he isn't worth it."

137

James Madden, with a horrid white cap like the soft drink advertisement, and a white apron, tossing pancakes at the ceiling and she on her knees in a charwoman's apron washing the floor. Over the counter the sign said, "Jim's Cafe". No, no, no, no, she cried, pushing her face deep in the pillow and then she began to cough and the cough tore at her. I must have something to stop it, something to stop it, to cut the phlegm. I must. Just a little one, it won't be more, I promise Thee, O Sacred Heart.

She slithered off the bed, twisting her stocking, putting a ladder all the way up to the knee. She scrabbled in the bureau drawer for the keys to the trunk and took them out with a hand that shook so the keys rattled. She unlocked it and found one bottle, wrapped in cheap brown paper. Then, apologetically, she clambered up on the bed and turned the Sacred Heart towards the wall. He looked at her, stern now, warning that this might be her last chance ever and that He might become the Stern Judge before morning came, summoning her to that terrible final accounting. No awakening to see James Madden, to walk ever in the city, to ever see him again. Tonight I may cast you down, He said. My Patience will not last for ever.

But the rage had started inside her, the pleasant urgency to open it, to fill a glass and sip it slowly, to feel it do its own wonderful work. So she turned the Sacred Heart to the wall, scarcely hearing the terrible warning He gave her.

Then she scrambled off the bed, shaking, took a glass from the trunk and scrabbled with her long fingers at the seal, breaking a fingernail, pulling nervously until the seal crumbled on the floor and the cork lay upended on top of the bedside table. She took off her clothes quickly, wise in the habits of it, because sometimes you forgot, later. She pulled on her nightdress and dressing-gown, sat quietly by the fire, shaking a little still, but with the rage, the desire of it. Then, while the bottle of cheap whiskey beat a clattering dribbling tattoo on the edge of the tumbler, she poured two long fingers and leaned back. The yellow liquid rolled slowly in the glass, opulent, oily, the key to contentment. She swallowed it, feeling it warm the pit of her stomach, slowly spreading through her body, steadying her hands, filling her with its secret power. Warmed, relaxed, her own and only mistress, she reached for and poured a tumbler full of drink.

# CHAPTER
# EIGHT

Bernard stopped outside Miss Hearne's door and knelt down. He put his eye to the keyhole and saw her. In her dressing-gown. He listened for the sound of voices. Nothing. Behind him, someone whispered:

"Bernie?"

Mary, half dressed, looking over the banister.

"Is he in there?" Bernard whispered, pointing to Miss Hearn's door.

"No. He went in his own room — Bernie, I want to see you."

"Go back to bed. I haven't got time."

"But Bernie, you promised."

"Go to bed. I've got to see *him*. It's important."

Dejection, she waited as he went up and crossed to Madden's room. "Go on," he whispered. "Get up to bed."

He watched as she went slowly up to the attic. Satisfied, he knocked quietly on his uncle's door.

"Who is it?"

"Me. Bernard."

Madden opened the door. He wore long white underwear, shirt and shoes.

"What?"

"Can I come in for a minute?"

Madden turned his back on Bernard and walked slowly to the bed. He sat down on it, his back propped up by pillows. He grasped his left thigh with both hands and swung his crippled leg up on the bed. Bernard came inside and closed the door.

"I'm sorry to disturb you, but I wanted to explain about tonight."

"What?"

"I mean mother saying those things about you taking Miss Hearne out. I hope you don't think I had anything to do with it."

Madden did not answer.

"Honestly, Uncle James, it was as much of a surprise to me as to you."

"Relax," Madden said. "Sit down. I'm not going to squeal on you, if that's what you mean."

"No, no, I just wanted to let you know my position."

Madden pointed to a pack of Camels on the bedside table. "Have a good cigarette and give me one too." He enjoyed making Bernard wait on him. He took his time about lighting the cigarette, letting Bernard hold the match until it had almost burned his fingers.

"What's wrong with May, anyway? What's the matter with her?"

"Well, it's the rent, Uncle James. She thinks you should pay her something for the room."

"Her own brother?"

"Well, you know what Mama's like. Between ourselves, she thinks you're better off than you've told her. And she thinks Miss Hearne has set her cap for you."

"I don't get it."

Bernard sighed. "She thinks Miss Hearne wants to marry you."

"Ah, she's crazy."

"I know. But she's always getting ideas like that. Honestly, I can't move hand or foot, but she thinks I'm planning to leave her. Every time I try to do something on my own, she stops me."

"Hah! You never wanted to."

Bernard shrugged.

"Want to ask you somethin'," Madden said. "You think she's got dough?" He pointed his thumb at the floor, like a Roman senator calling for death.

"Who, Mama?"

"*Judy Hearne*"

"I don't imagine so. Why?"

"You don't imagine so. Jesus Murphy, you and May are two of a kind. Where d'you think she got all them jewels? She's a real lady, Miss Hearne, a fine woman. And smart too, she's interested in what goes on in this world. She's not like you and May and the other jerks in this house. She's got class. And dough. And what's more, she's the

142

kind of woman if she likes you, there's nothing she wouldn't do for you."

Bernard's face was showing signs of weary irritation. But he still played diplomat. "Think so? Well, you might be right."

"I *am* right. I'll tell you something. Tonight, when we were out, I was explaining an idea I got. You know what she said? You've got yourself a partner. Her very words. I'd put money into that, she said. Smart business woman, though, wanted to know the details, costs, overhead, capital. Okay, I said, I'll give you a report. What do you think of that?"

Bernard make a mock salute. "Congratulations. Does the deal include marriage?"

"Lay off! Who said anything about marriage?"

"No one. I only thought . . ."

"Well, don't. I'm not marrying anybody, get that straight. What do you think I am? This is a business deal, purely business. Hell, I haven't made any passes at her, there's nothing like that between us. That's why I was mad at your mother. There's nothing between us, not a thing. And you can tell your mother I said so."

Bernard stood up. "All right, I understand. Good luck to you."

Madden swung his bad leg off the bed and began to pull his shirt over his head. Watching him, Bernard stuck his tongue out. "Good night, Uncle James."

"Good night," Madden said from the folds of

his shirt. "Close the door when you go out."

When Bernard had gone, Madden took off his long underwear and put on pyjama pants. Then he heard whispering in the corridor. He put on a bright blue robe and jerked his door open.

Bernard fled down the stairs. Mary scuttled barefoot up to the attic. Madden saw that she was wearing her shabby grey tweed overcoat over a short pink slip. He stared her out of sight. Short slip, white creamy legs, O Christ, a pleasure it would be.

He closed the door: forget it, only leads to trouble. What kind of guy are you, anyhow, at your age, you should be ashamed. Lie down, forget it. Now, that restaurant deal. Might go up to Dublin for a couple of days, look the place over, make a few inquiries. After tonight, I got a backer. After tonight, I can get going again, make a new start. Business. And May — ah, May, what does she know about business, sticking her nose into my private affairs.

He carefully removed his left shoe and got into bed. He put the light off. But in the darkness, images came.

Young — Christ, is there a Mann Act in Ireland? She's just a kid, scared of me since it happened, can't look me in the eye. That morning I went out for a crap and she was on the stairs. Up her legs, all the way. Ahh, I'm rotten — why can't I stop it? A country kid, if they knew back in her home town, they'd tan the arse off her. No, she wouldn't talk. But if they found out, her father, some big country bastard breathing murder. Forget it, can't you?

Still — she'd be nice. Scared of me. Nice, I haven't had a piece since . . . Don't get it, that's why I'm all worked up. A guy like me, used to it regular, needs it, keeps you healthy, at my age that's important. That counts. Ah, forget it, get to sleep.

But the images came. Flashing, fading, coming close, close. Breasts, thighs, bellies. Moving, asking — give it to me.

And her overcoat on the floor, the slip torn down off her back. Yes.

Christ, he groaned. Let it be. Let it be.

But nobody would know, no harm. *Nobody would know*. She won't tell.

Just this once. Just . . .

He stood up, hot excited, his legs trembling. Listened to his heart beat out a loud dead march. With a shoe horn he adjusted his specially built shoe. He put his other foot in a slipper, wrapped his blue robe about him and went to the door. Quiet and dark. He went out.

Snores from Lenehan's room. Then up the half-flight of stairs to the attic. Easy does it. My heart, for christ's-sakes, you can hear it. No light in her room.

He opened the door gently, closed it behind him. Moved towards the bed. She was awake.

"Who's that? Is that you, Bernie?"

He said nothing, found the edge of the bed and sat on it, jangling the worn and twisted bedsprings.

"O, Mr Madden, is that you . . .?"

"Quiet," he whispered, his voice trembly and hoarse. "You'll wake the mistress."

"O, mister, don't. Mister, please!"

He searched for her on the bed now, his hands feeling her face, her breasts, like a boy playing blindman's buff.

"Quiet now, quiet and there'll be no trouble."

"Don't, mister. I'll yell, mister . . ."

"Easy there. Be nice. It will only take a minute, honey. Be nice, be nice, easy — easy." Patiently he fumbled with the neck of her nightdress.

And she was quiet. Her body shrank away from him, her fretful hands gave him the pitiable resistance his ageing senses needed. He fumbled patiently but all coherence was gone. He had found her; in the darkness he tore and shook her like a dog at meat.

"Easy, easy. Be nice, be nice, just a minute, a minute."

He heard himself moaning, heard her muted terrified pleading. The bedsprings whirred and jangled in the darkness like an old-fashioned clock readying the stroke of one.

In a surprisingly short, a surprisingly timeless moment, he lay sweating, seeking memory by her side.

It came back, as memory will, coupled with

fear. "It's okay now," he whispered. "Okay. You be nice to me, I won't tell the mistress. Okay? Okay?"

She was weeping. She did not, would not answer. He rolled stiffly off the bed, wrapped his blue robe right around him, found the draw-strings of his pyjama pants.

"Nothing," he muttered. Nothing happened. Just a little fun, eh Mary? Just a little fun. Now, you be nice, be nice."

He heard her turn to the wall. Ah, what the hell! He left the room as carefully as he had entered. Dragged down-stairs to his own bed.

O Christ, what did I do that for? What a shit I am, a nogood shit, will I never stop? Why did I, why did I, why did I . . .? And only a kid, she is younger than Sheila, what age is she? I don't know, she looked older to me. Older than that, sure, sure. Christ, they should lock me up, I can't control myself. Like those guys you read about who — no, no, I'm all right, just normal, any normal man would take it if it was offered like that. And she won't tell. She knows what's good for her. She won't tell.

But fear ran through him like a sickness. Remembered fear. Somehow or other, sooner or later, they always did.

# CHAPTER
# NINE

At half-past ten on the following morning there was a knock on Miss Hearne's door. Miss Hearne woke from a thick, confused doze and called: "Who's there?"

"It's me, Miss. Mary. I've come to clean the room."

"Never mind. I'll do it myself. Leave me alone."

She screamed this out in an arrogant manner, slurring the vowels in such a way that her voice sounded altogether different. But Mary, pre-occupied with her own troubles, was in no mood to worry about other people. It had been like a bad dream, what happened, but her torn nightdress told her it could not be dreamed away. And she was afraid to face *him* again, now or ever, the dirty ould slabber. She couldn't even tell Bernie what had happened because Bernie would want to know why she didn't let a yell out of her. An' ruin myself, she answered the question, easier to let him feel away for a bit, an ould gaum like him, it was all over in a minute an' besides, if my dad ever found out, he'd kill me an' if I yelled, Mrs Rice would come an' then I'd be sent home. The dirty ould slabber, he knew I couldn't tell on him. I'll lock the door tonight, so I will, an' if he comes back, I'll throw the chairs about an' wake the whole house.

"Go away," Miss Hearne repeated. "Go away."

Ah, for all you have to worry, y' ould cod, Mary thought, looking at the closed door. She bent down, picked up her broom and pail, and went into Miss Friel's room, which was empty.

Wakened, Miss Hearne looked dully at the gas fire. The room was hot and very dry. The bottle beside her was empty and a second bottle, almost full, stood beside it. She had no idea of the time. The curtains were still drawn and the lights were burning. She turned the stove off, pulled the curtains and let the daylight in. Then feeling light-headed, but full of high spirits and power, she poured herself another drink.

A drink would put things right. Drink was not to help forget, but to help remember, to clarify and arrange untidy and unpleasant facts into a perfect pattern of reasonableness and beauty. Alcoholic, she did not drink to put aside the dangers and disappointments of the moment. She drank to be able to see these trials more philosophically, to examine them more fully, fortified by the stimulant of unreason.

Thus, she did not shirk consideration of the fact that she had sat up all night in a chair, that she might have made a lot of noise, that everyone might know her secret. She was drunk, so she found these possibilities amusing but unlikely. She did not forget her unpleasant conversation with Mrs Henry Rice. She remembered it with relish and her mind triumphantly altered the facts to a more bold, more heroic pattern.

What if he is a doorman? Yes, I put her in her place, the fat hussy. Don't you dare insult me, I said, don't you realize you're merely a common lodging-house keeper? Don't apologize, my good woman. You're forgiven.

Forgiving, she sat down in her chair, tumbler in hand, and turned to her aunt for confirmation. But her dear aunt was turned towards the wall. Poor aunt turned to the wall like a naughty little girl. O, she wouldn't have liked that at all.

All right, I'm coming, she told her aunt condescendingly, lurching to her feet again. I'll set you right, aunt dear, but you must promise not to be nasty again. Promise now! She turned the picture over and set into minor convulsions by the outraged look on her aunt's stiff face. Smile, she said, and the photograph smiled weakly. That's better, aunt dear. That frown — we've had too much of it.

The frown was familiar. Remember, Judy said, when I came back from convent? In nineteen thirty-one and I wanted to go to the Swiss finishing school? Ah, you frowned then, better stay here in the good home provided for you, you said, and we'll see what we will see.

So she stayed. Where else was there for her to go? Aunt D'Arcy was very musical and there were musical evenings at home with dear old Herr Rauh and little Evaline de Courcy as soloists. And the hours of daily piano practice, a pity, Aunt D'Arcy said, that Judy has so little talent for anything; with this depression in industry, eligible young men are hard to find, and the few there are want a *dot* and if there's no money, then they want a great beauty, a beautiful woman can improve a man's chances, especially if she comes from a good family. A pity, her aunt said, that Clodagh, Judy's mother, married a bit unwisely in that respect. Family, she meant, but of course it's not your poor dead father's fault that he was born a Hearne. And then, speaking of great beauties, you'll never have a quarter the looks of your poor mother. No, you take after the Hearnes, more's the pity. And they were nothing to write home about. Plain.

A plain girl with no *dot* has little choice but to reconcile herself to God's will, so Judy began to study shorthand and typing with Edie Marrinan, a convent classmate, a jolly chum and a plain girl herself. Edie got a civil service job out of it, passing the exam and settling down with a nice salary. But Aunt D'Arcy frowned on the idea, they're bigoted in the civil service, she said, if anything goes wrong, they'll blame the Catholic.

Still, fair's fair, and Aunt D'Arcy was a great one for fairness and when Judy had worked and reworked the Pitman's shorthand book until the binding came apart and was letter perfect in typing, her aunt phoned up Dan Breen, the solicitor, and a friend of the family, and asked him if he would have a vacancy for her niece.

He didn't, but he sent her to old Mr Donegan, another Catholic solicitor, and for three months Judy worked in his office, typing law documents and taking letters. Three months to the day, until her aunt came down with a stroke and Judy would have been downright ungrateful if she didn't give up her job and look after her aunt until things got better.

The stroke passed, but Aunt D'Arcy never moved out of the house again. She set up a system of bells in every room in the house, with strings running out of every door and up the sides of the stairs, all going to the front bedroom and joined at the head of the sickbed, so that Aunt D'Arcy, a huge old woman now, with a yellow face, a hawk nose and masses of white hair tumbled about her shoulders, could ring at all hours of the day and night for attention. And ring she did, driving them distracted, especially old Bridie, the house-keeper, who had a heart attack and died of it, at five o'clock one morning, running downstairs when the bells went off. And after Bridie's funeral, Aunt D'Arcy frowned and said, goodness knows, she couldn't be expected to break in a new girl, with herself bedridden, it was the least Judy could do to stay at home and see her through the few days left to her. So Judy stayed. It was lonely, nobody paid social calls any more. A few old friends came, talked in whispers to Judy in the hall, and left with the exaggerated quietness of people who have visited a house of sorrow.

When the second war started, Judy was twenty-seven. She made up her mind to study hard at the shorthand again and if she got a job, to use the money to get a good nurse for her aunt. And study it she did, despite the fact that her aunt, as though she sensed she was being deserted, rang her bells all day and every time she woke at night. But Judy worked the shorthand up until she was letter perfect and one day she went downtown with a newspaper advertisement in her handbag and came back with a job at three pounds a week in a big new contracting firm. That evening, she went up to the nuns at the convent and asked them to hunt high and low for a good woman to look after her aunt. God answered her prayers over the week-end and by Monday morning, the woman, a Mrs Creely, was settled in and running the big house like clockwork.

When she heard the news, Aunt D'Arcy said not one word to her niece for three whole weeks. Then she began to complain about the way Mrs Creely was ruining her treasures and her house. But Judy put her foot down, once and for all, and she went off to work every day, taking down letters and typing them out on a big new typewriter. And she hurried home in the evenings to give poor Mrs Creely a rest.

In 1941, the air raids came. The night the first big raid started, her poor aunt refused to go down to the cellar. It took Mrs Creely, Judy and an air-raid warden to get her out of bed, with her screaming and shouting and talking to people Judy knew were dead years ago.

She never came out of that stage. Dr Bowe, who came the next day, took Judy into the hall afterwards and said: "Miss Hearne, your aunt's mind has been affected by her illness and she will need a lot of nursing. She isn't a responsible person any more." In all fairness, Judy felt obliged to tell Mrs Creely and Mrs Creely said she was sorry, but Miss Hearne had better look for another woman, because she was giving her notice.

Miss Hearne never found another woman. Some weeks later the construction company sent her a letter with the money owing to her and told her her place had been filled. There were no maids to be had at that time, all the country girls had factory jobs, and Miss Hearne settled down to look after her aunt on her own.

It got worse. Her aunt gave her no peace. She rambled in her talk, she shouted at the top of her voice, she pulled and pushed at her niece and, when she was angry, she sometimes threw the chamberpot at her. But she was big and strong and she ate everything that was put in front of her, and when Dr Bowe looked at her he said she might live to be a hundred. Then, one day, he came with another doctor and they talked things over with Miss Hearne. They advised her to commit her aunt to a private home, a private asylum really, because she was so hard to handle and too much for Miss Hearne to look after alone. Miss Hearne had to admit she didn't know if they could afford it, her aunt had always been very secretive about money matters, all she knew was that Dan Breen, the solicitor, handled her aunt's affairs and sent a housekeeping cheque once a month. Dr Bowe said he would try to arrange something, there was always Purtysburn, the asylum, and the care was very good there. Then he and the other doctor went in to see Aunt D'Arcy. They came out after half an hour and said they were satisfied and would sign the papers. Miss Hearne would have to sign too, and it would be as well if she could find another relative to sign consent.

After the doctors had gone, Miss Hearne wept. She thought of the poor soul lying in the front room, not knowing what was being done to her. Will she know, she wondered, will she ever know even when they come and take her and put her in that place? But it was all for the best, her aunt would need special care, Dr Bowe had said that.

She dried her eyes and smoothed back her hair, for the sick woman had suddenly set all the bells jingling.

She went in. Her aunt's bed was near the

window in what had once been the drawing-room. The furniture, tallboys, sideboard, stuffed armchairs, antimacassars, knick-knacks, none of it had been moved out. A gas fire burned in the grate. Her aunt was sitting on the edge of the bed, big and sagging in her soiled nightgown, and Miss Hearne saw with horror that the poor thing was trying to put her stocking on.

'What are you doing, aunt dear? You must get back into bed at once, you'll catch your death of cold."

But her aunt continued to dress herself, putting on her slippers, looking around the room for her clothes, which were in a cupboard upstairs.

"You've hidden them, you've hidden them," she mumbled. "Ah, I can't get away at all, plotting behind my back, telling the doctors I'm mad, O, yes, yes, I know it all, Judy. I'm not daft, even though you're trying to have me shut up."

Miss Hearne knelt down beside the bed and caught the sick searching hands. "Please, aunt dear, please get back into bed. Whatever gave you that idea?"

"Taken out of my house by guards, yes, and locked away in a madhouse like a criminal. How would *you* like that, Judy?"

She wrenched her hands away from her niece and flung herself, hugh, despondent, across the bed. Her white hair hid her face, her fat old shoulders shook with weeping.

"Now, aunt, whatever gave you . . ."

"Ah, never mind lying to me, Judy, I hate a liar. It's a judgment on me, Judy, me that took you in an orphan child that nobody wanted."

She turned, raising her bloated, tear-ruined face from the pillow. "Yes, a judgment, for God help me, I didn't want to see you put away in an institution and now to think that you, of all people, would lock me away like that, me that sheltered you and gave you a home and your parents dead in their graves."

Miss Hearne bent over the sick woman and put her arms around her shoulders. She pressed her face close to her aunt's cheek and began to sob, harsh noisy weeping that shook her body and tore at her breath. "You're not going anywhere, aunt dear, I'm sorry, I won't let them take you. I won't, I won't, I won't."

The sick woman's hand's, maniacal in their strength, twisted her niece around. Her yellow hawk face came close. "Promise me now?" she said in a desperate monotone.

"O, I promise, honestly, I do. I promise, I promise."

The strong arms crushed her, sweeping her into the folds of soiled nightgown. She wept, wept with her head on her aunt's breast, wept until there were no more tears. When she lifted herself up, the sick woman's eyes were closed and there was a faint smile on the tired, yellow face. She tiptoed out and when Dr Bowe called next day, she said she had changed her mind and that she wouldn't hear of it.

She had given her word: she did not go back on it. Her aunt lived five years after that promise, fighting and raving her way through every ghastly day, until one Sunday morning in 1947, Judy found her sitting straight up in bed, eyes open, her bloated hawk face fixed in its habitual frown of reproof as life suddenly deserted her.

After the funeral, there was very little money. Dan Breen, who settled everything, told Miss Hearne that her aunt had lived the last seven years of her life off a dwindling capital. Miss Hearne was left with an annuity of one hundred pounds a year. She was thirty-six and looked older. She had very few friends. The O'Neills, Moira in particular, had been very kind, asking her to come and see them, and there was Edie Marrinan, her old chum, and the Breens. She enrolled in a secretarial college and took a furnished room. She found it impossible to get back her former speed in shorthand, it was more tiring nowadays, but after a few months she began to apply for jobs as a typist. She was told they wanted young girls. And living in Belfast on a hundred pounds a year was impossible. She would have to think of something else.

Father Farrelly, her old parish priest, spoke to one of his parishioners, a Mr Meron, and she was engaged to teach embroidery at the O'Connell Technical School. But she still could not make ends meet. Then one day she met little Evaline de Courcy, who used to sing at her aunt's musicales long ago. Evaline said she was not well, and would Miss Hearne like to take some pupils for beginner's exercises. And so Miss Hearne went to Evaline's house every day to practise on her piano and soon she had three pupils of her own. Beginners, not much joy to it, but it helped. Evaline died the following year and there was a legacy of five more pupils as a result.

It was about this time that the bronchitis which had plagued Miss Hearne for some years began to get bad. She had an awful bout of it one evening when she was visiting her friend Edie Marrinan, and Edie innsisted that she take a few glasses of tonic wine to soothe the cough. Miss Hearne had often noticed that Edie drank quite a lot of tonic wine. In fact, she always seemed to have some ailment or other that needed a glass to soothe it. Although she seemed a big, healthy girl, full of high spirits, not the sort that needed building up.

"Come on, Judy, down with that," Edie said, pouring half a tumbler full of wine. And Miss Hearne drank it down. The coughing stopped.

"Put another away for good measure," Edie said. "There's nothing like it in the whole wide world when you're feeling rotten."

The second glass really soothed the attack, and Miss Hearne was persuaded to a third. And then the two of them sat there, finishing the bottle, chatting about old convent days and the funny goings on in Edie's branch of the civil service. Edie could tell a story, she really had the gift and when put to it, she would act it out, how this one walked, how that one talked, and the look on the face of the other one. She really was a caution. Miss Hearne had quite a fit of the giggles listening to her.

And the next time she had trouble with her bronchitis, she bought a big bottle of the tonic, drank it alone, and felt wonderfully well on it. It warmed her, it made sad things seem funny, and if you were feeling down in the mouth, or a little lonely, there was nothing like it for cheering you up. She said as much to Edie Marrinan afterwards, and Edie laughed and said, it's good, but whiskey's the best . . .

She and Edie drank several glasses of whiskey one night in Edie's digs. The next day Miss Hearne felt awful. She phoned Edie and told her and Edie laughed and said the only thing that will cure you, Judy, is a hair of the dog that bit you. Edie came over that same night with a Baby Power in her bag and Judy had to admit that it did wonders.

After that, she used to buy cheap whiskey in a shop in North Street where they were very discreet. Gin was cheaper and it didn't smell, but it hadn't the bite of the whiskey that was good for her bronchitis. And sometimes, when she needed it badly over a week-end, she would take the long tram ride out to Ballymacarret and buy it in a place that Edie showed her. There was nothing like it, medicinally, of course, to make you feel better. And goodness knows, Miss Hearne often thought, I need something to cheer me up.

For as the years wore on, there was not much to be cheerful about, old friends dying off, young men a thing of the past, and even Edie Marrinan, poor Edie, ill in a nursing home run by the nuns at Earnscliffe. And all the things Miss Hearne used to dream about in those lonely years with her poor dear aunt: Mr Right, a Paris honeymoon, things better not thought of now, all these things were slipping farther away each year a girl was single. So she cheered herself up as best she could and if she overdid it, it was a private matter between herself and her confessor, old Father Farrelly, and he was understanding, he liked a drink himself, right up to the end, in 1952, when he had a stroke one Friday night before devotions. But after him there were harsh young confessors, young men who didn't really understand the circumstances. So Miss Hearne made a novena, after she lost three of her pupils because that Mrs Strain said she smelled of it one day when she met her in the street. She stopped drinking then, didn't touch a drop. She bought two bottles and kept them in her trunk, a temptation which nightly it gave her comfort to resist. Truth to tell, she used to say to herself, I cannot afford even one bottle a month now, with things going as badly as they are and so little money about. The economies will help me struggle through.

So, no matter how down in the dumps, no

matter how the attacks of bronchitis racked her, no matter how much the mysterious shaking started whenever she was upset, she did not let a drop of liquor cross her lips. She prayed, and despite the fact that her prayers were not answered, she persevered. When she changed her digs and met Mr Madden, she felt a sense of victory, a partial fulfilment, a blessing of God upon her for her sacrifices. Not a drop for six months. Six long months. And now, staring at the stern form of her aunt, she realized this: that she had sinned again, that she had not only touched it, but had really gone at it like a madwoman, like somebody possessed.

"Tut, tut, tut," she said drunkenly reproving, wagging her finger at the little shoe-eyes which stared at her from across the room. The little shoe-eyes winked back, friendly, sharing the silliness of it all.

For this was what it did to be cheered up: nothing seemed bad, nothing at all, not even sitting here all night in her dressing-gown in front of the fire, not even Mrs Henry Rice and her insinuations, not even the fact that James Madden, ah — James Madden might not have been all he was supposed to be in America. It didn't matter, everything could be solved. She sipped her whiskey, feeling the oily yellow liquid burn her throat, warming her all the way. Yes, it didn't matter, one single little bit. It was all unimportant. Unimportant. Everything would be all

162

right. James Madden would ask her and she would say yes. And then she would show him how to behave. New York, the picture-postcard city, they would go off to it together, sailing away.

"Sailing, sailing over the ocean waves," she sang, smiling as she remembered Mr McSorley, the big fat basso who used to sing that song although he knew her dear aunt didn't like it.

"You didn't like it," she said to her aunt's photograph. "I wonder why? It was a jolly song, light of course, but a sort of sea chanty. I liked it."

Then she saw her aunt's frown. "Smile," she commanded. "Just this once: smile."

And the photograph, converted by the delightful logic of intoxication, smiled. Miss Hearne smiled back, and poured herself another drink.

Smiled the photograph, smiled her dear aunt, the picture smiled, yes, it smiled when she told it to smile, it was cheerful, cheerful, not a worry smiled the photograph, smiled the . . . sleepy-smiled the . . .

Slept.

# CHAPTER
# TEN

"Miss Hearne. Miss Hearne. Hello there? Miss Hearne?"

She was on the floor. OmyGod, where? Where? My room.

She raised herself on an elbow, staring in panic at the shaking door. Och, och, och, it cried.

"Yes," she said. "Yes. Who is it?"

"Mrs Rice. Are you sick? Are you all right?"

"Yes." O, that cracked-sounding voice. She cleared her throat. "Yes, I'm perfectly all right, thank you. I was sleeping."

"Are you sure?" the door said. "Would you like me to get you something? May I come in?"

"No, no, I'm all right. I just want to sleep."

"Well, let me know if you want anything," the door said.

It waited.

She waited.

Silence.

Then the footsteps going down the stairs. She

dropped her face back on the worn carpet. The trembling started in her arms and spread upwards to her shoulders and face. What did I . . .? When did it start? How long have I been lying here?

Through the window she saw the night sky silhouette the house across the street. Her little travelling clock screamed confirmation: eight-fifteen.

And this morning, last night, all afternoon, where and what did I do?

Events unrolled themselves then, like a reel of film spinning backwards in flickering confusion. Mrs Rice, yes, and then this morning, the maid came, last night I drank, I was upset, yes, Mrs Rice and what she said. James Madden a door-man.

But what had happened in the lost time, the dead time of drinking? What awful thing? The anxiety of not knowing began, set her trembling, brought sharp needle pains to her forehead: sweat trickled like tears along her cheeks. She stood up, looked at the spilled glass, the empty bottle, the other bottle kicked in a corner (I must have made a noise when I did that), the drink stain on the floor, the rumpled bed, the stale room.

There was none left. She looked at her trunk, but she knew it was hopeless. Both bottles were empty. She must manage the trembling, the nausea, the awful hours of conscience, without any help at all. For the moment, don't think, just get the place tidy.

In her dressing-gown, her hair rumpled and falling about her shoulders, she began shakily to set things to rights. The bottles she wrapped in old newspaper and hid in a dresser drawer. The stain in the floor would not come out. She abandoned it and then, cramming her parched mouth with sweet nauseating cachous, she began the frightening task of dressing.

It took ages. Badly rouged, over-powdered, her hair done up in a bun, she sat down in her chair at last, and let the shaking take its course. The fears came. How much noise, did I talk to myself the way I did in Cromwell Road, did I go out of the room or let anyone in? Or was it all quiet, sitting in my chair, oversleeping, medicinal drink to help me sleep?

She was so weary, so worn with the raveges of her sin. But God was weary too. He had suffered through her carelessness, her sinfulness. She knelt beside the bed and made an act of contrition.

"O, my God, I am heartily sorry for having offended Thee and I detest my sins above every other evil because they displease Thee my God Who are so deserving of all my love — and I firmly purpose — by the help of Thy Holy grace — never more to offend Thee — and to amend my life."

But this seemed too impersonal. She looked up at the Sacred Heart for guidance and saw with shame that He was turned towards the wall. She stood on the bed and turned Him around to face her. His eyes, as always when the sin was committed, were hurt and reproving.

"I am sorry, I am terribly sorry and I promise Thee that it will never happen again."

But He did not believe her. His eyes said as much: she half expected Him to shake His head and turn His sad face away. And who could blame Him? Why should He believe me when I'm such a backslider, such a weak, useless, hopeless sinner?

Useless and hopeless, she straightened the bed, lit the bedside lamp and went to the mantelpiece to stare at the photograph of her dear aunt. A good thing God took you away, she thought, a mercy. For if you could only see me now, how could you have borne the shame of it?

Penitence gave strength. The open admission of error helped to drive it out. Still trembling, but with new confidence, she lit her gas fire. She warmed her hands for some minutes, then went to the wardrobe and put on her old green tweed coat and a dark red hat. She turned the stove and lights out and locked the door. She felt light-headed and terribly weak, it was the want of food, she was sure. If she hurried, the teashop at Bradbury Place would still be open. A cup of tea and a sandwich would do wonders.

But there was to be no slipping out. When she reached the hallway, the curtained door opened to reveal Mrs Henry Rice, fat and curious, her bland eyes showing nothing of what went on behind them. She stepped close to Miss Hearne, took her arm and put her face very near. At that moment, Miss Hearne blessed her foresight in eating so many of the nauseating scented cachous.

"Feeling better now?"

"O, yes, thanks."

"Catch a chill or something? You certainly slept a long time."

"Well, I wasn't feeling up to the mark." (Woman to woman, I must find a bond.) "O dear," she said, holding her handbag tight against her stomach to stop the trembling. "We women have to put up with a lot. Men are so lucky."

Mrs Henry Rice raised her eyebrows. "You feel sick with it? Some do. I used to get awful headaches myself, every thirty-three days, regular as clockwork."

"I know," Miss Hearne said. "Headaches are even worse than being sick. Still, I do feel rotten."

But her lie had not taken. Mrs Henry Rice had opened a trap for her victim. She closed it now, with a smile of full-bloated malice. "Well it seems to affect you pretty merrily. Why, you were singing away all afternoon."

". . . No — I mean . . ."

"Yes, singing and talking away to yourself as happy as a lark. It's a wonder nobody complained, you were louder than the wireless."

"I — I used to sing a lot. I was — practising. I give music lessons, you know. I'm awfully sorry, I didn't realize I was disturbing anyone. I — suppose the walls are thinner than I expected."

168

"The walls in this house are not thin, they're old walls, very thick as a matter of fact. You'd have to shout at the top of your voice to be heard."

"Well, a person singing — you know the singing voice carries. The tones penetrate. I'm awfully sorry if I disturbed you."

"O, singing's loud, I know that. Why, there was a drunk man in the street last week, you could hear him a mile away. It's terrible noise a drunk man makes."

She knows. The bad, black-hearted slimy voice of her. O, I could kill her. "Well, I must be on my way. Good night, Mrs Rice."

"Good night, Miss Hearne. And — Miss Hearne?"

"Yes?"

"You will be careful, won't you? About singing. I wouldn't like people to get the wrong impression."

"Well, people are funny. Even Jim, my brother, he got the wrong idea about it. Why he said to me this afternoon that it sounded as if you were having a party in your room. I said no, that was silly, you were just singing to yourself."

"*Good night*, Mrs Rice."

"Good night."

The night air helped. It tasted clean and fresh and she breathed deeply as she walked, trying to stop the trembling which had now become a sort of shivering as the cold crept into her bones. She felt nauseated. Singing, talking to herself, awful, it was awful. And in front of other people. In front of *him*, what could he think of her? He had waited to see her, his horrid sister had rubbed that in, the sly one.

The Bon-Bon teashop was still open, thank heavens. She picked a table near the radiator. A slow, shuffling waitress took her order and served a pot of tea and an egg sandwich. With her eye on the slightly soiled tablecloth, Miss Hearne forced herself to get the food down. She drank the tea and when the pot was empty, she asked for more hot water. But the waitress had seen her before and knew that she never tipped. The kitchen was closed, she said, she was sorry, but the teashop closed in five minutes, at nine o'clock.

She paid and went out. The thought of going back to her room was hateful. It was too late to go anywhere else, the pictures, for instance, and besides, even the pictures couldn't stop the shaking. There was only one other place to go, and perhaps an hour there, an hour of quiet prayer, would give her strength to resist the temptation that was coming fast upon her.

It was shameful, shameful. Singing like a crazy woman, lying on the floor of her room, drunken, dirty, sinning, while God in His Heaven looked down at her. And then being forced to humiliate herself in front of a person like Mrs Rice, telling that lie about monthlies *and being caughted in it*. Could anybody blame her if she despised me? I deserve it. I'm rotten, rotten, just a useless

170

woman, all alone.

But there in front of her was Saint Finbar's, its Gothic spire uplifted like two praying hands, a grey religious place, the house of God in the peace of night. She went in, dipping her hand in the dirty Holy Water font, making the Sign of the Cross as she pushed open the door leading from the vestibule to the nave.

The church was dark: here and there, a small lamp or a cluster of candles burned in lonely devotion before a picture, beneath an altar. The church was empty: cleared of its stock of rituals, invocations, prayers, a deserted spiritual warehouse waiting new consignments. One old woman kept watch for the community, sitting in the darkness with her back to a radiator. Was she praying as she watched the altar, or had she come in to keep warm?

This quiet, this gloom, this immense repose, soothed Miss Hearne as she stood in the deep shadows at the back of the church. She walked up the highway of the centre aisle, past the side aisles tormented by the Stations of the Cross, up to the great golden and white sweep of the main altar. She genuflected, and sat down in the front bench, feeling faint, weary, but at peace.

O Sacred Heart forgive me, she prayed, her eyes on the small golden door of the tabernacle. God sat behind that door, God in the form of bread by the sacrifice of the Mass, God sat alone behind that door in His empty church. Deserted God, she thought, You wait alone each night while men forget You.

The tabernacle glowed red-gold from the small light of the hanging sacristy lamp. She remembered that when the lamp is lit, God is in the tabernacle. When it is put out on Good Friday, He is absent.

The sacristy lamp winked. In the shadows the old woman stood up, genuflected, and turned her back on God. Miss Hearne watched the tabernacle, heard the dragging footsteps, the muffled slap of the swinging door, as the old woman went out into the streets. Alone in the immensity of His house, she gazed at the unseen Presence behind the little golden door. Alone with her God, she knelt down and begged Him.

O Sacred Heart, please, I need Your strength, Your help. Why should life be so hard for me, why am I alone, why did I yield to the temptation of drink, why, why has it all happened like this? O Sacred Heart, lighten my cross. You know it was hard, aunt dying after all those years of caring for her and You, only You, know the things I wanted, the home, children to raise up to honour and reverence You. O Sweet Jesus, You have shared my suffering, You know that I love you, please dear Lord, give me a sign, give me strength.

Tears wet her eyes. She raised her head. But the tabernacle was silent. Behind the door, God watched. He gave no sign. And around her the statues, unlit and unlovely, stared coldly across the church, unhearing, uncaring. Our Lady, her eyes and hands uplifted in her own private prayer; Saint Patrick, a gaunt old man in a green chasuble and a golden mitre, his right hand gripping a staff, unmindful of the snales which coiled around its base; Saint Joseph, his meek eyes downcast, a good greybeard few people prayed to. Plaster saints, no entreaty could move them. Alone, rejected, Miss Hearne looked again at the tabernacle, behind whose tiny door bread made into the Body of God lay hidden. The Holy of Holies.

Behind the altar an old sacristan appeared, a minor mummer on God's stage. Perfunctorily, he paused, genuflected in front of the tabernacle, then mounted the altar steps. His old eyes sought the tabernacle, dismissed it and he went wearily around the back of the altar. She heard him fumble with a switch and the lights in the side aisles went out. Then he came around the front again, walked down the steps and opened the little gate at the Communion rail. He did not genuflect but walked straight down the main aisle.

"Closing now, closing," he said in an angry voice as he passed her bench.

But she sat stiffly, terrified by the thing she had felt. For when the lights went out, it seemed as though the tabernacle were empty, a little golden house, set in the middle of a huge mantelpiece. It was as though the old sacristan, keeper of secrets,

**173**

knew he had no need to genuflect again. The lights were out, the people had gone home, the church was closing. In the tabernacle there was no God. Only round wagers of unleavened bread. She had prayed to bread. The great ceremonial of the Mass, the singing, the benedictions, what if it was show, all useless show? What if it meant nothing, nothing?

O God, God forgive me! she cried, falling on her knees. Forgive me, O Sacred Heart, for the terrible doubt the devil put in my head. O my guardian angel, shield me, protect me. Forgive me, O God, for I have sinned. I have blasphemed.

The footsteps returned. "You'll have to leave now, missis," the old sacristan said. His soutane was unbuttoned, showing a dirty brown pullover underneath. She looked into his old discoloured eyes, searching for secrets. But saw only that he was tired, that he wanted to close the church, that he wanted her to go.

She stood up, bowed her head to the tabernacle, genuflected and went quickly down the aisle to the door. She made the Sign of the Cross in dirty Holy Water (if it is only ordinary water and the priest is wrong . . . ?) and went out of the church, hearing the swinging door slap shut.

Outside the church gates, people passed. People busy with the immediate things of life. People making a living, bringing up children, planning, talking, sharing each other. Alone, Miss Hearne looked back at the church, an unhaunted house of

174

God, an empty place, stripped of the singing, the ritual, stripped of men; men who brought it to sudden glorious life.

Empty. And above her, the night sky, curved and vast. An empty sky, nothing beyond it but the stars, the planets, with the earth spinning among them. Surely some great design kept it all moving, some Presence made it meaningful. But what if the godless were right, what if it all started back aeons ago with fish crawling out of the sea to become men and women? What if not Adam and Eve, but apes, great monkeys, were our ancestors? In that world, what place had a God who cared for suffering?

She began to walk. Supposing, just supposing, her heart cried, supposing nobody has listened to me in all these years of prayers. Nobody at all up above me, watching over me. Then nothing is sinful. There is no sin. And I have been cheated, the crimson nights in that terrible book from Paris, the sin, permissible then. Nobody above. Nobody to care. Whiteness hers, he seized, revelled in. Virile he, his dark flashing eyes, they lifted beakers of wine and quaffed them, losing themselves in the intoxication of love, homage to Bacchus, lusts of the flesh. That handsome boy bathing that day at Greystones, standing up in his tight bathing trunks, his bump of virility sticking out, he would enfold me, he would run gracefully with me up the strand to the dunes. No sin in it. It would be passion, sublime freedom. And my

175

breasts bare, that day in Dr Bowe's surgery, his assistant, McNamara his name, me lying on the examination couch, my arms hanging over the edge, and he came close, yes, close, his stethescope cold on my chest, he bent over and against the back of my hand his trousers pressed, I felt it, his thing, swelling there soft, he didn't notice, an accident, but behind the material it was there, soft, swelling, the hot flushes I had, daren't move my hand, soft, hard, warm, supposing he had noticed, it swelled, all caution gone, he had turned, the rough beast, tearing all his clothese off, black hair all over him, lusting after my whiteness, yes, I could too, give myself, gipsy girl, hair about my shoulders, my breasts bare, rolling on the greensward, Romany marriage, blood mixing blood, while he, his male blackness enfolds me. It would be nature, not sin. For remembers the night old John Healy said to aunt that if he weren't a Catholic and did not believe, then what would there be to prevent him living as a profligate, cheating his neighbours, owing slaves, living like a great Roman in the golden days of Rome. Rome, Samson and Delilah, his great powerful half-naked body in the picture. What would prevent him, what indeed? No hell, no purgatory, no responsibility to God. If all the priests were wrong and you died and slept into nothingness, what point, then, in all of that? The community, it can go hang, what did the community ever do for me that I should help my fellow man?

No god. But the Protestants would never be saved and still they went on making laws stopping people from doing sinful things, canting about sin and corruption. And if we Catholics were wrong too? she thought. Then we'd be no better off than godless Russia, free love, no morals, rape in the streets, men killing, strangling, defiling women like the sex maniacs in the *News of the World*. Who'd stop them? What use in the courts if there was no moral code, no bible to swear on? A woman like me, defenceless against the beast in men, what would I do? No, no, there has to be a god and if there was no god, men would make one. Idols, like that great idol, in the picture, the Temple of Dagon, Victor Mature pulled it down, a god of clay. And those people back in ancient times, superstitious they were, afraid of the sun, of snakes, of things of clay. Omens and portents. And us? The golden door, the circle of bread in the monstrance. What if . . .? O forgive me Sacred Heart, the devil's thoughts, forgive me. But — tearing at my dress, ripping it away, his toga thrown aside, his huge hands feel me, press me close, his body, muscled, hard. And drunken, that wonderful cheerfulness, gay laughter, quaffing the wine, forgetfulness, Sweet oblivion. O Thou. A loaf of breaad, a jug of wine and Thou beside me in the wilderness. Paradise enow.

A car, headlights like yellow angry eyes, brakes screeching in rage. She stumbled, drew back, fell. Strong hands lifted her.

"Are you all right, Miss? You nearly got kilt."

And a man's head from the car window. "The lights were against her. She just walked out, not looking. Get herself killed."

Then the noise of engines backing up, moving again. The passersby stared, resumed their progress. The man who had lifted her, touched his hat. "Sure you're all right? Are you ill?"

"No, no, thank you. Thank you very much."

Nearly killed me, not looking. *I was nearly killed.* Called to meet my Maker. And in mortal sin, sinful evil thoughts, sins of intent. Denying God.

She stood there shaking, saying an act of contrition. Struck down in the midst of my sinfulness, O Sacred Heart, forgive me. You gave a sign, a warning. Your patience will not last for ever. O dear Jesus, the drink, the sin that led to another sin. Hallucinations I had, and shaking like this. O my God, I am heartily sorry. I thank Thee.

Her eyes sought the night sky and she gave thanks. Then she crossed carefully when the lights showed green and continued home to Camden Street. She said a whole rosary on the way. A rosary in honour of the Sacred Heart. He had warned: Repent. Once again He had been merciful, He had shown the way.

# CHAPTER
# ELEVEN

Next morning when Miss Hearne appeared for breakfast, her earthly penance began. All eyes watched her as she came in and sat down.

Mr Lenehan opened the attack. "Feeling better now, Miss Hearne?"

"O, yes, thank you."

"Well, that's good news now. I'm sure we're all glad to hear that." He smiled deceitfully at the others. "It's a terrible thing, sickness in a house."

Miss Friel shut her book with a snap. "Some people have no consideration at all," she said loudly. "No consideration at all. Sickness indeed! Singing and carrying on at all hours."

Mrs Henry Rice poured tea. Now, it won't happen again, I'm sure."

Disgraceful, I call it," Miss Friel said. "A nice thing for a Catholic house."

Miss Hearne, her face burning, hardly listened to these words. She was watching Mr Madden. But he only opened his mouth to put toast in it.

"I like a bit of a song myself," Mr Lenehan said, grinning at Miss Hearne. "You have a fine voice there. A fine carrying voice."

Mary came in with fresh toast and put it in front of Miss Hearne. She fumbled with the toast-rack and one of the slices fell beside Mr Madden's cup. Miss Hearne saw Mr Madden look at the girl and the girl blushed red. He kept on looking, all the time the girl was in the room. Anything, so's he won't have to look at me, Miss Hearne thought. O, I don't blame him. She's shocked, and no wonder.

But there was no time to think about it: Miss Friel still wanted satisfaction. "I can hardly keep my eyes open," she told the table. I'm dead tired, so I am, after yesterday. Singing and carrying on, you could hear it all over the house. It's all very well for the rest of you, but I have to keep my wits about me, teaching."

"O, we all make noises now and then," Mrs Henry Rice said. "I know I often disturb Bernie at his work when I put the vacuum cleaner on."

"Vacuum cleaner? I wouldn't mind that. But caterwauling, no, it would drive you mad," Miss Friel said, glaring down the table at Miss Hearne..

O, the mortification of it. But she couldn't let that pass.

"Is is me you're referring to?" she asked Miss Friel.

"And who else?"

"And is it any business of yours what I do, I'd

like to know?"

"It's a matter of common comfort to the people who are living in this house. Singing and shouting away half the blessed night, and yesterday afternoon, I was correcting exercises, I cold hardly hear my ears. I hammered away on your wall, but not a bit of heed you paid. You'd think you were. . ."

(O, no, not that! Not said out in public!) "I'm very sorry," Miss Hearne said, cutting her short, "I promise you it won't occur again." She looked at Mr Madden. "I must apologize to all of you. I didn't realize the singing voice carried so much."

But Mr Madden kept his head down. He looks upset, poor man, she thought, how embarrassing it must be for him.

"I see," Miss Friel said, standing. "Well, I should hope not indeed." Her victory won, she tucked her book under her arm and marched out of the room.

"Ah, never mind her," Mr Lenehan chuckled, nodding towards the door. "Sure there's nobody doesn't have a bit of a jig now and then. Except for the likes of her, never had a night's fun in her life."

"Mr Lenehan!" Mrs Henry Rice was stern. "I'll thank you not to discuss people when they're hardly out of the room!"

"No offence meant. I was only sympathizing." He winked at Miss Hearne.

Keep your winks to yourself, you counter-jumper. Shameful, O shameful, being discussed like that, by such people, no tact, no manners. At least *he* had the sense to say nothing. Gentleman. One of nature's gentlemen.

Miss Hearne drank her tea and forced a piece of sickening buttered toast into her mouth. Her stomach rejected it. Sick bile rose in her throat. She swallowed it. O, not here, I couldn't be sick in front of him. Lie down, a good lie down and some broth tonight, and not another drop of liquor, not another drop ever. Go, I must. At once.

"I think I'll go to my room."

"Not feeling well?" Mr Lenehan inquired.

The sick bile rose again. She shut her lips tightly and nodded. Mr Lenehan smiled. "A good rest is the best cure."

I could kill him, the cheeky thing, as if it was any of his business. O, that shaking. Stop it. Stop it!

She ran upstairs to her room and reached the wash-basin just in time. Afterwards, she felt purged and weak.

She took off her dress and lay down on the bed. Nothing matters, she said. Nothing. I must sleep and get well. Can't talk to him in this condition. I must look dreadful. O, I feel sick. The sickness.

But sleep came quickly and she lay in light nameless dreams all through the forenoon. It grew very cold in the room and she woke to pull the blankets over her. She slept on dreamlessly into the afternoon, making no sound, hidden in the cocoon of unconsciousness. To sleep and never wake. Wake to face him.

Someone outside?

"Miss Hearne."

She started up. "Who is it?"

"There's a Mrs Brannon on the phone."

"Mrs Brannon? O Sacred Heart, the lesson, little Meg, today, Thursday it is!

"Did you tell her I'm not well?"

"She wants to speak to you," the door cried with the soft compelling voice of Bernard.

"Just a minute."

My dress, where? O, Mother Mary, my heart, the pain of it. O, what'll I say? Sick, yes, unwell, O Sacred Heart, help me. O Mother Mary, my good intention, help me now. I will not sin again.

Bernard, wearing a black turtleneck sweater, dirty flannels and slippers, was waiting on the landing outside. He followed her downstairs to the hall where the phone dangled like an evil fruit from its cord. Her hand shook as she put the black earpiece against her tousled hair.

"Hello?"

"Is that you, Miss Hearne?" Mrs Brannon's voice, twisted and harsh, leaped out of the little black cylinder. Mrs Brannon behind it, big, mean opinionated.

"Yes, Miss Hearne speaking." She looked back along the hall. Bernard, horrid fatty, was listening, sucking at a cigarette.

"Well, I'd like to know that's the meaning of this? Today's your lesson with my Meg, you know that. And the poor child sitting there at the piano this last hour, waiting for you."

"O, Mrs Brannon, I'm terribly sorry. But I was ill. I've been in bed all day."

"That's no excuse." the crackly mean voice roared out of the earpiece. "You might have phoned, it's the least you could have done. Not leaving the child waiting hour after hour like that, no consideration at all. I like people to keep their appointments. If you can't do that, I'll just have to get someone else."

"O, Mrs Brannon, I'm sorry, really I am, I'll come over right away, I'll be there in half an hour."

"So, you're *not* sick. Not sick, that's a fine thing. I never heard the like. No, Miss Hearne, that won't do. That won't do at all. I'm sorry, I'll just have to get someone else. I never heard of such a thing."

"But Mrs Brannon, I *am* sick. I mean that I'd come anyway. It skipped my mind, really, or I'd have phoned of course."

"Well, it didn't skip Meg's. I won't have a teacher who forgets her pupils. Good day, Miss Hearne. You can send me a bill for the last two lessons."

"Miss Brannon, really, I don't think . . ."

"Click!" said the little black earpiece.

"Bad news/" It was Bernard, fat, sucking his

184

cigarette, coming towards her.

"No. No."

"Are you a teacher or something? I heard you mention going over. And the lady told me her little girl was waiting for you."

"I teach piano," Miss Hearne said, trying to walk round him and get back to her room.

"I'm very fond of music myself. I have some good records and a record player, if you'd ever like to listen to them."

"That's very kind of you, I'm sure. Now, I really must get out of this draughty hall. If you'll excuse me . . . "

"Horowitz, Schnabel, Gieseking. I've got a lot of good piano. Some lovely stuff." He leaned over the rail of the bannister, watching her go up. "Lost a pupil?" he asked.

O, the brute! Listening in on every word, the sneaky thing.

"I said did you lose a pupil?" He had raised his voice to a shout. She turned and looked down the stairs.

"I'm not deaf, thank you, Mr Rice. The answer is yes. Although I don't see that it's any business of yours."

"I didn't mean to be nosey. I just know some people who want a piano teacher for their little girl, that's all. Maybe you'd be interested."

"Perhaps we can discuss it some other time."

"As you wish." He went off down the hall whistling.

Whee-whe-whee-who . . . piano, pianissimo. I wonder now, a tidbit for little old New York upstairs? Yes, uncle dear, a piano teacher, a failed piano teacher at that. Heard her myself on the phone, not half an hour ago, terrified because somebody'd cancelled a lesson. How'd he take that, eh? What the hell do you know, roaring it out, but it's true, I'd say, I *will* say, and he'll know it. And talking of the lady's special peculiarities, uncle dear, has it every occurred to you that the evidence presented in the past twenty-four hours leads indisputably to a certain conclusion? Item: two empty whiskey bottles in her room. Item: loud solitary songs. Item: generally hung-over appearance at the breakfast table this morning. Yes, uncle, the verdict is that the lady, to put it crudely, is a boozer. Watch his meat-face rage, nonna my business, in Hollywood tough-talk out of the side of his mouth. Ah, I know him, the sod, he'll bluster and bluff out with another mad scheme, he'll be off to Connemara to drain the bogs of Ireland for uranium, handing out the big talk, but I'll stop that, watch the fear when I point out, all reasonableness, mind you, that hell hath no fury like a spinster scorned. And that she's been — led up the garden shall we say — by one James Madden and that he'd better watch his step now for she'll be after him, thirsting for holy union. That should shift him.

But wait. Think about it. Messire Niccolo. Is

this the way to proceed? There's the affair of the serving girl, m'lud. And if he talks? No, in it himself, up to his neck, don't worry. Yes, proceed as planned. And why not? If I tell him now that she is what she is, a piano teacher, a woman of straw, not a penny, then the business designs will stop, his interest will abate. He'll avoid her. And then? A word in the other direction, a hint to the lady that all is not lost. She pursues, he flees, he cannot flee and continue to live here. An intolerable situation. Demands decisive action. Retreat. Pack. Bag and baggage. Out. Bye-bye blacksheep. Yes, worry him. Handle it diplomatically. Iron hand in velvet. Yes. Do it now. He's in.

Whee-whe-whee-who . . . whistling once more, Bernard turned, climbed the stairs to his uncle's room.

# CHAPTER
# TWELVE

The male must pursue. Miss Hearne believed this. If Mr Madden did not seek her company, she would be abandoned. The woman's place was to resist advances, to grant the favour of her company, to yield little by little.

But on the following day Mr Madden again preserved a total silence at the breakfast table. She tried to make him talk. He would not. Their cosy chats might never have been. He confined himself to the business of eating and drinking, and as soon as he had finished, he put on his hat and coat and went out. He was out all day. She waited for him, but the night came and sleep came and still he had not returned.

On the third day of Mr Madden's silent retreat, she sought him out. Accidentally, as it were. But she pursued him. At breakfast he made her feel positively foolish when she drew him into conversation. Afterwards, she went to her room, put on her hat and coat, and sat down on the old straight-backed chair, facing the bay window. She allowed nothing to distract her: a moment's inattention could mean another day of unhappiness. At eleven, she saw him come out on the front steps beneath her, dressed for the street. She jumped up and hurried down the stairs as fast as her legs would carry her. He was walking down the street. She ran after him.

"O, good morning, Mr Madden," she called. "Lovely day for a walk, isn't it."

"Yeah," Mr Madden said, looking at the sky. She fell in beside him.

"Are you going downtown?"

"I've got some business," he said.

"O. Mind if I walk with you? I've been thinking a lot about you, you know."

Mr Madden stared straight ahead. She tried again. "I mean, I've missed our little talks, you — you seem to have been very silent these last few days."

"Um."

"I was wondering, I mean, I wonder is anything wrong? You — ah, you haven't had bad news or anything?"

"Hey," Mr Madden said. "There's my bus. I got to get it. I'll see you later. I got to run now." and run he did, limping on his game leg, jumping on the back platform of the bus as it pulled away from the kerb. He waved goodbye. Then was lost in traffic.

Avoiding me, O, it's shameful of him, running

away like that, as if I had the plague or something. You hurt me, James Madden, if you knew how much, you'd come back on your bended knees to apologize. Clutching her handbag to her stomach, she stared down the road. Ran from me. When I ran after him. Humiliated myself for him. He rejected. He turned away. But my own fault, yes, I'm the only one to blame, no I'm not, that horrid sister of his, telling him heaven knows what awful tale. Rejected, she looked at her long pointed shoes with the little shoe-eyes winking up at her. Little shoe-eyes, always there. But the magic didn't work. The shoe-eyes were just buttons. Just shoe buttons.

O, she said, a woman in love can't afford to be proud. He must be made to see, he must be made to come back. And I must do it myself, no matter how silly it looks. Tomorrow is Sunday, we first walked together on a Sunday. Tomorrow he must go to Mass and I will go with him, I will have it out, yes. I'll come right out with it, no matter how much it hurts, ask him to explain himself. Because anything, anything is better than sitting here alone at night, not knowing. And what will I say? Subtle, yes, lead up to it gently, find out his intentions. O, maybe he would say it himself, not have to be asked, gentle, tender with me again. And he will, he will, he's just put off by the things his horrid sister said against me. I'll explain, the first time it ever happened, I'll say, and it was because of you, you made me unhappy. Show him, I will, he is responsible for it, come right out with it, I was upset for you, I only fell into it because you made me unhappy. And now you are cold, tell me why, I have a right to know.

She did not go to confession, although it was Saturday. Although drunkenness was a mortal sin. No, after tomorrow, after the Sunday talk, it could all be told to this new priest, Father Quigley, why it had happened. And maybe she might ask for advice on marriage. As her confessor, her new one in her new parish, he must be consulted, he would have advice to give.

The next morning she was up at six. She dressed carefully and sat by the window until nine. But he did not go out. So she went down to breakfast. The others were there, even Bernard, but he was not. She couldn't eat a thing, she was so nervous. At a quarter to ten, he appeared and she dawdled with her cup of tea until he had finished eating. He did not speak to her. He lit a cigarette and stood up to leave. She went after him into the hall and saw him put on his coat.

"Are you going to eleven, by any chance, Mr Madden?"

"Well, " he hesitated. "I might do that and I might go to twelve."

"Anyway, you're going out?"

"Yeah."

"Well, I'd like to walk along with you. As a matter of fact, I'd like to have a word with you."

"Well — sure."

They walked side by side down the street. "I think I'll go to eleven," he said. "Have you been yet?"

"No, I'll go to eleven too. We can go together, if you've no objections."

"That's fine."

They turned out of Camden Street, passing the university. "You seem to have been very busy lately, Mr Madden."

"I had some business to attend to."

Well, *really*. If he thinks he's going to put me off like that, he's got another think coming. Out with it, out with it, and shame him.

"I — you'll think it forward of me — but I had the impression you were avoiding me." Her face coloured scarlet as the words came out.

"Where did you get *that* idea? I was busy, that's all. I'm going to Dublin on business."

"O?"

"That restaurant project. A friend of mine is coming back to Ireland for a holiday. I want to discuss it with him."

"I see. And when are you planning to run off to Dublin, may I ask?"

"Well — uh, I haven't decided yet. Soon. My friend will be here soon. I got a letter from him yesterday."

"You might have told me. After all, I'm interested in what you do."

"Well, uh, I got two letters. I mean, I got a letter a while ago and then another one yesterday.

It isn't sure though, when he's coming."

"But I don't see what two letters have to do with it. You made up your mind to go to Dublin and you didn't even have the decency to tell me."

He stopped walking and stared at her. "What's it to you?" he said harshly. "That's my personal business. If I want to go to Dublin, or New York, or anywhere, that's my business. I might even go to New York. I tell you it's not sure yet."

"New York? But you said you were going to stay her. Why, you told me yourself — why only last week you said . . . "

"Last week was different."

"I don't see how."

He began to walk again at a terrible pace. She had to run to keep up with him. "Last week I thought I had a partner for that restaurant deal," he said, his head down, his rough-red face angry. "This week, I find you've been stringing me along."

"*Me*? But Mr Madden — Jim — I don't understand. If you mean what happened, your sister told you I drink, I mean, it's not true."

"Never mind that. I hear you're a piano teacher, is that right."

"I don't see what that has to do with it."

"It has everything to do with it. I need a partner for this hamburger joint I got in mind. I thought you were on the level. Well — are you? If you've got a couple of thousand pounds we can talk business." he stopped walking, took her roughly by the arm. "Well, how about it? You want to be partners with me?"

"But — but that's impossible. I haven't got any money. I . . ."

He let go of her arm. " See what I mean? I thought not. Phoney, same as everybody else in this town. Okay, I'm, going to Dublin, see what I can do. And if it doesn't work, I'm going back to the States. I never should of come here."

"But I thought you were going to stay in Ireland. I thought that was why you retired from business over there."

"Ireland!" He stared at the rain-threatening sky. "Who'd stay in Ireland, unless he had to? Tell me that?"

She was silent. As though by common consent, they began to walk again.

I don't understand why you thought that I — I mean, I thought you were interested in me, Jim. As a woman, I mean. I don't think you've behaved very well."

"*Well*, what d'you mean *well*? What I do's *my* business."

"*Your* business? And what about me, Mr Madden? What am I to think? You took me out, you might say you confided in me, you gave me certain ideas, you led me on to think all sorts of things and then you just ignore me. I have to humble myself to run after you and then you have the nerve to tell me you were only courting me because you thought I might put some money in your silly restaurant."

They had reached Saint Finbar's. The people were coming out from the ten o'clock Mass, meeting the people who were waiting to go in for the eleven o'clock. He looked at the crowd and then looked at her.

"Come on with me," he said. "I want to talk to you. In private."

He walked past the church, down a side street. She followed, her face mottled with blushes, her whole body quivering with indignation and shame. In the side street, he stopped and looked back at the crowds.

"Now listen, Judy. You've got this all wrong. I took you out — sure. You had nobody else around. I liked you, I thought you were a fine woman. I thought you and me were interested in the same things. But I didn't make any passes, did I? I didn't give you any ideas. Let's get that straight."

"It's that horrid sister of yours," she cried, her voice shrill with fear. "She turned you against me. She told lies about me."

"May? May's got nothing to do with this. Besides, I didn't need May to tell me you were drunk, that day. I've got ears."

"O, but you mustn't believe it. It was because of you. She upset me with what she said, I couldn't bear it. I had a drink, medicinal, purely medicinal. I took it to soothe my nerves."

"Well, that's *your* business. I didn't ask you

your business, did I?"

"I know what's wrong," she screamed, clutching at his sleeve, standing out in the street with the tears blinding her. "You think I'm a drunkard, *you do*, that's why you're going away, that's why you've been so cold. The other thing is only an excuse. But it's not true, Jim, it's not true. I hardly ever touch it, that's why it affected me, I'd make you a good wife, Jim, really I would. I'd be a help to you, I don't care what you were, I don't care. I don't care."

Carefully, he lifted her hands off his sleeve. "Who said anything about getting married? Did I? I never even considered it. Listen, Judy, get a hold of yourself. I like you, I thought of you as a good friend. That's all, *that's all*. Marry? Are you crazy in the head, or something? Marry! At my age. At yours. What is this?"

"O, my God!" she wailed, shielding her face with her arm. "O, merciful God!" She ran away from him, stumbling, her head down: to get away, away anywhere from his face, his harsh voice, his hate. Running, weeping, she reached the street corner and the gate of the church. The people were now going in to eleven o'clock Mass. Hide! Hide! She joined the crowd, mopping her face with her handkerchief. She dabbed Holy Water on her brow and went blundering to a side aisle, to the great mass of kneeling people, hiding herself among them, getting away from him.

"*Introibo ad altare Dei!*" cried the priest.

"*Adeum quilaetificat juventutummeum*," the altar boys mumbled.

Where is he, he wouldn't come in after that, he wouldn't dare to face me after the way he spoke. O, the horror in the street, me shouting like a servant girl and him bellowing like a soldier, his voice, his face, cruel, enjoying the hurt, how could he do this, how could he, so hurtful, has he no kindness, no mercy in him, telling that story about a letter, going to Dublin, a fairy tale, a pure invention, it rolled off his tongue as deceitful as a bad confession, I should have asked him to see it, proof, I had a right to, yes, because it wasn't true, else why did this happen now, after he was so nice, no, it was the drinking, the stories that horrid sister of his told about me, she's the one who's responsible, she did it, and me too, I made a fool of myself, I should have been polite and firm, giving myself away like that, shouting and weeping and I rushed at him, accusing him, they say that puts a man off, you could see he was embarrassed, that's why he went down the side street, so's people couldn't see us, yes, I put him off, a pushing woman, it hurt him to say those things, he still called me Judy, even then, Judy, you can see he's still fond of me, he's sorry now, sorry, he *was* hurtful though, the cruel way he said it, 'at your age,' what does he know about my age, yes, and he said 'are you crazy in the head,' crazy, O, aunt dear, no, no, it couldn't be, O, my God, help me, save me.

She began to pray, her eyes on the altar, her mind far from the sacrifice. The Our Fathers and Hail Marys stumbled through her mind, repeating themselves until they were meaningless, as hurried and without devotion as the mumbled responses of the altar boys. They died half said as she slowly retraced the agony from its beginning, from the humiliating moment she had run out of the house after him. The walk, the things said, the cruel way he said them. They could not be washed away by repetition, those cruel words. Unlike prayers, they could not be dulled by restatement. They were the negation of prayer, the antithesis of hope.

She did not hear the sermon. She only wondered if he were in the church, sitting cruelly in the house of God after destroying her faith. When the Mass was over she sat until everyone else had left. Let him leave first, hide from him. He had said those things, they could never be unsaid. And he was the last one, James Madden, the last one ever.

People were already taking their places for the twelve o'clock Mass. She must leave. Impossible to go back to Camden Street now. He'd tell the whole thing to his horrid sister and then in no time at all, others would know about, that Friel woman and that sleekit birdy Lenehan. They would all have a good laugh over how she had made an utter fool of herself. No, I can't go back now among them, among enemies. Thank God I have some real friends left, the O'Neills — and it's Sunday.

I'll go somewhere and have a small bite to eat and afterwards I'll got for a walk until three.

At a quarter to three, Shaun O'Neill looked out of the drawing-room window and saw Miss Hearne coming up the avenue.

"Daddy," he said, "J.H. sighted on the horizon. Prepare to abandon ship."

His father nodded, picked up his newspaper and made for the door.

"I'll be in the study if you want me," he said to his wife.

"Una and Kathleen. It's your turn to stay." Moira O'Neill said. "And I don't want any arguments about it."

"But I have to prepare my stuff for tomorrow's lecture," Una said.

"No. When you went to the dance last night you told me you'd stay in today. I want you here. After all, poor Judy Hearne looks forward to seeing you. It's the biggest event in her week, the poor soul, and I'm not going to have her snubbed by you children."

"Anyway, I'm off," Shaun said. "I've done my sentence."

"Go on then. But I don't want any more jokes about this." Mrs O'Neill said sternly. "Kevin, you stay here."

"O, holy smoke!" Kevin wailed.

"That's enough. And Kathleen, I want you to stay too. After tea, you can all go off if you like.

But someone must see Miss Hearne to the bus."

"There she is," Shaun said as the bell shrilled below in the hall.

Una, Kathleen and Kevin pulled long faces.

"Where did I ever get such a selfish bunch of children?" Mrs O'Neill asked the ceiling. "Not an ounce of Christian charity in them. Poor Judy, she loves every one of you. And to think you couldn't show her a little Christian kindness."

"It's Miss Hearne, Mam," said the maid.

"All right, show her up, Ellen."

They waited. Young Kevin kicked at the rug. Shaun had already disappeared.

Someone rapped gently on the drawing-room door.

"Yes."

"It's only me," Miss Hearne said, coming into the room with a sad attempt at a smile.

"Hello, Judy dear."

"Moira." They embraced, making the mock kiss of women, careful not to disarrange each other's hair. Una, Kathleen and Kevin came forward to shake hands.

"Sit down, Judy dear. Una, move those books off the chair."

"Thank you. And how are all my little nephews and nieces?"

This was her little joke: she liked to think of them as young relatives. But they turned indifferent faces towards her, their eyes cold, rejecting the hint of kinship.

"O, we're all right," Una said. "And how's Baby Rice?"

"Don't talk to me about that horrid thing. Although, now that I'm settled in, I can see where the trouble lies. It's his mother. O, Moira dear, Una darling, you don't know what a horrible woman she is."

Mrs O'Neill looked at Una: they both knew Judy Hearn's familiar pattern. Landladies always started out by being very nice, the nicest people possible, but after the first disagreement, they began the slow transition to deep-dyed villainy. With this new one, Mrs O'Neill thought, she's skipped the preliminary stages.

"O," she said. "Why is that?"

"Well, Moira dear, she's terribly common for one thing. Not that I'm a snob, Moira, you know me better than that. But she's the nosiest woman I ever set eyes on. Do you know she's killed with curiosity to know what I'm doing all the time. And malicious, well, you wouldn't believe the things she says about me."

"Malicious?" Una said. The thought of anyone finding subject for malicious gossip in the doings of poor old Judy Hearne . . .

"Well . . ." Miss Hearne looked significantly in the direction of Kevin and Kathleen. "Not in front of the children."

Una preened herself, smiled triumphantly at her younger sister. Seventeen had its few rewards.

"Kevin and Kathy, would you like to go off

upstairs and play?" Mrs O'Neill said.

"Wow!" young Kevin cried, jumping up. "Race you to the landing," he called to Kathleen. And they fled out of the drawing-room, banging the door behind them. Una watched them go, a little downcast.

"Such obedient children," Miss Hearne said. "Well, as I was saying, this Mrs Rice is the sort of person you could take into court and sue, the things she says."

"What things?"

"Well, this is in the strictest confidence, mind you, but last week she as much as accused me of being a bad woman."

Una found this impossible to take seriously. She howled with laughter. "A *what*?"

"A bad woman," Miss Hearne said firmly.

"O Judy, you're exaggerating."

"No, Moira, it's the truth. You see, she has a brother living with her, an American, who's back in Ireland on a visit and is thinking of settling down. A Mr Madden. A very nice man, at least he seemed to be. Well-behaved, an older man, you know. And he seemed very interested in me. He was always pestering me to go out with him, to go to the pictures or a walk or something."

Una's eyes were circles of disbelief. Mrs O'Neill chuckled. "O Judy," she said. "Is it a flirtation you're having?"

"Not at all. It's just that he — well, you know I have a lot of time on my hands now, the piano lessons have dropped off a bit as a matter of fact. And the embroidery classes not being renewed at the Technical School, as I told you last week. So, just to be polite, I went out with him a couple of times."

"To the pictures?"

"Well — yes. And he took me to dinner one night at the Plaza. A very nice man, purely friendly, you know, and I was very interested to hear what he had to say about America. He's a Donegal man originally, from your mother's part of the country, Moira."

"O, there's lots of Maddens in Donegal," Mrs O'Neill said. "And what happened then, Judy?"

"Well, one night last week we came home from the pictures and there she was, waiting for us like a policeman. She asked us in for a cup of tea. I saw nothing odd about it at the time, but as soon as my back was turned — she sent me into the scullery to wet the tea, mind you I offered to do it — well, when I came back into the room, he — Mr Madden — was gone. After some row, I didn't hear what it was."

"And then what?" Una asked. Holy Moses, could you imaging old Judy Hearne in a romance?

"Well, she just said she didn't want any misunderstandings and that she was running a respectable house and so forth, and that her brother didn't have much to do with himself and that was a pity. I've never been so insulted in my life, you could see what she was hinting at, I just told her who did she think she was talking to? I declare I nearly gave her notice right on the spot. Of course, you could see she was jealous of the brother, worried about fortune hunters or something."

"Why? Is he well off?"

"Well, I haven't the faintest idea. As if it was any concern of mine whether Mr Madden is well off. I think he's quite comfortable, but that's by the by. The important thing is this woman, the cheek of her. Can you imagine, as much as telling me to my face that I was carrying on with him?"

Despite herself, Moira O'Neill was seized with a fit of the giggles.

"O, it's not funny, Moira dear, I can tell you it was humiliating. Humiliating. I made up my mind today that I'll not stay another week in that house."

"And was that all there was to it?" Una asked.

Miss Hearne hesitated. I said too much, boasting again, I should have held my tongue. I'm making a fool of myself. "Yes, that's the whole story. Did you ever hear anything so ridiculous?"

Mrs O'Neill frowned. "Now look here, Judy," she said. "You shouldn't jump to conclusions. I feel the time has come for us to talk frankly, as old friends. These digs are cheap and well situated, and you said yourself you were quite comfortable. I think you'd be foolish to move again over a little tiff like that."

She doesn't understand, Miss Hearne thought, how can she, when she doesn't know the whole story? When I never can tell her the truth. Like the time I left Cromwell Road, it wasn't the row about cleaning the room, it was the other, the night I burned the mattress when I fell asleep with the bottle beside me.

"Well, I feel I have to move," she said. "I wouldn't be happy there."

"Now, Judy, be sensible. This is about the sixth move you've made in the last three years. No digs are perfect. And you've been complaining that moving is expensive. Now, why don't you stay where you are. You can always ignore things like these."

"What's this Madden like?" Una said. "Is he a real dyed-in-the-wood Yank?"

"O, he's all right, I suppose. Anyway, he's going off to Dublin soon. The trouble with him is he believes everything his sister tells him."

"Don't tell me you had a row with him too."

"No — not a row exactly. But ever since then he's been cool. And this morning, this very morning, I had to ask him what was the matter and he mumbled something about going to Dublin, a lie obviously. I wouldn't be surprised the sister put him up to running away like that. Because before that he was all over me, you know."

She looked at them, the grey-haired matron and the young girl. And why shouldn't I, they don't take me seriously, those two, laughing like that. She leaned forward: "As a matter of fact, he proposed to me," she said.

"He *proposed* to you?"

"He did. Of course, I didn't take him seriously for a moment. After all, I told him, I hardly know you."

"What did he do in America?" Una asked.

"O, he was in the hotel business in New York. I believe he had quite a big hotel there."

"Well Judy, for heaven's sake, he sounds quite a catch."

"O, mind you, I thought about it for a minute. After all, men don't grow on trees. But I just didn't feel we were suited to each other."

"And how did he take it when you said no?"

"Well — men are so funny — He didn't say a word. Of course, it might be that, that's driving him off to Dublin."

Mrs O'Neill and her daughter exchanged glances. They're interested in me now, all right. With a tale like this. This is the way it should have been. Telling it, reversing the events to fit a more dignified pattern, she was uneasily conscious of the obligations of the lie. Told once, it must be retold until, in the blurring of time, it became reality, the official version, carefully remembered.

"Well, Judy dear, I still think you'd be foolish to leave," Mrs O'Neill said. "Although I can quite understand that it was embarrassing for you. But if he goes away, it will all blow over. Who knows, she'll be grateful to you, the sister, for turning him down. You two might even become the best of friends."

206

"O, it's impossible. Friends with that fat thing! I'd be hard up for friends indeed."

And you are hard up, Mrs O'Neill thought. Something about this rigmarole doesn't make sense. And there was something fishy about the tale you told the last time you changed your digs. God knows, all landladies couldn't be as black as you paint them. Ah, poor Judy, there's no use arguing with you, you have a touch of your Aunt D'Arcy there. Stubborn as a mule.

"Let's have some tea," she said. "Una, go and call your father."

Friends with the likes of Mrs Rice, Miss Hearne said to herself. O, Moira doesn't understand things at all. How could I be friends with that fat thing and how could something, a serious thing — a love affair — just blow over like that? O, Moira wouldn't know, sitting here in the middle of her chickens like some contented hen. And Una, just a child, what does she know about men and women? They don't understand, they never will, they've never been me.

Professor O'Neill entered, his monocle flashing opaque against the light. "Hello there, Judy. And how are you?"

"Hello, Owen, I'm well, thanks. And how are you?" Owen, such a distinguished-looking man, he went straight up to Madden, looked him square in the eye: "I'll have you know, sir, Miss Hearne is a very dear friend of mine, how dare you talk to her in that tone of voice? Many a man would have

207

given anything to marry her. And an angel, she devoted her whole life to her sick aunt." Ah, Owen, Owen, and to think that a woman like Moira got you. Moira, she doesn't understand, how could she, common herself, I don't like you, Moira, never did, and God knows I'd love to tell you straight out.

"Sherry?" Moira said.

"Thank you, Moira dear." She drank it down in one swallow, to still the hatred that was starting inside her. I need it, I'm upset, I've had a very upsetting day.

Mrs O'Neill watched this. She lifted the decanter again. "Have another, Judy. It will warm you up. There's quite a nip in the air today."

Miss Hearne agreed. She noticed the way I drank it, Moira, she doesn't miss much, it's the countrywoman in her. I must go slow on this one, I must make it last. She looked down at the pale sherry in the glass and saw that it shook like a tiny sea. She tightened her grip pressing her fingers against the rim of the glass. But her hand still trembled. She drank it down in two swallows.

The second drink helped. No sooner had she swallowed it than she felt it send delicate fumes to her head, flushing her cheeks, easing the tension. One more drink would bring the good feeling. But meantime she must wait; she must let it do its work. She refused sandwiches and biscuits; they would spoil the effect of it. But when Moira ritually offered the decanter, expecting the familiar refusal, Miss Hearne smiled and held out her glass: "Yes, I think I will. It's awfully good sherry, so light and dry."

The room was bright and cosy, the children were grouped around the fire. Professor and Mrs O'Neill sat in their armchairs on opposite sides of the grate, befitting parts of the family picture. Miss Hearne leaned back on the cushions of the sofa, her eyes misty as she watched the changing pictures made by the flames. A happy family, how lucky they were. In the bosom of my family, O, if it were really true.

She asked young Kevin what he was doing at school and did not listen to his answer. Instead, she ran her fingers through Kathleen's curls. Ugly little Kathy, she likes me still.

And she drank the third sherry. It was pleasant, harmless, and goodness knows, she could have another, it tasted so mild.

"A cup of tea, Judy?"

"No, I couldn't spoil the taste of this delightful sherry."

"Well — would you take another?"

"D'you know, I think I will."

Mrs O'Neill poured a fourth sherry. I always knew she liked a little drop, but this is going to make her tipsy, she thought. The poor soul, I suppose she's upset about what happened. What *really* happened? Well, I suppose we'll never know.

"Why don't you play something for us, Judy?"

she asked as she saw Miss Hearne greedily swallow down half of the new glass.

"I couldn't. O, no, you don't want to hear me. Besides, I haven't any music with me."

Una smiled at her. "O, please, Miss Hearne. Play some Chopin."

"Yes, Judy, we haven't heard you play for a long time," Professor O'Neill said.

"But I'm out of practice, really I am."

"Please. Just one piece," Moira O'Neill said. It would at least keep her from finishing the bottle of sherry all by herself. Besides, she liked being asked to play and playing might take her out of herself a little.

So Miss Hearne stood up and Una cleared the bric-'a-brac and books off the top of the upright piano which stood against the wall. She opened the top of the piano and Miss Hearne sat down on the stool. The O'Neill children smiled to each other, anticipating the show which their brother Shaun had often mimicked for their entertainment. Then, as though she in turn were mimicking Shaun's burlesque of her playing, Miss Hearne furtively slipped on her glasses, struck a few chords and began to play, firmly, ferociously sounding the first bars of Chopin's *Polonaise*. The brass candlesticks on the piano did a frightening jig accompaniment as she bent forward, her eyes intent, her ringed hands jerking up and down the keyboard as though controlled by puppet strings.

When the piece was finished they all applauded.

She turned around, smiled and made a little bow from the piano seat. As she straightened up, her glasses fell off. Una retrieved them and handed them back, waiting for her to return to the sofa. But Miss Hearne swivelled the stool around again and poised to play.

"Chopin," she said. "The immortal Chopin." And her fingers struck a great chord on the keys. Off she went, ripping through a prelude, her face intent, forgetting all in the rise and fall of the music. But the chords faltered, fumbled, and the notes stumbled into silence.

"O, I wish I had my music," she said sadly. "I'm becoming terribly forgetful. I used to know that piece as well as anything. O, dear."

A little embarrassed, the O'Neills waited. "Well, never mind, Judy," Mrs O'Neill said. "You'll play it the next time you come. Now sit by the fire here, I'm sure you're tired after the playing."

"Ah, Chopin," Miss Hearne said, her shifting black eyes sad and misty. "And that woman, Georges Sand, what sort of a woman can she have been at all, Owen?"

"Well, I haven't read her books," Professor O'Neill said. "She's on the Index, I believe."

"And no wonder. Could I trouble you for another glass of that delightful sherry, Una? Thank you, dear. Ah, no wonder, Owen, that she's on the Index. A vulgar person who dressed like a man and smoked cigars. I don't know how

211

Chopin put up with her."

"A-hem!" Professor O'Neill said. He did not consider such matters fit subjects for discussion in front of the children.

"And he a Catholic at that," Miss Hearne said. "Living with a woman who smoked cigars. Still, he was a great artist, Chopin, wasn't he, Owen? And we must allow great leeway for the artistic temperament."

"Being an artist does not absolve a man from his religious duties, Judy," Professor O'Neill said firmly. "And besides, I don't think we should discuss it."

"O." Miss Hearne looked at young Kevin and Kathleen. "O, excuse me, I don't know what I was thinking of." She raised her glass and drank the fifth sherry. Something was happening, she could feel it. Maybe I'm just a teeny bit tight. O, no, I mustn't be tight here, of all places.

She stood up, spilling her handbag out of her lap. "I must be going now. I've just remembered that I've got an awful lot of things to do this evening. You know what it's like, Moira, washing and little sewing jobs, you put them aside . . ."

"You dropped your bag, Miss Hearne," young Kevin said, handing it to her.

"It's early," Mrs O'Neill said politely. "Stay a while."

"No, I really must go now." Miss Hearne straightened her hat with the coloured flowers on the band. "I really must."

212

"Kevin, get your coat and take Miss Hearne to her bus."

They all stood up then, like people getting on their feet after a family rosary. She said good byes and went downstairs with Mrs O'Neill and Kevin, and Kevin took her arm as she walked along the avenue to the bus stop. (Afterwards, he told his mother that Miss Hearne was very jolly and talked all the way. When she got in the bus, she turned and blew him a kiss. "Gosh, it was awful, everybody was watching us," Kevin said. "Why are women so sloppy?")

After she blew her good bye kiss, Miss Hearne watched young Kevin run back up the avenue. What a lovely family, what lovely friends to have. He might be her own little boy, running off like that after saying good bye to his mummy. Her own little boy. Not now. Not ever. Saddened, she went up the aisle of the bus. She sat down, paid the conductor, and stared at the neck of the man in front of her. A fat neck, with hairy pimples. People were so horrid sometimes. She looked down at her shoes, little shoe-eyes, always there.

The bus stopped and two young people, dressed in their Sunday best, got in and sat near the driver. Miss Hearne noticed that they were holding hands. Newly-weds? The girl's clothes, in such terrible taste. Magenta, with that blue scarf, O dear.

The young couple saw her look. Like Siamese twins, they turned their heads and stared back at her. They had pale sweaty faces, fed on cheap pastries, bags of sweets, tea and bread and jam. Their light-blue eyes were vacant, unblinking as children's. They stared at her without interest, as though they were too tired to look anywhere else.

Do I look tiddly, or something, what's the matter with them anyway, is my hat on crooked, I wish they'd stop, they're making me nervous again, and after I was feeling better too; O, look at them, what's the matter with them? Why are they so rude?

The young man said something out of the corner of his mouth. The girl snickered and nudged him with her elbow. But their eyes, those vacant blue eyes, never wavered. They watched Miss Hearne.

Well, you'd think I was something in a cage, what can be the matter with me? O, I'm trembling, honestly I am, they're upsetting me, I need something medicinal, something to settle me. And there's nothing in my room. Sunday too, none of the public houses open, only that place in Ballymacarret, against the law too, so far away.

But the shaking would not stop. The good feeling of the sherry was going fast and it had been an awful day, a day to end all. Nobody could blame me, she thought, not even Moira O'Neill, she was pouring them as fast as she could, a great shock, I'm not over it yet, I need something medicinal to steady me. In moderation, it will help me sleep.

214

So at City Hall, she changed buses and began the long ride out to Ballymacarret. This time, the bus was almost empty as it rushed through the gritty gloom of evening, down grey drab streets, fringed by row upon row of mean little working-class houses, brick red, stone grey, each and every one the same. At each window, between fraying lace curtains, a coloured vase, a set of crossed Union Jacks, or a figurine of a little girl holding her skirts up to wade, sat like little altars, turned towards the street for the edification of the neighbours.

She got off at the usual place, a stop near a factory. She walked along a street of tiny houses, tiny gimcrack shops, all of it stage-lit by the harsh orange glare of new street lamps. Dispirited children played hopscotch in the gutter and a starving cat walked delicately around a pile of refuse. Milk bottles adorned the doorsteps in preparation for Monday morning. Inside the tiny, smelly upstairs bedrooms, lamps were already lit.

Alone, tired, trembling, she reached the public house on the corner.

F.P. MCAVINEY. *Licensed to sell wines and spirits.*

It was closed. The blinds were drawn but slivers of light shone through the curlicues on the Victorian plate-glass windows. The heavy door was padlocked. But in the cobbled entry behind the pub, men stood and talked in whispers. Under the street lamp, a Woodbine dangling from his lips, a

215

shabby youth stood sentry. He wore a cheap brown suit with padded shoulders and his tie was a mass of stained, multi-coloured triangles. When Miss Hearne stopped outside the pub, his eyes moved in his narrow, pasty face. He watched.

Three men came out of the entry, hiding bottles under their coats. A door opened behind them, emitted a clamour of laughter and talk, then closed into blackness. The men became quiet when they reached the street. They looked up and down, worried working men, then made off home in a hurry. The pasty-faced boy rubbed his shoulder-blades against the lamp-post. He flicked the butt of his cigarette against the brick wall, watched the sparks fall in the dusk. Then his eyes found Miss Hearne. He waited.

Miss Hearne went to the head of the entry and stood there, undecided. What a dark place, you could — anything could happen to you down there. Last time there was a little boy who did the errand. But it was in the daytime then. Still, I must have it, I've come so far.

She opened her bag and felt the pound notes inside. Maybe if a nice respectable man came out I could ask him, tell him it was for a sick person, he would understand. But go down that black entry, no. Men down there.

The pallid youth detached himself from the lamp-post. His ferret eyes blinked. Then he made up his mind. He grinned at Miss Hearne.

"Luckin" for sompin, missis?"

"Well, eh, yes, I was wondering, I mean, I have a friend who's sick."

He put out a hand that hadn't seen a tap for days. "Is it gin, missis? Wiskey, porther or stout?"

"Well, how much is it? Say whiskey?"

"Three poun"."

"O, but a cheap one would do. Three pounds, why that's exorbitant. Gin, how much is gin?"

"Three poun"."

"O, but look, what do you take me for? The best whiskey is only about two pounds. Two pounds two and six. And my goodness, gin couldn't be more than thirty-five shillings."

"Okay. I kin get ye wiskey for two poun' five."

"Well, that's still a lot."

He paid no attention. He looked up and down the street and smiled. "The peelers," he said. "They might be here anny-time. Then wat?"

Shakily Miss Hearne took two pound notes and a ten-shilling note out of her purse. "Would you mind getting me the whiskey then? And it had better be Jameson at that price, young man."

His dirty hand closed on the money. "Fix yew up in a minnut," he said and ran down the entry. The door flashed open for a moment. Miss Hearne, abandoned, looked up and down the mean street. Those street lights are so bright. What if the police *did* come?

The door banged again and the boy was back. He took a bottle wrapped in brown paper from under his coat.

"Put it away quick. I kin get jail for this," he said.

"What kind is it?"

"John Jameson. Hurry up, missis."

"Well, thank you," she said, putting the bottle in her bag. The neck stuck out. "It's for a sick friend, you see."

"Okay now. Bye bye." And he walked back to the lamp-post.

"Wait," Miss Hearne called. "The change. You owe me about seven shillings. Or at least five."

But the boy laughed. "Yer head's cut," he cried scornfully. "G'wan home. The peelers'll catch yew."

It was no use. She turned away, shaking more than ever. O, the terrible little gutty, the little gouger! At the bus stop she carefully unrolled the brown paper. The label on the bottle said "Dunrovin's Best old Scotch". She had never heard of it.

# CHAPTER
# THIRTEEN

When she reached Camden Street, Miss Hearne remembered that the neck of the bottle was sticking out of her bag. She removed the bottle and hid it under her coat. It was early, nine o'clock, and there was always the chance of meeting somebody on the stairs. But as she walked down the street, she saw that the house was dark. And when she let herself in, nobody seemed to be at home, not even Miss Friel. So much the better. She hurried to her own room, unlocked the door and put on the lights. Then she locked the door from the inside. Trembling, she put the bottle on the bedside table, drew the curtains and made her preparations. She undressed, put on her robe, lit the gas fire and drew a jug of water from the wash-basin tap. Then the seal on the terribly expensive bottle was broken and she poured the first drink. It made her cough, cheap nasty stuff, the kind of whiskey a person would pay thirty-five shillings the bottle. But it was whiskey; it was good to get it. She poured a second one, half a tumbler, and put some water in it. Drink this slowly; let it do its work.

But she had forgotten to . . . O, such a nuisance. She put down the glass, unlocked the door and tiptoed along the corridor to the lavatory. As she went in, she heard footsteps, soft footsteps. She waited until the footsteps had gone; then tiptoed back to the half-opened door of ther room.

O, it was good to get back in the heat again. She closed and locked the door.

"Good evening, Miss Hearne."

Miss Hearne pulled the lapels of her dressing-gown tight. A lightness took her in the head, making her sway. She turned around.

"What are you doing here? How dare you?"

"Please!" Bernard said. He stood with his back to the mantelpiece, looking quite unlike himself in a dark-blue suit, a clean shirt and a black knitted tie. His long blond hair was carefully combed and his shoes were black and shiny.

"I saw your door open, so I looked in. No harm in that, is there?"

He wouldn't dare, she thought. But they say that effrontery is a mark of such men. She went back to the door and unlocked it. "I was going out to a dance," he said. "But I decided to stay in and have a chat with you instead. There's something we should discuss."

"Mr Rice, really, I was going to bed. Some

220

other time, perhaps. If it's that pupil for piano lessons, we can talk about it in the morning."

"No, it's not that." He drew out her armchair. "Sit down, won't you? It's something rather private."

What does he mean, he couldn't want to attack me, I'll scream . . .

"I'll only stay a few minutes, Miss Hearne. Surely you can spare me a few minutes?"

"Well . . ."

"What about a drink? I see you have some Scotch."

"All right if I use this tooth-mug?"

She nodded and sat down in the armchair, her nervous dark eyes shifting from him to the door.

Bernard replenished her glass and filled his own. Then he pulled the old straight-backed chair up to the fire and sat down opposite her. "I'm going to be frank," he said. "I'm going to put my cards on the table. I want to talk about Uncle James."

"I — I don't understand."

"Uncle James is disturbing my work. He's made Mama upset and he's made life miserable for you. I've been watching you at breakfast. It shows."

"What do you mean?"

He held up a fat hand for silence. "You know very well what I mean. Now, take me, for instance. I don't mind telling you that I consider my work the only important thing in this affair. I'm writing a great poem. A *great* poem and it may

221

take years to finish. And in the meantime, I'm forced to live here and let Mama support me. Which is as it should be."

"O?"

He refilled his glass, and handed her the bottle. He looks a bit mad, she thought, I've noticed that he has a queer look about him. If he — I could scream. Somebody would hear, somebody. I need another drink. To steady me.

"People don't understand," he said. "But you should, you're a woman of some discernment. I need peace to work and Uncle James has destroyed all that. You see, Mama has changed since he came. She thinks he's got a lot of money and she wants to get it. She's greedy, poor Mama, not that I blame her, of course. There are no financial rewards in writing great poetry, you know."

"I suppose you could always get a job. I'm sure most poets have to work."

"No, no you don't understand. This work I'm doing, it's an epic poem, a great epic. This is just the first phase of it. It may take five years. Why should I prostitue my talent?"

He jumped up from his chair and began to walk about the room. "Why?" he said. "Why shouldn't my mother invest in immortality? After all, that's what mothers are for."

What a funny duck he is, half crazy, the artistic type, I suppose. She handed him the bottle and he poured two drinks. Why, I am not afraid of him at

222

all, he's harmless. Just a funny duck.

"No water, thanks," she said.

Bernard clasped his hands behind his back and struck a Napoleonic attitude, head thrust forward. "I'm forced to be ruthless," he said. "I can't let my work suffer from this situation. It's only right that Mama should support me. But now she's supporting Uncle James too, and that's not good for her morale. And he's got money, he doesn't need to be kept. Now, that's where you come in."

"Me?"

"You want him. Why don't you take him away from here?"

"How dare you? What on earth . . ."

"He loves you. *He loves you*, do you understand? He wants you and he thinks he's not good enough for you. Did you know that?"

"But — that's ridiculous. Why, only today he told me — he said some very harsh things, he hasn't the slightest intention of marrying me, I can tell you that."

"That's Mama's fault. She's been putting in the black word against you. Like that drinking business."

"*Well* — O, I know she's your mother and so forth, but *really*!"

Bernard nodded. "Yes Mama's a bitch, poor dear. Do you know what she told Uncle James about you? You'll not believe this, but she actually told him that you said he wasn't good enough for you. That you'd had enough of him!"

"But I didn't. I wouldn't dream . . ."

"I know. But Mama said you did, and he believed her. He's a very proud man, you know. That's why he was cruel to you today. His pride was hurt."

"But it couldn't be that. Why, I made myself perfectly clear. I — well, anyway, it isn't that at all. He's going to Dublin to do some business. That's why he was rude."

"What business? There's no business, believe me. The only place he wants to go is the States and he can't think of a good excuse to go back after boasting to all his friends over there that he was coming to Ireland to settle down. But if he got married, that would be another thing. He could go back then. To show his wife America, so to speak."

"It's true," she said. "He wants to go back."

"Of course he wants to go back. With you. He told me. After all, I'm his nearest male kin. But that was in confidence, you mustn't say I said it."

"No, no." She held out her empty glass. What if it could be true? It would explain so much, his cruelty, a fraud, you could see he was hurt the way he spoke, maybe, maybe . . .

Bernard tilted the neck of the bottle into her tumbler. "And he's not a bad catch financially," he said. "That's another consideration."

"But even if he wanted to marry me — which is not the case — even if he did, your mother has poisoned him against me."

224

"If you want him," Bernard said. "You'll have to go after him. You'll have to fight for him. And you will. Because you want him, you want him badly."

"How dare you!" she cried drunkenly. How dare you. Want him indeed, whatever gave you that idea?"

"I've watched you these last weeks. You're in love with him. But you allowed Mama to walk roughshod over you. Didn't you?"

"Well, she certainly had no business . . ."

"That's right. She had not. Now, what are you going to do about it?"

"Well, I — there's nothing more *to* do."

"You won't catch a man by sitting in your room sopping up whiskey, Miss Hearne. No, I'll tell you what you're going to do. You're going to tell him you love him. That you want to marry him. You're going to keep on telling him, no matter what he says. Because at first he won't listen . . ."

"But I couldn't. I wouldn't dream . . ."

"Yes, you could. And you will. Ask him, ask him, don't take no for an answer. He'll balk, he'll fuss, but he'll do it. Because he wants to. And you've got to."

"But it's unheard of — I couldn't bring myself. . ."

"You must," Bernard said quietly. "You need him badly."

"How dare you!"

"It's either that or drink yourself into a

225

madhouse. And you know it."

"Get out!" she screamed. "Get out this instant!"

"I'm sorry, Miss Hearne, I didn't mean to upset you. Keep your voice down, there's a good girl. You don't want Mama to come up and find you half seas over again, now do you?"

"No," she sobbed. "No, no."

"Or Uncle James. If he found you like this, he might believe Mama's stories. And that would be terrible, wouldn't it?"

"O, dear God," Miss Hearne sobbed, holding her face in her hands. "Leave me alone, leave me alone. Please!"

"Don't get hysterical, Miss Hearne, I'm trying to help you. Let's be sensible. You and I are going to hook him, if you do what I tell you."

She stopped crying then and sat up straight in her chair.

"What do you mean, *hook* him? Have you no morals? Have you no shame at all? And me, I'm as bad as you, listening to you, you horrid sneaky thing, poking your nose into other people's affairs."

"Come off it," Bernard said blithely, picking up the bottle.

"Put that bottle down! Taking what doesn't belong to you, have you no manners? A boy like you, what were you taught at school, where's your religion, you good-for-nothing little sneak, plotting the way you do?"

He laughed. "Religion is it? And what has

religion ever done for you, may I ask? Do you think God gives a damn about the likes of you and me? I don't know what got you into this mess. I can guess — you're no beauty and this is a hard country to find a man in — but I know what's keepng you this way. Your silly religious scruples. You're waiting for a miracle. Look at yourself: a poor piano teacher, lonely, drinking yourself crazy in a furnished room. Do you want to thank God for that?"

"So, you're an atheist!" she cried. "A rotten atheist. No wonder you think the way you do."

His fat face suffused with blood, his long blond hair falling over one eye, he leaned forward and caught her by the elbows. "I *think*, Miss Hearne. At least I do some thinking. I ask myself a few simple questions. Perhaps you can answer them for me. Your god is omniscient and omnipotent. That's what the Church says. Do you know what that means, omniscient and omnipotent? Knows everything and can do everything. All right. Then how can we hurt Him? Why does He allow all this suffering in His world? Why doesn't He answer your prayers, my mother's prayers? Has He ever repaid your faith in Him? Has He some secret reason for behaving the way He does, some reason He can't tell us? All right! Then why should I be expected to know His secret reasons? Why should I be expected to understand Him when an omniscient, omnipotent God can't give me the answers? It's stupid, stupid! Why are you alone tonight, if

227

it isn't for your silly religious scruples? Answer me that, Miss Hearne."

"Don't you dare take the Holy Name in vain," Miss Hearne cried. "God's ways aren't our ways. This life is a cross we have to bear in order to store up merit in the next. Don't you know your Catechism at all?"

"Is that your answer?" He looked at the picture on the wall. "You and your Sacred Heart. What the hell good has it done you? It's only an idealized picture of a minor prophet. It won't work miracles. You've got to make your own miracles in this world. Now, listen to me. I can help you, if you'll forget this nonsense and do what I say. You want a man. You can have Uncle James. But don't bore me with this nonsense, with these silly scruples. Your God is only a picture on the wall. He doesn't give a damn about you."

"Stop it!" Miss Hearne screamed. "Stop it, taking the Holy Name in vain. Get out of here this instant!"

"Shh! Bernard said. "You're waking the whole house. Sit down and keep quiet. I'm sorry I lost my temper. I'm sorry."

"I will not sit down," she cried. "You rotten atheist!" She struck at him. "Get out of here, get out of here."

But he had moved aside and her flailing arm met no resistance. She blundered against the bedside table, spilling the remains of the whiskey bottle on to the floor.

"*Look what you've done!*" she screamed. "*You've made me spill it!*"

His fat white hand caught her throat. He pressed her close as a lover. "Shut up," he whispered. "Shut up, for God's sake. You'll wake everybody up."

Caught in his flabby grasp, she fought to get free. Her fists beat against his face, his chest. He swayed back, catching his heel on the worn fibre threads of the carpet. He fell and she fell with him, close to the fire. Something hurt her head. But she became warm, sleepily warm, as her mind slipped into unconsciousness.

★　★　★

When she opened her eyes, she heard Mrs Henry Rice's voice, saw Mrs Henry Rice's feet in carpet slippers, a few inches from her face.

"A nice thing in a respectable house," Mrs Henry Rice said.

"I just came in to see what was wrong and she was lying there. She must have hit her head," Bernard said.

"It's a wonder she didn't kill herself. O, come on in, Jim, I want you to have a look at your dear friend, Miss Hearne."

"Accident?"

"Accident, my eye! Drunk as a lord and screaming all over the house. Well, it's my own fault, I should have asked for references. Out she goes, bag and baggage, first thing in the morning.

you look at the cut of her, Jim!"

"Put her on the bed," Madden's voice said. "She might have hurt herself. You can't leave her lying there."

Then hands, Madden's hands, slipped under her shoulders. Other hands lifted her feet. She kept her eyes shut, her mind shut as they lifted her on the bed. The shame of it, the shame. I must say something. Something.

But her arms would not obey when she tried to sit up. She fell back.

"Thanks be to God, Miss Friel is out, or I'd have lost two boarders instead of one. I never saw such a sight."

Somebody was bending over her. A man. *Him*? She opened her eyes a little and saw Bernard, his fat face near, his eyes worried.

"Go away," she cried. "You rotten atheist, go away?" She managed to sit up, her hair about her shoulders, her dressing-gown loose. "Filthy little liar," she cried.

Mrs Henry Rice, menacing, bent over the bed. Her great white arms reached out to seize Miss Hearne by the shoulders. She began to shake her. "Sober up!" she shouted. "Sober up. Have you no shame, carrying on like that?"

"Easy there, May," Madden said. "Let her be. Let her be."

But Mrs Henry Rice continued to shake until Miss Hearne jerked up and down like a rag doll.

"Leave her alone," Madden said, louder now.

"She's loaded, she doesn't know what she's saying."

Released, Miss Hearne turned her head, weeping, and pointed straight at Madden.

"You!" she cried. "And I thought you were a man. A man who could do his own asking, not a man that would send a rotten fat atheist to talk for him. You're as bad as the rest of them."

"What did she mean by that?"

"Never mind her. Never mind, she's off her rocker," Bernard said.

"Just a minute. *Just a minute*! What d'you mean by that, Judy? *Judy*?"

Miss Hearne fell back on the pillows, her hand over her eyes. "You know what I mean," she whispered. "You know."

"What?"

"He said you want to marry me. Tonight, he said it. He said you were afraid to ask." She looked up at him, her face a ruin of tears. "Why?" she cried. "Why?"

But Madden had grabbed hold of his nephew. "Leave me alone, Uncle James, leave me alone."

"What's this? What the hell's going on? What you up to, you creepin' jesus?"

"Leave me go, leave me go. It's nothing. Nothing."

"Leave my Bernie alone this minute. Leave him alone, you big bully."

"Please, Uncle James, you're breaking my arm!"

"Don't hit him. *Don't*, Jim, *don't!*"

"You sonofabitch, I got your number. Trying to get rid of me, eh? Telling her lies so's she'll chase me, eh?"

"No, *no*"

"I'm going, don't worry. But I got a few things to say before I do."

"No!" Bernard shrieked again. "*You were in it too, remember!*"

"Sleeping with the kid upstairs, your darlin' boy, that's what's worrying him. Shacking up every night with Mary. Look at him, May, look at him, if you don't believe me."

"Don't listen to him, Mama, he's telling lies. It was him, it was him that did it."

Mrs Henry Rice sat down on the armchair and keened back and forth. "No, no," she moaned. "You wouldn't do that, Bernie. You wouldn't do that to your poor mother."

"He would and he did," Madden shouted. "And then sneaking in here, trying to ruin me with that poor woman."

"Don't listen to him, Mama. Mama, please! He nearly tore Mary to pieces himself. Ask her, ask her, she'll tell you."

"I don't want to hear it," Mrs Rice shrieked. "I don't want to hear it, that child's only sixteen, O my God, the police could have you up, Bernie — Bernie, why did you do that to me?"

"Sixteen?" Madden said.

"Mama, you don't believe what he says? Mama

232

darling — ”

"Sixteen?" Madden said. "Christ!"

"Mama, listen, Mama — ”

"I don't want to hear about it," Mrs Rice cried. "I don't want to hear it. For the love of God, keep quiet, the pair of you, you'll have us all ruined, so you will. Away to bed with you, I don't want to hear any more. And for God's sake don't say a word to a single soul, promise me now? Promise? O Merciful Mother, what I have done to deserve this?"

"Come on,"Bernard said. "I'll put the lights out. Mama darling, don't worry, it's not true. it's not true."

"What about her?" Madden said, staring at the bed.

"Let her lie," Mrs Rice cried. "Let her lie, she's asleep. O, it's that woman brought bad luck on this house. Away to bed now, away to bed, both of you."

"Mama . . ."

"O Jesus, Mary and Joseph, *let me alone!*" Mrs Henry Rice cried.

The lights went out. Madden closed the door. The red glow from the gas fire flickered over the walls of the room. The woman on the bed lay quiet, staring at the ceiling. She did not hear the whispering as Mrs Rice, Bernard and Madden finally separated and went to their rooms. After a long time she turned her head and her nervous dark eyes searched for the bottle. It was lying by the grate. Spilled. All spilled.

# CHAPTER
# FOURTEEN

Next morning, when Miss Hearne did not come down for breakfast, Mrs Henry Rice went to see her in her room. She found Miss Hearne sitting by the fire, neatly dressed, wearing her hat and coat. The room had been tidied and the bed had been made.

"Good morning," Mrs Rice said, rumbling into the room like a tank with all guns at the ready.

Miss Hearne nodded. She was shivering, although the room was very warm. The effects of the drink, Mrs Rice said to herself, it's a miracle I never noticed it before.

"Miss Hearne, I'll have to ask you to leave. After last night, you understand, there can be no question . . ."

Miss Hearne nodded again. It's as though she doesn't understand what I'm saying, Mrs Rice thought. I wonder could she be a bit off? Some of these single women, the change of life comes early.

"I'd prefer to see you go as soon as possible. After what happened, I think it would be better."

"I'll go today," Miss Hearne said, without interest.

"Well, then, I'll refund the balance of the month from today, if that's satisfactory. I want to be fair."

Miss Hearne was looking at the gas fire. "Yes." she said.

"Well . . ." Mrs Rice hesitated. "If you're leaving, you'll have a lot to do. I won't keep you. You haven't had any breakfast. Would you like a cup of tea sent up?"

"No, thank you," Miss Hearne said, still staring at the gas fire.

Mrs Henry Rice shut the door with a bang. She might at least have apologized, after what happened last night, I wonder does she remember what was said, about Mary? I hope not. No, she was too far gone in drink. An apology, it's the least she could do after the way she carried on.

When she heard the door slam, Miss Hearne began to weep. Within a few minutes, her face was wet and her whole body shook with sobs. She wept very easily these days, but weeping did not help. It was exhausting though, and after a while, she closed her eyes and fell asleep, sitting in the chair.

She woke up when Mary put her pail down with a clatter on the landing outside. She got out of the chair and locked her door to keep the girl from coming in. Then she sat down again and looked at the gas fire.

If only I could stay in this room for ever. Never have to go out, never have to see anybody at all. Meals? They could leave them on a tray outside. No, better if I were sick, sick with something tragic; cancer or heart, then everybody would be sorry. The priest coming, whispers in the hall, same as aunt, people coming into the sick room, Moira O'Neill with calves' foot jelly and young Una, no smiles on her face, I would take her hand, my own hand white on the covers, and I would thank her for the grapes she had brought. And Owen O'Neill, asking me what the doctor had said, nodding his head, concerned. Mr Heron might come, making his small jokes about things at the Tech, telling me the class would be waiting for me, whenever I was up and about again. And Sister Imelda and the other nuns, a knitted bed-jacket, all in tissue paper, they'd lay it on the bed and tell me they were saying special prayers. The whole convent offering up a Holy Hour. And then Dr Bowe sitting by the bed, his gold watch in his hand, his fingers on my pulse. Keep her on a light nourising diet. Yes, wasting away slowly, everyone sorry. Everyone wanting to help. And her, Mrs Rice, all apologies, I'm tired now, Mrs Rice, would you mind? And *him*. His man-face weeping at my funeral. His only love. Standing in the rain at Nun's Bush while the others waited, a small sorrowing group and Father Quigley shovelled the earth. *Memento homo*, what is it? Remember man that thou art dust and unto dust thou shalt return. Then close the grave, close it quickly, the two men at my aunt's funeral, shirts and braces, shovelling the rest of the earth in. Owen O'Neill standing there to give them five shillings apiece for their trouble. The limousines at the gates of the cemetery with young Kevin O'Neill holding the pall-bearers' hats. Big black limousines waiting, Connelly's would do it, five cars and the hearse. And on the way back to Belfast, all saying how sorry, a devoted life really, fine woman, such a tragedy, spent the best years of her life looking after her aunt, yes, a saint really, a saint of heaven. And him, love-lorn, alone in a rented car, everyone wondering who he was and why an American at the funeral? A relative? No, they say he was going to marry her, poor man, you can see he's terribly upset. In grief, alone, year after year, never getting over it, never forgetting, never forgiving himself for his thoughtlessness.

Death. Beyond earthly cares. And then? Summoned before the judgment seat of heaven. The brilliance, the light, the Presence. Remember the last end. Remember the four last things, the missioner said: death, judgment, hell and heaven.

Thy sins. This: the body is the temple of the Holy Ghost. My temple degraded by alcohol. No, I didn't , not really. But drunkenness, a mortal sin, a sin of commission. O, my God, I am heartily sorry. Too late for that then. Judgment Day. Other sins? Seven, deadly: *pride, covetousness, lust.* Lust, the sins of the flesh. My sinful dreams, my evil thoughts. Sins of intent. O forgive me. Mortal Sin. *Anger, gluttony,* my sin, drinking. *Envy,* O, yes, I have committed that sin, yesterday, Moira O'Neill, I envied, I hated her. And how many other women have I envied? Many. *Mea culpa, mea culpa, Sloth,* the last sin. Sloth, remember, I asked old Father Farrelly about that once, no, my child, he said in the darkness of the confession box, I do not think you are guilty of that sin.

*Lust, envy, gluttony.* Three on which I will be judged. And — worst of all — the sin against faith. *Pride.* I doubted. Only last week in Saint Finbar's, the greatest sin of all, I denied God, like Peter, the tears wore grooves in Peter's cheeks. And last night, that horrid Bernard what does He care about you, he said, and I thought, yes. He does not care. Mortal sin. Cast into outer darkness. Loss of faith, loss of God, the greatest sorrow any human soul can feel, the missioner said. *Mea maxima culpa.* Perhaps that is why I sit here weeping, not knowing why I weep.

Three mortal sins I have, blackening my soul at this moment. Lucifer, daring to pit himself against God, to challenge His being. O, it's no wonder terrible things happen to me, I deserve them and worse, sitting here, feeling sorry for myself while I am lost in the sight of God. No, I must put it

239

right. Right with Him. For until then nothing can be right, nothing can succeed.

She turned the gas fire out. Hell-flames faded to white corpse bones in the dying heat of the mantles. She washed her face with cold water, no rouge now, no pomps of the flesh. In sackcloth they went, the penitents. O, you can understand it. She trembled, she felt ill, vomit rose, but it was a cross she was glad to accept. She went out then, downstairs, welcoming Mrs Henry Rice's prying peep from behind plucked lace curtains. A rebuke, deserved.

She walked all the way to the church, although she felt it an effort to put one foot in front of the other. No mercy, now, she said, no mercy for my sinful flesh. And she prayed as she walked, she talked quietly to God, God above who did not hear, and no wonder, she said. He cannot hear until I take my black rotten soul to be shriven.

God's confessor, His anointed priest would hear it all, he would give comfort. Father Quigley, I'll go to, a general confession, the kind I'm going to make should not be said before a young curate. Hollow-cheeked, he came before her, his accusing voice calling his parishioners to repent, to forget the world and its follies, to get down on their bended knees and prepare for their last end. He will be glad, a man of God, seeing the sinner sworn in God's ways, the erring sheep shorn of her sins. And at Mass, that day when I saw him first, I knew he would take poor Father Farrelly's place,

a real shepherd, and maybe even better than
Father Farrelly, more stern. For poor Father
Farrelly had known her and her aunt, had had tea
there many a time, and goodness knows, he was
the easy-going man in confession, nothing seemed
to shock him. Too easy, she said, walking down
the street that led to Saint Finbar's. Too easy on
me.

Her plan was to find out the hours of the confessional at the new parish. There were usually
confessions at six in the evening, and she had not
thought what she would do until then. But when
she went into the vestibule, small children ran past
her, swinging on the door handles. She entered
the gloom of the church, expecting to find some
schoolchildren's devotions in session. but instead,
there were lines of children, one or two to a bench,
forming two fidgeting, inattentive crocodiles on
either side of a confessional. She went up the side
aisle and read the name on the confession box. *Rev
D. Hanratty. CC.*

No. A young priest with a skin the colour of
grapefruit and a pompous Maynooth manner. She
had heard him preach at Mass a few Sundays
back. Young. Not wise in the ways of the world.

Then she saw the other two-tailed crocodile on
the far side. Little boys in one line, waiting to go
in behind the door marked MEN. And little chittering girls kneeling in the other line to tell their
sins under the door marked WOMEN. Their
confessor had not yet arrived.

She crossed the altar, genuflecting before the tabernacle, and hurried down the far aisle. The little half-door where the priest sat, was open, the curtain flapped in the wind of her passing. Over the door she saw his name. *Rev. F. X. Quigley. Adm.* Relieved, she knelt down at the end of the crocodile of little girls. The chittering ceased and the children turned frank, curious eyes on her. A woman, praying. Then, seeing no danger from her, they resumed their whispering, their squirming. All awaited the priest.

Ten minutes later he came out of the sacristy, making a busy genuflection as he passed the altar, his black soutane swirling around his large black boots, the end of his stole fluttering. His dark eyes glared at the children as he came through the gate and into the body of the church. Warning: be quiet. You are in God's house. With the possibility of a good clip on the ear to enforce reverence. Or tell your teacher. No nonsense.

Wise in the moods of authority, the children practised silence, leaned their heads against the benches in front of them and feigned prayer. Quickly, Father Quigley strode past the line of boys and reached his half-door. But turned then and looked along the line of little girls. That woman at the end of the line, didn't she know these were children's confessions? Or was she at the ninth station of the cross? Maybe, most likely, yes. Satisfied, he slammed the door shut behind him, pulled the red plush curtain across to hide his upper half and sat his bony buttocks on the horse-hair cushion covering the wooden seat.

Penance-giver, he prepared for the penance of listening. Expiator, he hurried to his task of washing away the twin sinful crocodiles. He shot the little slot open with a plock! on the first quivering boy who waited in the darkness on his knees, his small story rehearsing in his mind. Father Quigley bent his head, rested it on his hand. Rissoles, he thought, they give me the heartburn.

"Blessme Father forIhavesinned," the boy whispered.

"How long since last confession?" Father Quigley said, the efficient foreman, setting the belt of sins in motion. Rissoles, he thought, as the boy told of lies. I must ask Father Hanratty if he likes them. We could surely do better than rissoles on a Monday, with a whole roast chicken yesterday, there should be more than Monday rissoles out of it.

Outside the confessional, the children appeared to be engaged in a form of musical chairs. As each small penitent left the box, the remaining queue moved up one bench nearer. Thus, every few minutes the crocodile reared up, weaving in and out of the benches, and Miss Hearne, a tall vertebra in the crocodile's tail, was obliged to move in turn. It was distracting and she found little time for sustained prayer. She did, however, manage to say her *confiteor* and again examine her conscience. And so, head filled with ejaculations

243

and contrition, she at last found herself in front of the door marked WOMEN. The trembling had come back and her sickness was on her again. Just nervousness, she said to herself. But she knew it was also the after effects of drink.

A little girl ducked out through the door, ran to a bench, mumbled her penance and left the church. The queue behind Miss Hearne grew restless. The crocodile waited to rear forward again. A small fist dug in Miss Hearne's back.

"It's your turn, missis."

Shakily, Miss Hearne went in, closed the door behind her and knelt in the shadowy anonymity of the small cabinet. A cross with an ivory Christ hung above her head. Behind the iron grille with its wooden shutter, she could hear Father Quigley's grunting interrogation of a small boy. She waited, holding the edge of the grille for comfort. He would help her. He would know what was best. She heard his deep manly voice begin the words of absolution. Soon.

Plock! Light filled the dark box as he slid the wooden door aside. Framed by the grille, she saw his hollow-cheeked face, his head resting on one hand, the purple and white of the stole around his neck. He leaned forward, listening, not looking at her.

"Bless me, Father, for I have sinned."

"How long since last confession?"

"Three weeks, Father."

Father Quigley (Aha!) had waited. After all, if it

was a real sinner, come back after a year, maybe, that would be different. But you might know it, his mind raged, one of these old bodies that takes an hour to tell you nothing. "What do you mean, three weeks, my good woman, don't you know this confession period is for the children? For the children. The grown-ups' confession is at six and eight. Not now. Now, what's the meaning of this, coming here with the children, *with the children?*"

"O, Father, I'm sorry, Father, but I had to come now. I have to make a general confession, Father."

Blessus and saveus, Father Francis Xavier Quigley said to himself. A general confession, no less. And I promised to see Father Feeny for golf at half-past one. Well, you never know, maybe she's in trouble, this poor soul.

A general confession, my child, is there something that's bothering you? Something in particular? Some sin in particular? Is that it?"

"O Father, yes, Father."

"All right, my child, tell me about that sin."

"O father — it's drinking."

"I see. Drinking to excess, is it? How many times?" (I wouldn't have taken her for that.)

"O, Father, yesterday. And last week. I lost all control."

"I see. And have yu done this many times before?"

"No, Father. Well — yes — sometimes. You see, Father, I had a lot of things I was unhappy about, Father, and that started it."

"I see. You know, that's a very bad habit, drinking to excess, drunkenness, that is, it leads to all sorts of sins."

"Yes, Father."

"Yes, it leads to other sins. Do you understand that, my child?"

"O yes, Father. Father, I . . . "

"Now any other sins, my child?"

"Yes, Father. I doubted my faith, Father. I need your advice because I had moments of doubt, Father."

Father Quigley raised his head. His face was in profile and it seemed as though he were listening to some distant sound. "And what doubts were those, my child?" he asked in a quiet voice.

"Well, Father, I doubted that God was in the tabernacle. I doubted if He cared about me."

"I see. And did you have this doubt for long, my child?"

"O, no, Father. It passed almost immediately. But it occurs to me now and then, this thought, although I try to stop it."

"And did you pray to our Lord for guidance, my child? You should pray for guidance, pray to our Holy Mother and to the Sacred Heart if ever such a thing should happen again. Everyone has moments of doubt, my child, everyone, even the holy saints. But you must pray for faith. You will do that now, won't you?"

"O, yes, Father. But Father, why? I mean, why

246

should I be losing my faith like this? Why do I doubt? Why doesn't the Sacred Heart answer my prayers? Why?"

(These single women, I'm sure she's single, they'd talk your head off, every blessed one of them.) "Well, my child, God's ways aren't our ways. You should ask for guidance, pray every day to our Blessed Mother to help you. Will you do that now ?"

"O, yes, Father. Father . . ."

"Now, any other sins, my child? Anything else?"

"Father, I want to ask your advice about another matter."

"Yes?"

"Father, I've nobody to advise me. You see, Father, I live alone, I've lived alone since my aunt died. Father Farrelly used to be my regular confessor, before I moved to this parish. He's gone now, Father, I'm alone a great deal and I often feel a bit depressed, that's how I started to take a drop to cheer me up. And recently, I was nearly engaged to a man, but it — it hasn't worked out very well. And, of course, Father, when you're my age, that's a worry. I've got no relatives at all, just friends and — mind you, I'm not saying this man would have been quite suitable, I don't think so, as a matter of fact — but anyway, as I was saying, I'm all alone and I'm afraid because I don't feel well sometimes and a drink seems to help me. I know it's sinful, and I know I should

247

pray more, and . . ."

But she stopped speaking. She had seen his face. A weary face, his cheek resting in the palm of his hand, his eyes shut. He's not listening, her mind cried. Not listening!

He began to speak: "Now, my child, we all have burdens put upon us in this life, crosses we have to bear, trials and tribulations we should offer up to Our Lord. And prayer is a great thing, my child, a great thing. We should never be lonely because we always have God to talk to. And our guardian angel to watch over us. And we have a mother, our Heavenly Mother, to help us and intercede for us. Yes, we have a Holy Family, each and every one of us. All we need to do is pray. Pray, my child, ask God's aid in fighting these temptations."

"Yes, Father." (O, he doesn't understand, he doesn't.)

"Now, I want you to say five Our Fathers and five Hail Marys as penance for your sins."

And then his voice, mumbling the Latin, giving the sacred words of absolution, the words in which, acting as God's medium, he washed the soul white as purest snow. His fingers raised in the sign of forgiveness. The confession was over.

"God bless you now, my child. And say a prayer for me."

The slide shot shut. The box was black. Plock! The slide on the other side shot open and a boy's voice mumbled: "Blessme Father for I have sinned."

And she was alone in the darkness. Shriven, her sins washed away.

She opened the door and walked down the side aisle to kneel at the back of the church. Her penance said, she started a rosary to Our Lady. Perhaps through prayer, hard prayer, she could conquer her fears, her troubles. If what Father Quigley said was true, she had a family. The Holy Famlily. They would help her.

But as she said the second mystery, she stopped and gazed at the faraway alter. What good, if even God's anointed priest did not understand? He did not listen, he cut me off, nicely, of course, but he cut me off. And the rude way he told me I shouldn't be having my confession heard at this time. Instead of showing some understanding. We all have burdens, he said. As if he didn't want to hear them, don't bother me with your troubles. An ignorant man. God's anointed, with God's guidance, he should have known it was important, perhaps the most important confession of my life. But he didn't see that. And if he didn't see, why didn't You tell him, O Sacred Heart, why didn't You guide him, help him to help me? Why?

The tabernacle door was covered with a white curtain. It was screened, it gave no answer. She looked at the confessional and saw the last child leave. Then Father Quigley stepped out of his retreat. He looked up and down the church, took off his stole, and hurried towards the sacristy. He genuflected on the run as he crossed the alter. As if he's late, she thought. Late for an appointment.

Kneeling in the silence of the church, she remembered the night she had knelt alone and saw the old sacristan make his hurried genuflection. The Priest of God and the Keeper of God's Secrets, both passed God's temple as though they were unbelievers, performing a perfunctory obeisance, a matter of habit. As though they both knew there was no need to bow, as though the tabernacle were empty.

Was it? Was there nothing to pray to? Was the confession she had just made a form, something you went through to ease your conscience? If it was, then how easy to explain all the miseries, the follies, all the useless novenas, the prayers that never got an answer. And if it was true, then all the priests, all the bishops, all the cardinals are wrong. Deluded men, believing that they are being helped by a God who is not there. An unhelpful God. Why does He make men suffer? Bernard had said. Why should my sins hurt Him?

She saw the Pope, Christ's Vicar on Earth, tall, white-robed, his fingers extended in blessing. Surely he, a saint of God, would have helped her. But what if he could not? What if there was no God? What if he, the general of the great army of the church, knew there was none? How could the Pope, the bishops, the priests, tell the people? For they had always believed in a merciful Jesus. They could not be disillusioned. It would be too cruel.

250

The priest had no reverence in his genuflection. And the Pope? Supposing the Pope did not know for sure, supposing the Pope did not really know if there was a God, or if . . .

Bread, only bread in the tabernacle. I am losing my faith. O merciful God, do not leave me, do not abandon me, hear me; O Sacred Heart, hear my prayer. Give me faith, Sweet Jesus, give me strength, give me Thy Eternal Love.

And if it is only bread? O my God, protect me. O Holy Mary, intercede for me.

Mary, hands raised, a painted statue.

And if it is only bread?

If no one hears?

No one.

No one. The church, an empty shell, nobody to hear, no reason to pray, only statues listen. Statues cannot hear.

And if I am alone?

If I am alone it does not matter what life I lead. It does not matter. And if I die I am a dead thing. I have no eternal life. No one will remember me, no one will weep for me. No one will reward the good I have done, no one will punish the sins I have committed.

No one.

If it is only bread.

O Merciful God, save me. O Mother Mary, protect me. O saints and angels, intercede for me. O Sweet Jesus, save me. O Blessed Virgin, protect me.

Tower of Ivory,
House of Gold,
Ark of the Covenant,
Gate of Heaven.
And there, behind that gate, behind the tabernacle door?
Gate of . . .
Only bread.
She stood up, staring at the tabernacle. She stepped out of her bench. She did not genuflect. She turned away from the alter and walked slowly out of the church. Her hand, from the habit of a lifetime, found the Holy Water font, dipped two fingers in it. But she did not make the Sign of the Cross.

Show me a sign, she said.

# CHAPTER
# FIFTEEN

Mr Mick Malloy, cashier at the Ulster and Connaught Bank, draped his grey sports jacket neatly on a hanger and put on his black shantung work coat. He unlocked the door of his small cage and whistled a few bars from Offenbach's *Tales of Hoffmann* as he went in. Discreetly, because old McStay hated that. Lunch at the Bodega, an occasion, it had put him in fine fettle. With two halfuns of whiskey and a glass of beer afterwards with the roast beef. By God, Mr Malloy said to himself, and all because of a horse I never saw and never will. Flammarion, my beauty, I must watch for you the next time you're out.

John Harbinson, the messenger, was opening the doors to the public and removing the lunch card. Mr Malloy set his little cage in order. I wonder now, he said to himself, I wonder would there be a bit of gold going this week-end? He rubbed the bald spot on the back of his head speculatively. There might, there might indeed, if the weather held up at all.

Mr Mick Malloy, tall young secret gambler with devil-may-care eyes and a long humorous nose, became Mr Malloy, tall cashier with a dignified face, a gentlemanly bank clerk, a nice sort of fellow. He smiled politely at the funny-looking duck.

"Yes, Madam?"

By the holy, thought Mr Malloy (the rake), that one wouldn't be an occasion of sin for any man. And indeed she was a sight. On the wrong side of forty with a face as plain as a plank, and all dressed up, if you please, in a red raincoat, a red hat with a couple of terrible-looking old wax flowers in it. And two, it's the mortal truth, two red rings on the one hand.

No mint of money there, thought Mr Malloy, the cashier.

"I'd like to draw some money," said the red coat.

Mr Malloy took her book and checked it with his ledger.

"And how much would you be wanting, Madam?"

"Fifty pounds."

The lot, damn near. £58 16s 2d. Minus, equals £8 16s 2d. Clerkly, Mr Malloy rechecked. Book compared. Approved. Signature on cheque. Rubber stamp. "And how would you like it, Madam?"

"O, five-pound notes and one-pound notes."

"Fives and singles." Mr Malloy remembered happily the pleasant pay-off he himself had received down Union Lane just after the bank closed for lunch, two quid each way, Flammarion, there yew are, mister, the dirty bookie's clerk said, sliding no less than sixteen quid across the counter, remembering his own good fortune, Mr Malloy paid out the money cheerfully.

She took it and her hands were trembling. Would that be a disease, is it Parkinson's they call it? Mr Malloy (student of mankind) wondered. She has the look of a sick person, he decided, watching her count it.

Right you are. Book back. Entries made. Check. Recheck.

"Thank you," she said, taking the book and the money, sweeping them into her big old purse.

"Thank you, Madam. Good day to you."

Not a single good-looking, let alone smashing, girl has walked into this bank all week, Mr Mick Malloy (philosophic philanderer) thought, watching the funny-looking duck walk away.

Ah, well! Lucky at cards. Or rather, horses. My bonny Flammarion.

Next customer!

Mister William Creegan, wine and spirit merchant, came out from the back and caught young Kelly reading a magazine. *Movieland*, it said in bright blue letters across the top.

"Is that what I'm paying you for?" Mister

William Creegan said.

"Nosir."

If I catch you at it again, you can take your cards and go."

"Yessir." Young Kelly skittered away to the other end of the shop, making believe he had some bottles to put up for an order. Mister William Creegan consulted the gold half-hunter watch his own father had worn. Ten to three. He had to buy an ironing board. Later. He put the watch back in his vest pocket and arranged the gold chain across his middle.

Jing, jing, jing! the bell cried. Mister William Creegan looked over at Kelly. Never mind, his grey eyes said, I'll take it myself.

A bit old for that sort of get-up, he thought as he cracked his solemn jaw into a smile. A red coat and she must be about the age of my Agnes.

"Good afternoon," he said. "And what would you be wanting?"

"Two bottles of John Jameson, please. And a bottle of gin. Gordon's, I think."

A lady by the sound of her. He looked at the trembling hands. Ah, dear, my fine lady, I know your trouble.

"Mis-TER Kelly!" Proprietor William Creegan called. "Two Jameson and a Gordon's."

"Would that be to be sent now?" he asked solicitously. For she'll never have the strength to lift it herself.

"O, dear."

"It's a bit of a weight to carry," William Creegan, wine merchant, said. He knew his wine, his spirits.

"Well, perhaps I could take one with me and you could send the others."

Pencil. Order pad. All attention, he looked up.

"And what's the address, please?"

"Well . . ."

Ah, I know your trouble. No priest knows better. A man gets to be a mind-reader in the business of selling spirits.

"Now, I could give you a shopping bag, if you like," he said. "It mightn't be so heavy after all."

She smiled at him. She looks as if she'd been crying, God knows the troubles people have. And the trouble they bring on themselves. He looked at her left hand. No ring. Have I seen her before?

"Good afternoon, miss," young Kelly said, putting the two Jamesons and the Gordon's down on the counter.

O, he knows her, does he? A regular customer, I wonder. Well, thought Proprietor Creegan, she buys the very best.

"That'll be five pounds, eighteen shillings and ninepence," he said.

She opened her old purse and pulled a clutter of notes out of it. William Creegan, wine and spirit merchant, looked at the white fives, the green ones.

"I'll put it in a bag with a handle on it," young Kelly said. "Then you'll be able to manage."

Mister William Creegan made change. "Do you know her?" he said out of the side of his mouth.

"Sure. But she must have come into money," young Kelly whispered. "Most of the time it's fifteen bob tonic wine. One bottle only."

Mister William Creegan slid the cash drawer shut and turned gravely.

"Five, eighteen and nine." He paid three coppers into her trembling hand. "That's five nineteen. And a shilling is six."

"Thank you."

"And here's your parcel. Can you manage it, do you think?"

She took the bag, lowered it to the floor and lifted it again. "O, yes, it will be all right, thank you."

"Thank *you*. Good afternoon now."

"Let me see now," the clerk said. "You're the lady who telephoned from the station. Yes, here it is. A single room. Would you mind signing the register?"

He looked at the two bell-boys. They waited the word. They wore little round caps with PLAZA HOTEL across their brows.

"Number two-one-four," the clerk said, handing them the keys.

"Can I take that bag, ma'am?" the bell-boy said, reaching for the paper bag which the lady held in her arms.

"I, I think my trunks will be quite enough for

you," she said, smiling weakly. "They're quite heavy, you know."

"We can manage the bag as well, ma'am."

"No, I'll carry it." And she went shakily to the elevator.

Bottles, the hotel clerk said to himself. Bottles, by the sound of them, when she picked it up. She has the look of a schoolteacher on a spree. Well, it takes all kinds. A hotel is your home. In your home, you are master, unless you offend the neighbours. Mindful of the precept, he promptly forgot the matter. He picked up the afternoon post and began the slow labour of filing it in pigeon-holes.

★ ★ ★

"Thank you, ma'am," the older bell-boy said, pocketing silver. "Would you like the window open a little?"

"No. Just draw the curtains."

"And there's your key, ma'am," the second bell-boy said.

"Thank you. Good night."

"Good night. Good night. And thank you."

They closed the door. The lady went to the wash-basin, took a glass from it and sat down in an armchair, still wearing her red hat, her red rain-coat.

"How much?" the older bell-boy said to the younger as they sauntered down the corridor.

"Five bob, would you believe it?"

"Me too."

"She doesn't look that type."

"Ah, sure you never can tell. Some of these ould dolls are rollin' in it. And to look at her, you wouldn't think she had tuppence."

"Where?" asked Mr Lenehan.

"To the Plaza Hotel, no less," Miss Friel told him. "You could have knocked me over with a feather when she told the taxi driver."

"The *Plaza*? Did she win the football pools or somethin?"

"Win nothing! Mrs Rice packed her off, bag and baggage, today. But the best of it is, she came back this afternoon to get her things. And would you believe it, she had a shopping bag full of whiskey bottles under her arm. O, I had the measure of *her* a long time ago!"

"Off on a toot, eh?"

"Butter wouldn't melt in her mouth, the bad article, but I was passing quite close to her door a few minutes after she came back and what should I hear but the sound of a bottle hitting a glass."

"You've got good ears," Mr Lenehan said, grinning.

"Do you want to hear the rest of it, or don't you? I'm not going to stand here and be insulted."

"Now, no offence meant. So you heard her guzzlin' it up?"

"Heard her? Two minutes later you could hear her all over the house, singing away like a flock of parrots. I couldn't do a stitch of reading, so I put my book down and went to her door and gave it a rap."

"That shook her, eh?"

"Well, you should have seen her. She had on a red dress, bright red, you've never seen the like of it. And a red hat, I tell you, it was comic. "Are you leaving?" I said. "Yes," she said, "I'm leaving. I'm sorry if the packing has inconvenienced you. Now, I've got things to do," she said, bold as brass. "Would you mind?" The cheek of her! Well, I gave her a look as much as to say, I know what's the matter with you, my lady, drunken old, cheeky old, thing. And then I just looked at the bottle. A bottle of whiskey right there on the table. And a glass half full of it, without benefit of water. I just looked at it and said, "Well, I hope you'll keep sober until you're ready to clear out. Because we won't be able to carry you down the stairs.'"

"And what did *she* say?"

"What could she say? Half an hour later she was out in the street with Bernie Rice helping her to load her trunks on a taxi. And the cut of her! Holding this shopping bag full of booze in her arms as though it was a baby."

"Wait till Madden hears this," Mr Lenehan said. "That'll put the ould Yank's nose out of joint."

"Is she gone?"

"Yes, Mama."

"Did she say anything?"

"No, Mama."

"And what about him?"

"He's upstairs packing now. He says he's taking the train tonight for Dublin."

"He'd better. I'll be glad to see the back of both of them. And there'll be another at the end of the week. I gave that girl her notice this afternoon."

"But Mama, it's not true what he said."

"Don't you add the sin of telling lies to what you've done already. I had it out with that child this afternoon, I don't want to hear another word, O, men are filthy beasts, every blessed one of them."

"But Mama, it was him, not me."

"I know it was him, the girl told me, what do you think I gave him his marching papers for? To think that a brother of mine — O, don't say another word, it doesn't bear thinking of."

"But Mama, please! Mary will tell you, I did nothing."

"I didn't ask her. And I'm not going to. I just don't want to hear it mentioned again. And Bernie, I want you to promise me one thing."

"What, Mama?"

"There's confessions tonight over at Saint Finbar's. I want you to promise me to go. That's not much to ask, now is it?"

"No. I'll go. Mama, I'm sorry about all this."

"Don't try to get on the soft side of me now. It

just goes to show what I've been saying to you all along, Bernie, if you paid more attention to your religious duties, these things wouldn't happen. Because, Bernie, it doesn't matter what you do in this world, it's the next world that counts. Mass and Holy Communion would suit you better than trying to get back on my good side again. Make your peace with Our Blessed Lord, that's what counts."

"Yes, Mama."

"You'll do that now, won't you, Bernie, for my sake? When I think of all I've gone through in the last week, first that woman, and then your Uncle James, a scandal, and that slip of a girl that I treated as well as if she was in her own home. Nice gratitude, I tell you."

"I know. But it will be all right now."

"I'll *make* it all right, so I will. I'll not have the whole town talking about us. I don't want to hear another word about this, now or ever, do you hear me, Bernie?"

"Yes, Mama."

Barman Kevin O'Kane, his red pompadour of hair bright as a brilliantine advertisement under the light, bent over and drew a glass of Guinness Double X. He sliced the head even with a ruler and placed the glass, white on rich black, in front of Major Mahaffy-Hyde. "So the Yankee's gone," he said. "Well, he was a good customer, no doubt about it."

"A grand fellow," Major Mahaffy-Hyde said, drawing the glass of stout towards him. "A grand, open-handed, big-hearted fellow."

Kevin O'Kane looked along the deserted expanse of mahogany, wiped himself elbow room, and leaned forward confidentially: "I hear tell he's going into business in Dublin," he said. "What do you make of that, major?"

"That'll be the day," the major said, brushing foam from his straw-coloured moustache. "Far be it from me to doubt a man's word, but I don't put too much faith in *that* tale. You'd think the police were after him, he was so glad to get on that train."

"Aye, he made up his mind quick enough. Yesterday, there was no word of leaving."

The major smiled a wicked parrot smile: "Or had it made up for him, Kevin lad. Did you ever think of that now? Y'know he let slip something this evening that could be a clue. It could be a clue."

"Just a minute, major, I'll be right with you."

Kevin O'Kane went down to the end of the bar, put a double Johnny Walker Black Label in front of a commercial traveller, name of Craig, made change, and returned to hear the clue.

"Remember that woman he was going into business with? The one that turned out to be poor as a pauper? You remember that, Kevin?"

"Aye, many's the time he talked about the way she led him up the garden path."

"It could be the other way around," the major said. "Did you see his face when he came in tonight?"

"A real thundercloud, major."

"Eggs-actly! Well, tonight he informs me that she's just moved into the Plaza Hotel, if you please."

"Oho!"

"And that's not the best of it, Kevin lad. Y'see, it's my bet he was a bit of a scoundrel, the bold James Madden. And it's my bet he diddled her out of a bit of cash and then threw her over. And now, when he's getting ready to skip off to Dublin, he finds out that there's more where that came from. But not for him. D'you follow me?"

"Aye, I wouldn't put it past him."

"Eggs-actly! A real Yankee-doodle blather! Too smart for his own good, do you follow me?"

# CHAPTER
# SIXTEEN

It was a lovely room, the kind of room she never could afford in her aunt's day, or after. A heavy broadloom carpet, golden brocade hangings and the finest soft double bed you could imagine. And central heating, comfy armchairs and no sound from the corridor. And the dinner, served on a tray, with heavy silver dish-warmers over each course, was lovely too. But there was no pleasure from the room and she left the dinner almost uneaten. What good was it, if there was no one to show it to, no one to share with?

And it was so expensive. So terribly expensive. The habits of years, the constant counting of the cost, the careful measuring of pounds, shillings and pence, wondering if there will be enough to last the week, these things become part of you; it is hard to wave them all away in a single day. Each time money had to be paid out, it had been as hard to give more, to disregard the cost, as formerly it was to make do on too little. So expensive, and really not worth it. But no, she would not count it to see how much had gone. That was not part of the bargain. She would just pull it out of her purse when it was needed, until every penny was spent. And then?

Miss Hearne stood up, drink in hand, and went to the window. She pulled aside the heavy curtains and looked out. Here, in the best hotel in the middle of Belfast. Me. But Royal Avenue was asleep, a wet grey belt studded with garish street lamps. A policeman turned his back against the wind and huddled in a doorway. A lonely tramcar clattered by, bright-lit, empty, its conductor standing alone on his platform, fareless and forlorn. Traffic lights flashed red, amber and green in empty futility. Two late-goers passed below on the pavement, the voices loud, unreal in argument.

What time at all at all? My clock, she turned balancing the drink dangerously on the window-sill, and hurried to her bag. The little travelling clock her dear aunt had received as a gift from Paris was on top. Five in the morning! How? Where did the evening go?

The bottle said: I am almost empty. It stood on the floor, near the bed, a small black accusing smoke-stack. Empty, it said, your fault.

No, she said, smiling at the bottle. You're behind the times. There is, she told the bottle, no earthly reason to feel sorry. Because there is no heavenly reason to feel guilt. At least, nobody has shown me that there is. And I'm waiting to be shown, dear bottle. I'm waiting patiently. It's five o'clock already.

Too much, the black bottle said. Nearly empty. You are drunk. You drink too much.

Drunk? Any why not, nobody's to mind, nobody minds if I'm anything. Nobody, not a single soul, I'm free. I'm — falling.

The bed, not mine at all. The hotel. The drink spilled on the bedspread. I'll have to pay, who cares? Only money as Dan Breen used to say. Only money. And meanwhile, as long as I've fallen on this bed, I might as well sleep. My shoes, I should take off. Off with my shoes. Sleepy shoes.

Sleepy smiling shoes.

Sleep.

★ ★ ★

And then, later, the clock says it's after nine and the noises outside on the street, such a noisy place. Royal Avenue. Put the lights off and draw the curtains I feel quite rocky.

A drink, That will put me right. Stop this giddy feeling. There, it's horrible tasting, the first sip. Right as rain. Well, not really, but it helped. And today is a gay day, in a fine hotel, money to do whatever takes my fancy and nobody or nothing to worry about. Except *him*. Maybe if he heard I've left Camden Street, he might come after me. Down to the hotel here. No, he won't, he said those things. Don't worry about him. I have other friends, good friends, the finest friends any girl could ask for. The O'Neills, they adore me. And Edie Marrinan. And Sister Imelda and all the other nuns; O, I have no lack of friends. Now, Edie, for instance, Edie and I used to have rare sport together. Poor Edie.

She thought of Edie, lying in bed at Earnscliffe Home, looking old and sick, arthritis it was, poor Edie, in among all those old people and nuns. Edie that used to be such a gay one, and now to tell the truth, I hate to go and see her, so depressing and such a long way out, it takes you fifteen minutes to walk up to it from the main gate. Or it did. Delightful thought. A taxi can get you there in no time. And why not? Edie was the gay soul, why a drink is just the very thing she needs.

Wearing her red raincoat and her red hat, with her cheeks heavily rouged and with a bottle of Gordon's gin in her handbag, Miss Hearne waited in the lobby of the hotel until the commissionaire told her he had a taxi. She gave him three shillings. The taxi driver was very respectful and he seemed to know where Earnscliffe was. It was a nice big taxi with little jump seats folded down so that they acted as foot-rests, and grey upholstery, very clean and comfortable. Pleasant to have one's own car and chauffeur like some of the people who lived on the Malone Road, driving down into the city every morning to do your shopping, the liveried man waiting to open the door of the car and help you with your packages.

A *grande dame*, Miss Judith Hearne of Bellavista, Malone Road, Belfast, relaxed among the soft cushions as her Daimler purred politely past lesser cars. Musical, she thought of the musicale she would give that evening. Gieseking had promised to be present and there would be a small recital. 'Cello and piano, the Steinway grand in the large alcove of the drawing-room. The butler would announce the guests, yes, they were all there, the handsome soldier she had admired so much in the advertisements for The Greys' cigarettes. A diplomat, French, but with a face like Lord Louis Mountbatten, bowing over her hand, an old lady who wore a strange sash, Maude Gonne MacBridge, once the most beautiful woman in Ireland, Judy, how delightful to see you again. And in a corner, dressed properly in evening clothes, affable in the manner of his race, James Madden, impressed, hardly daring to speak to her. Gracious, she smiled at him over the Lord Bishop's hand. Your Excellency, scarlet robes, princely priest. Father Quigley, the bishop said, O my dear Miss Hearne, I don't seem to recall his name. Quigley? O, yes a very good man, no doubt. But my dear Miss Hearne, I will advise you, I should consider it an honour. Only my duty. Princely, the bishop passed, made way for Moira O'Neill gushing, O Judy dear, what a wonderful evening! Eyebrows slightly lifted: O, did you enjoy it, Moira dear? And how are the children? So long since I've seen them, yes, it was Paris this time, the Duc de Guise simply insisted I stay another week. I've been so terribly rushed. Yes, I must try to get over some Sunday.

"Is this it, mum?" the driver asked, stopping the car before a set of heavy iron gates. He sounded the horn.

A man, a weary old pensioner with a bald dirty head and a stained brown corduroy waistcoat, appeared at the door of a small gate lodge. He saw the car and opened the gates. Slowly the driver accelerated and like a royal limousine entering some great demesne, the car squished forward over the gravel and went whirling up the avenue under the tall trees. Miss Hearne looked out, saw the sky above her in gulps of speed. Earnscliffe. Poor Edie!

Earnscliffe Home had been built as a private mansion by a mercantile family in the spacious days at the turn of the century. The main building with its Grecian columns on either side of the door reminded Miss Hearne of the Georgia mansion she had seen in *Gone with the Wind*. But the stone was granite and the symmetry of the house was destroyed by long red-brick pavilions which stretched like crucified arms on either side of the main building. The gravel approach was covered with rotting leaves and the withering trees behind the home sighed and crackled like old abandoned newspapers. The windows were small and dark and those on the ground floor were equipped with iron bars. The trees, the large sweep of the grounds and the country quiet of the air, gave Earnscliffe the look of a deserted house. But the iron bars, the crucifix which hung over the door, and the smoke from the ugly red-brick pavilions said that this was an institution, that people lived here, and that some lived here against their will. Miss Hearne was always saddened and frightened when she came to this place.

She rang and waited. Wondered how long she should wait before ringing again. Time always seemed longer in a place like this. Better not be impatient. Carefully she clutched her big bag, holding the neck of the bottle inside the cloth. Then there was a sound. It was a sound of keys and linen and, although Miss Hearne did not recognize it, of the heavy black rosary beads, large as liquorice lozenges, knotted around the waist of the nun who opened the door.

She revealed herself slowly as the door swung back; first, her hand, old , clean and withered; then the black stuff of her habit, and finally, her face, framed by the black veil with crimped white linen edging, her cheeks scrubbed clean and reddened to an apple brightness by years of vigorous ablutions with hard cheap soap. A lay sister labouring for ever at humble tasks.

"Yes?"

"I'd like to see Miss Marrinan."

"But it's not visiting time."

"O? But couldn't you make an exception? I'm a

very dear friend of hers, and I've come specially."

The old face shook from side to side like the trees outside. She had her orders. No. No use to appeal. Orders of the Order. No exceptions. No.

"But this is ridiculous." Miss Hearne cried. "Let me talk to Reverend Mother then."

"What is it, Sister?" A softer voice, behind the door.

"O, Sister, a lady." The old lay nun opened the door wider in the face of superior authority. Her head bobbed respectfully.

The other nun wore white. White from head to foot, a nursing sister. Starched white robes, broken in the middle by a thick black leather belt with big beads dangling from it. Brass Christ on black wood crucifix agonized against her bosom.

"Yes?"

"Good morning, Sister. I wanted to see Miss Marrinan, on a personal matter. I've come here by taxi, a long way. Couldn't you make an exception, Sister?"

The nursing sister's pale blue eyes catalogued the red raincoat, the rouge, the distracted manner. Still, she seemed respectable, if odd. And the taxi there. Hmm!

"All right," she said. "But you mustn't make a habit of this, you know. We have to keep to our visiting hours, otherwise we'd never get any work done. Marrinan, you wanted. Yes, on the second floor. Turn to your right when you go up."

The old lay sister opened the door wide and

Miss Hearne stepped into a clean, unornamented hallway, smelling of Jeyes Fluid, floor polish, the perfumes of an institution. The white-robed nun nodded and turned on her heel. Alone, Miss Hearne crossed the hall, hearing her footsteps echo on the mosaic of yellow and white tiles. She reached the staircase. Ah, these nuns here, they weren't like the Sacred Heart nuns at all. What was it old John Harvey once said: the Sisters of Mercy have no charity, and the Sisters of Charity have no mercy. And it was true.

A senile woman passed on the stairs, not looking at her, her old eyes on the ground. Watching her step. It puts me off, Miss Hearne thought, this place. All those old women, poor old creatures, nobody to care about them, nobody.

At the top of the first flight of stairs she reached a ward. Some of the women were lying in the ugly white institution beds, reading or knitting. Most of them, wearing grey institution dressing-gowns, were clustered around the stove in the centre of the room. Their hair was bundled upon top of their heads. They wore no powder, no make-up at all. Women together, living where they were seen only by other women, they felt no need for beauty. And old, most of them, they had reached an age where illness is all engrossing and comfort the only standard, the only desire. They sat around the stove with its big black funnel rising to the ceiling and she heard them whisper, their voices like the sound of mice behind the walls of an old house.

Giddiness came upon her as she climbed the second flight. Her heart had a nasty trick of acting up lately, plucking inside her chest like a bird in a bag. A drink, she said. I need something to steady me. And Edie? She stopped on the stairs for breath. Why did I come? she cried mutely. It's depressing, depressing, and Edie will only be depressing too. Why? Why?

Because she is my friend. And I need a friend.

She went on. When she reached the second floor, she turned right and walked into a ward. There were about fifteen women there and they stopped all talk at once. Those in bed dropped their knitting and the group around the fire turned their heads to look. Like browsing cows, they stared at the strange animal in their midst. One of them tittered.

Edie? Miss Hearne's shifting dark eyes sought her friend. But the women all looked the same.

"Is Miss Marrinan here?" she said, stopping by the stove.

"She's ova' tha'," a toothless old woman said, pointing.

"Thank you."

The bed nearest the corner. And under the yellow blankets, someone asleep. Miss Hearne put her handbag carefully on the bed-table.

"Yes?" the woman on the bed said. Her face was turned to the wall. She did not move.

"Edie?" Miss Hearne bent over and saw Edie's profile, wan, lacklustre, against the pillow. "It's me, Edie. Judy Hearne."

Slowly, with infinite care, the sick woman turned over on her back. The greying widow's peak of her hair was wet with perspiration. "Judy. Nice of you to come and see an old wreck like me. O, it's killing me, this pain."

"The arthritis?"

The sick woman nodded. Miss Hearne sat down by the bedside. Jolly Edie Marrinan, always a plain girl, but such fun. Such a hearty, good-natured soul, you knew she'd never get married, but that was because men were so foolish, for she was a wonderful cook and she adored children. A jolly cousin to all the other Marrinans, and she had a big circle of girl friends too, girls who worked and girls like me, Miss Hearne thought, who lived at home with relatives. And now: a sick pained woman, crippled by the disease. Bent over double, they said, when she stood up.

"O, Edie," she said. "And I thought of you this morning the minute I woke up. Early and all, I decided to come over and have a little chat, we could cheer each other up. I brought a little 'tonic', just a secret, the two of us, I thought it would be cheerful."

The sick woman smiled. Her twisted hand stiffly caught at Miss Hearne's sleeve.

"You brought something?"

"A little gin," Miss Hearne whispered. "I thought it would be best. They wouldn't smell it."

"Good, good," Edie said. She pulled Miss

Hearne closer. "Be careful. They're watching. Don't look now."

But Miss Hearne peeked. The dressing-gowns had moved into a wider circle around the stove, the better to observe. There was conversation, but their eyes and minds were not on it.

"Take the glass," the sick woman said. "Put it in the glass and give it to me."

But this is not right, Miss Hearne screamed silently. This is like giving drugs to a sick person. Poor Edie, why shouldn't she enjoy herself? O, these silly rules that nuns invent. They think everybody should live the way they do. But the rest of the world didn't take the veil, don't they know that?

She put the water-glass on top of her bag. Then, without taking the bottle out of the bag, she uncorked it and bent its mouth towards the glass.

"More, more," the sick woman said.

"But you want me to put some water in it?"

"No."

Miss Hearne, acutely aware of the inquisitive dressing-gowns, held out the half-filled glass to Edie.

"My hands. I can't hold things any more. Just lift me up."

Skilfully, remembering her dear aunt and the stroke, Miss Hearne lifted the sick woman, slipping her arm under the head and neck. She held the glass to Edie's lips. Edie coughed and choked at the first sip, but then she sucked at the gin like a man after a day's work in the hot fields.

"Was that good?" Miss Hearne asked, letting her friend rest back gently on the pillows. The sick woman closed her eyes. "Ah, you're an angel, Judy, a perfect angel. I'm so glad you came, I was wondering if you'd ever be back. It seems so long here."

"But it was only last month, Edie."

"They all stop coming, sooner or later. Who wants to come all the way out here to see a creature like me?"

"O, now, Edie!"

"My own brother, Eamon, yes, my own brother, he hasn't been here for two months. Too busy, he says. Judy dear, you'll never know how lonely it is here."

"O, now, Edie, you mustn't say that. Why, you've got heaps of friends. You were the most popular girl in Belfast, really you were. And you still are, don't you worry. People are always asking about you."

The sick woman moved her stiff neck like a tortoise. "Popular, my eye. When you're sick, you're popular with nobody. You'll see, Judy, you'll see. And when you're sick and alone in the world the way I am, everybody'd be glad to see you dead."

O, why did I come here? Miss Hearne asked herself. Poor Edie. She took the glass from the table and filled it up as if the gin was water. "I'm going to have a sip to keep you company, " she

278

whispered.

It burned, it burned like fire. But she drank it all down. "O, Edie," she said. "I miss you, really I do. When I think of the good times we used to have together, you and I, in your old digs on Cedar Avenue. And what fun we had, laughing and joking about all the things that happened, the little funny things that used to happen in your office. Do you ever see any of the people you used to work with, Mr Henry, or Mr Flannery, or any of the girls?"

"Would you have a sup more gin?" the sick woman said. "It does wonders for the pain."

"Yes, dear, just a moment now." Miss Hearne pulled the neck of the bottle out of her bag and tilted it into the glass.

"Nurse!" an old woman called in the background. "Sista! Sista!"

"What is it?" A nun, white robed, with flashing steel spectacles, appeared at the ward door.

"Them two women is drinkin'," the old woman cried. "Them two. That one over there wi' the red coat."

"O, you dirty sneak. Wait till I get you," Edie Marrinan cried. Perspiration ran like rain down her face. "You see, Judy, you see what I have to put up with? Dirty old hags, filthy, back-biting old sneaks."

"Now, what's this, Miss Marrinan?" the nun said, coming up the ward with a swish of stiff white skirts. "What's this I hear?"

"Nothing, Sister, nothing," Edie Marrinan said, turning carefully towards the wall. "My pains are bad, Sister, leave me alone."

"How did you get in here?" the nun said, turning angrily to Miss Hearne.

"By the front door. With permission. I never heard of such a thing," Miss Hearne said. "You'd think I was a thief or something."

"Well, you'll have to leave now," the nun said suspiciously.

"Goodness me, Sister, you'd think I was a criminal, the way you talk to me. I was just visiting my friend."

She stood up, clutching her big handbag with a tottering attempt at dignity. But the bottle had not been corked. Under the nun's shocked stare, she looked down and saw the gin seep through the bag and fall in splashing wetness on the floor.

"Well! " the nun said, her pale face flushing. "Did you ever? Do you know this woman is sick? Do you know the seriousness of coming in here and feeding her that vile stuff, whatever it is, without a doctor's permission? O, you should be ashamed of yourself, really it's scandalous. I don't know who let you in but I'll report this to Reverend Mother immediately."

The grey dressing-gowns, joyful at this break in the dull daily routine, had clustered around the nun.

"Luk at her, luk at her wi' her red coat," a woman said in a broad Belfast accent. "That 'uns's a bad woman, Sista."

"I beg your pardon," Miss Hearne said icily. O, my God, I must get away.

"Edie," she said. "Good bye, Edie."

But the sick woman stared at the wall.

"Out you go this minute," the nun cried in anger, taking Miss Hearne by the arm. "Outside at once. I've a good mind to call a policeman."

And she marched Miss Hearne down the ward, followed by the slippered clop-clop of the grey dressing-gowns.

"A booza, booza," a woman chanted. "She must be on the wine, Sista."

"Out with you," the nun cried, giving Miss Hearne a rude push at the head of the stairs. "Out with you, this minute."

O, the mortal shame of it. And the cheek of that nun, pushing at me as if I was a fallen woman or something. With giddy drunken dignity, Miss Hearne descended the stairs. A kind act, a corporal work of mercy, visiting the sick, and look what happened. You got treated as if you were trying to kill poor Edie, instead of cheering her up. And Edie, she might at least have stuck up for me. Turning away like that as if it was my fault she's sick.

By convent telepathy, the old lay sister who guarded the door seemed to know the whole sorry story. "Humph!" she snorted as Miss Hearne approached. "There you are. Ah, I knew Sister was foolish to let you in. No visitors. No visitors!

It's the rule."

But there was the taxi, consoling in its size, waiting, the meter ticking. The taxi driver courteously opened the door and helped her in. I'm leaving in style anyway, she thought, I hope they're watching.

The driver got in the front seat and started the motor. "Where to, please?" he said as the car crunched off down the avenue.

Where?

O, I'm in trouble, in awful trouble. And nobody to help me. Where? I've got to talk to somebody, some friend, someone who can advise me, the faith, I've lost my faith, I've burned my boats and it will happen soon, it will happen. Now, if You're there, she screamed wordlessly. Now show me. Anything, a bolt of lightning, strike me down, anything. But don't leave me, don't leave me alone.

"I didn't hear you, mum." the driver said. "Where did you say?"

"O, anywhere. The Plaza. Take me back there."

And what will I do there? That room, the mess I made last night, the maid will have been in by now. And this. She looked down and felt her legs wet under her skirt. The bottle, I must throw away. Wasted. No, not the Plaza. Lonely there. Somebody I must tell. Who?

Moira. Moira always liked me. She always tries to be my friend.

282

"Wait," she said to the driver as the car passed the little gate lodge and moved into the traffic on the road outside. "I've changed my mind. Take me to twenty Melrose Avenue."

# CHAPTER
# SEVENTEEN

"It's Miss Hearne, ma'am." Ellen said, coming back into the kitchen.

Mrs O'Neill closed the oven door and gently adjusted the gas. "Now what on earth brings her here?" she said, untying her apron. "And the children will be home for lunch in half an hour." She handed the apron to Ellen and went out of the kitchen, along the dark back corridor to the hall, where Miss Hearne waited, her red hat askew, her big bag clutched to her stomach.

"Judy dear. And how are you?"

"Moira." Miss Hearne pecked at Mrs O'Neill's cheek. "I know you must be busy, but I had to have a talk with you."

Well, I swear she reeks like a booze factory, Mrs O'Neill said to herself. Could it be possible? Squiffy. Better not let the children see her.

"I'd ask you to come up to the drawing-room, Judy, but the fire's not lit. Let's go in here." She opened the dining-room door. "There's a stove in here and it's nice and warm."

"We'll be alone?" Miss Hearne asked, looking around her in a frightened way. She sat down on one of the dining-room chairs and put her bag at her feet. Mrs O'Neill saw the neck of the gin bottle sticking out of the bag. Somehow, it was like seeing Miss Hearne with her clothes undone. She did not dare look at her caller.

Miss Hearne did not notice her *gaffe*. She stared moodily at Mrs O'Neill's arms bare to the elbow and with traces of flour on the skin.

"You were cooking," she said. "I interrupted you."

"O, not at all," Mrs O'Neill lied. "Ellen can finish it as well as if I was there. It was all done, anyway."

"I went to see Edie Marrinan this morning. Poor thing, she hardly knew me."

"Yes, poor Edie. I must go out and see her some day soon. It's such a long way out." Surely she didn't come here to talk about Edie Marrinan? Of course, if she's as tight as she looks, there's no telling. The poor soul, it's that disappointment about the Yankee, the one she mentioned last Sunday. You have to feel sorry for her.

"I wanted to get some advice from Edie, do you see?" Miss Hearne said. "But she was too sick."

"O, that's too bad, Judy. Was it something special?"

Miss Hearne put her head down on the table and began to sob. Her red hat rolled off. Mrs

O'Neill, embarrassed, picked it up. "What is it, Judy dear?"

But Miss Hearne did not raise her head. She covered her face with her elbows and her shoulders shook with sobbing. "I have come to you," she cried. "You, of all people. And I never liked you, Moira, that's the truth, I never liked you."

*In vino veritas*, Mrs O'Neill said to herself. But then, for some reason which she could not understand, she too felt as though she must cry. For after all, she thought, drunk or not, it must cost her something to say that to me. Because now she can never pretend again.

"Well, Judy, I suppose you had your reasons. What can I do for you?"

Miss Hearne lifted her teary face from the shelter of her elbows. Her rouge was smudged into two blurred scars across the paleness of her cheeks.

"Moira. I've lost my faith. And I've left Camden Street and I'm living at the Plaza Hotel and everything's finished, Moira, everything."

"But why, Judy, why?"

"What am I doing with my life? I ask you," Miss Hearne cried loudly, leaning across the table and catching hold of Moira's bare arm. "A single girl with no kin, what am I doing? O Moira, you always were the lucky one, a husband and children around you, you'll never know what it's like to be me."

"Judy dear, I know it must be hard at times.

But just a little bit quieter, please, Judy! the children."

"But I have to say it. I have to tell somebody and you've always been kind to me, inviting me over here on Sundays, you'll never know what it meant to me, Moira, to come here and sit with a family and feel that I belonged here, that I was welcome. Do you know what I mean, Moira, do you know what I mean?"

Only you didn't belong, you poor thing, Mrs O'Neill thought sadly. "Yes, Judy, I think I know."

"And then, just a few weeks ago, I might have got married. Do you know how long I've waited to be married Moira? Do you know how many long years, every one of them twelve long months? Well, I'll tell you, it's twenty odd years, Moira, if you count from the time I was twenty. O, I know I didn't think about it all that time — when my aunt was ill, I gave up thinking about it for a while. But a woman never gives up, Moira, does she? Even when she's like me and knows it's impossible, she never gives up. There's always Mr Right, Moira, only he changes as the years go by. At first he's tall, dark and handsome, a young man, Moira, and then you're not so young and he's middle-aged, but still tall and handsome. And then there's moments when he's anybody, anybody who might be eligible. O, I've looked at all sorts of men, men I didn't even like. But that's not the end, that's not the worst of it."

Her fingernails dug into the flesh of Moira's arm. She leaned forward, across the table, her dark nervous eyes filled with confessional zeal.

"No, no, I'm going to tell you the whole thing, Moira, the whole thing. Because I have to tell it to somebody, somebody must listen. That's not the worst when he's just anybody who might be eligible. You might as well forget about eligible men. Because you're too late, you've missed your market. Then you're up for any offers. Marked down goods. You're up for auction, a country auction, where the auctioneer stands up and says what am I bid? And he starts at a high price, saying what he'd like best. No offers. Then second best. No offers. Third? No offers. What am I bid, Moira? and somebody comes along, laughable, and you take him. If you can get him. Because it's either that or back on the shelf for you. Back to your furnished room and your prayers. And your hopes."

Mrs O'Neill began to weep. "O Judy," she said. "Don't."

"Your hopes," Miss Hearne repeated, her dark eyes clouded and strange. "Only you've got daydreams instead and you want to hold on to them. And you can't. So you take a drink to help them along, to cheer you up. And anybody, Moira, who so much as gives you a kind word is a prince. A prince. Even if he's old and ugly and common as mud. Even if the best he can say for himself is that he was a hotel doorman in New

288

York. Would you believe that now, would you believe it?"

The American. The one she was talking about. A doorman. O, the poor soul!

"That would be bad enough, wouldn't it?" Miss Hearne cried. "Bad enough, yes, you'd be ashamed of yourself. And rightly so. But there's worse yet. What if that doorman turned you down? TURNED YOU DOWN!"

Miss Hearne stopped, open-mouthed, her face quivering. "Have you got a drink, Moira?" she said. "I need a drink."

Mrs O'Neill got up from the table and went over to the sideboard. She unlocked the liquor cabinet and took out a bottle of whiskey. (Afterwards she said she just knew instinctively it was whiskey she wanted, although, if she had stopped to think of it, she said, she would have realized that the poor soul didn't need another drink, seeing she had far too many in her already.) She took a glass from another shelf and poured a tot of whiskey into it.This she placed in front of Miss Hearne and sat down beside her. Not a word had been spoken.

Miss Hearne put the whiskey to her lips and drank it down neat. She put the glass back on the table and they sat there, side by side, in silence. At last Miss Hearne shook her head.

"That's what I've come to, Moira. Turned down by a doorman. And what's more, I didn't want to be turned down. I'd take him yet."

Mrs O'Neill patted her arm. There seemed nothing to say.

"Nobody wants me, Moira. I'm too old. And I'm too ugly. Yes, he was the last one and now I'm left on the shelf."

"Now Judy," Mrs O'Neill said. "There are other things in life besides that. You have lots of friends, you know."

"But I don't. *I don't.*"

"Judy, that's not so. And besides, just because life is hard at present, there's no need to think it will always be hard. Now, why don't you let me see you home and then you have a nice lie down for a while. You'll feel better about all this tomorrow. Remember, God has given us all heavy crosses to bear."

"God!" Miss Hearne said bitterly. "What does *He* care? Is there a God at all, I've been asking myself, because if there is, why does He never answer our prayers? Why does he allow all these things to happen? Why?"

"O, you're not yourself, Judy," Mrs O'Neill said, shocked. "You don't really mean that."

"I do. I do."

"Now, Judy, why don't you let me take you home? Tomorrow, when you feel better, you can go and talk things over with your confessor."

"He won't listen to me," Miss Hearne said, beginning to cry again.

"Now, that's nonsense, Judy. Of course he will. Have you talked to him already?"

"He didn't pay any attention!"

"Well, perhaps he didn't understand how seriously you felt. Go and see him again. Or you can go and see an Order priest. They're very understanding."

"Mama?" a voice said at the door. Mrs O'Neill hastily stood up, blocking Miss Hearne from the newcomer.

"What is it?" she said crossly. "I'm busy."

"Hello, Miss Hearne," the little girl said.

"Hello Kathy. My own Kathleen," Miss Hearne cried, getting up from the chair. She advanced, falteringly, her arms wide in welcome.

"Judy!" Mrs O'Neill detained her. "Run along, Kathy. I'm too busy to talk to you now."

She hurried the little girl out of the room. But the child had seen Miss Hearne advancing in a parody of affection, her outstretched arms trembling like a pilgrim's.

And Miss Hearne saw the fright in the child's face. And the way Mrs O'Neill came between them. She turned, clutching the dining-room table and searching Mrs O'Neill's face for the truth, seeing herself, a child, hurried on along the street when a drunk man passed. *Not in front of the children.* What have I done? she thought, allowing Mrs O'Neill to seat her in a chair. Coming here like this, in this condition, telling her all those secrets, telling her what I think of her.

And it came to her then that in all the years she had known the O'Neills, they had never really known her. In all the thousands of conversations with Moira, she had never so much as hinted at the things she had told today, openly, irrevocably. All the years of polite chatter, all the small Christmas presents exchanged, all the little courtesies accepted, the wine, the cakes, the tea, all of these things had been swept away for ever by this one small encounter. The child at the door; the mother hurrying to shelter it from these signs of an adult grief, an adult failing; the drink poured not in hospitality but to supply a shameful need; the confession of feeling, the admission that she disliked Moira, nullifying scores of Sunday afternoons of polite inquiry, hundreds of false pleasant welcomes; all of these things came to her mind now with brutal clarity. The choice of the dining-room as a place to talk had not been for the purpose stated: it had been to hide her from the children, to keep her shameful condition from their eyes. And Moira's kind words were only to calm her down, to shut off this shocking flow of unwanted confidence. In Moira's eyes I am drunk, that is all she sees, a drunk person, Nobody takes them seriously. Lie down and you'll feel better. Nobody listens.

I am drunk.

I must get out.

She bent to the floor to pick up her bag and saw the shameful neck of the bottle sticking out of it. O! Her red hat rolled off her head again and settled on the carpet. Mrs O'Neill picked it up.

"I must go now," Miss Hearne said, scrabbling to hide the bottle inside her bag. "I'm sorry, Moira, I must have been an awful nuisance to you. With your lunch ready and everything. I must go at once."

"That's perfectly all right." Mrs O'Neill said, handing her the red hat. "I think I'd better take you home in a taxi. Just wait a minute while I get my hat and coat."

"No, no. I'm going alone. No, you mustn't come."

"It's no trouble, Judy. I'd feel happier if I went with you. Then you can have a good nap and you'll feel better."

The red hat would not fit somehow. Mrs O'Neill straightened it. "There, that's better. I'll get a taxi."

"I have a taxi. It's outside now. And I'm going alone."

"A taxi? Waiting all this time?"

"Yes. Good bye, Moira." She did not kiss her. I couldn't. Not after what I said.

But Mrs O'Neill impulsively put her arms around Miss Hearne and kissed her on the cheek. "O Judy," she said. "Take care of yourself."

"I'm sorry, Moira." The tears, uncontrollable, began again in her eyes.

"Nothing to be sorry about." But Mrs O'Neill looked cautiously into the hall before she showed her out. They clasped hands again.

"Sure you'll be all right?"

"Yes. Good bye, dear."
"Good bye."

Moira watched as she walked to the waiting cab. Watching me, mustn't stumble. Mustn't stu . . .

"Here you are, mum." The taxi driver steadied her. "That's right."

He helped her in and shut the door. It was beginning to rain. Through the blurred pane of glass she saw Moira wave, standing at the door of her house.

"Where to now, mum?"

Where?

# CHAPTER
# EIGHTEEN

Reverend Francis Xavier Quigley was taking his ease in front of a roaring fire in the back parlour of his presbytery, his black boots propped upon the fender, a copy of the *Tablet* rising and falling gently on his lap. Nearby, on his cluttered desk, the monthly report on the School Building Fund waited his scrutiny as did the returns from the Black Baby Society. But Father Quigley's eyes were closed. It was the slack time of day, half-past one. Two whole hours of peace before his afternoon calls.

"There's a woman to see you, Father," said Mrs Connolly.

Father Quigley opened his eyes and stared at the ceiling. "What?"

"She come in a taxi," Mrs Connolly offered.

"Is somebody sick?"

"She kept the taxi-man waiting, Father."

Father Quigley closed his eyes.

"To tell the truth, Father, I think she has a drop

taken."

"Well, find out what she wants."

"I told her to come back later, Father, but she didn't heed me. She wouldn't let on what she wanted, Father."

Father Quigley swung his feet from the fender to the floor. The *Tablet* fell beside the grate.

"She's in the front parlour, Father," Mrs Connolly said, her mission accomplished.

Father Quigley pulled the ends of his black clerical waistcoat down over his hard narrow stomach. His hollow-cheeked face flushed by the fire, he left the cosy warmth and strode down the dark presbytery hall. The taxi driver, waiting by the front door, did not salute him. Father Quigley gave him a sharp look and went into the parlour.

"Good afternoon."

The women looked at him out of staring dark eyes that were swollen from weeping. Her red hat was awry, her red raincoat unbuttoned down the front. She came forward, through the maze of worn Victorian furniture, and fell on her knees at his feet, clutching his trouser legs.

"O Father, Father, help me," she sobbed.

Father Quigley disengaged her clutching hands from his shanks and surreptitiously hoisted his trousers. Then he bent down and dragged the woman to her feet.

"Now, now," he said. "Control yourself. What's the matter?" But as he said it, he smelled the drink off her. Stocious, she is, stocious drunk.

"O, Father . . ."

Father Quigley guided her to a chair. "Sit down," he ordered. He sat down opposite her. "Have you been drinking?"

"Yes, Father."

And you mean to say you've come here to see me, drunk?"

"I'm sorry, Father. But Father, I had to. I need your help."

"What kind of help?"

"You know!" the woman said.

Father Quigley shook his head in irritation. "How can I know, if you haven't told me?"

"But I told you in confession."

"My good woman, I hear a lot of confessions. And I don't know who's making them. You should know better than that."

"Father," the woman said, beginning to weep. "Father, I'm all alone. I need somebody."

She bent over. Her red hat fell off, rolled on the floor. Father Quigley picked it up.

"I need a sign," the woman said. "I need a sign from God."

"You need to sober up, that's what you need."

"But Father, I'm not — not drunk, now. Honestly. Father, I can't believe any more. I can't pray. He won't listen. Maybe it's the devil tempting me as you said, Father, but I just don't feel that God is there any more. Nobody is listening. All my life I've believed, I've waited — Father, listen to me!"

"I'm listening," Father Quigley said grimly.

"Father, why is it? You're a priest. Are *you* sure He's there? Are you really sure?"

"Now, get a hold of yourself." Father Quigley said.

"You're not sure, are you? Then how can I be sure? Father, if there isn't any other life, then what has happened to me? I've wasted my life."

"Now, what nonsense is this, woman? It's the drink talking in you. Aren't you ashamed of yourself, drinking like that, making a public spectacle of yourself, a well-brought-up woman like you?"

But the woman did not seem to hear. She sobbed, making short panting noises, like a tired dog. "Do you understand?" she said. "*Do you understand?*"

Shepherd, he looked at his sheep. What ails her? Father, he did not comprehend what his child was saying. Priest, he could not communicate with his parishioner. "No," Father Quigley said. "I don't know what you're talking about."

"Then nobody does. Nobody will," the woman cried.

"Now, you listen to me," Father Quigley began. "Go home and sober up and examine your conscience while you're at it. You can't think straight in this condition. And tomorrow evening I'll be hearing confessions from six to eight. Come and see me then, and we'll have a talk. Are you from this parish? What's your name?"

"Hearne, Father. Judith Hearne."

"All right, now, Miss Hearne. You have a taxi waiting I believe?"

"Father, I've got to get this settled. Father, can you tell me . . ."

"Now, Miss Hearne, I want you to promise me that you'll go straight home. Where do you live?"

"I have no home."

"Well, where are you living at present?"

She did not answer.

Father Quigley got up and went to the door. He beckoned to the taxi driver in the hall. "Do you know where this lady lives?"

"I picked her up at the Plaza Hotel, sir."

"I see." He went back into the parlour and closed the door. The taxi-man was a Protestant. Nice thing for him to see. "Now, where do you live, Miss Hearne? We've got to get you home."

"I'm at the Plaza."

Humph! That's funny. "Now look, Miss Hearne, will you promise me one thing on your word of honour? Promise not to touch a drop of drink until you've been to see me again. Will you do that for me now?"

She stopped crying. "But why, Father, why? What's the good of word of honour? What's the good of anything, unless it's more than bread. More than bread, do you understand, Father?"

"Miss Hearne, that's a terrible thing for a Catholic woman to say to her priest. That's a terrible sin, talking that way about the Blessed Sacrament. That's what you're talking about, isn't it?"

"Yes."

"You should be heartily ashamed of yourself, then. Coming in here drunk at this time of day and talking that way about Our Blessed Lord. O, what a terrible thing to let drink take hold of you like that, you should be down on your bended knees, praying for forgiveness. A terrible, terrible thing! Shocking! Now, you go straight home and say a mouthful of prayers. And not another drop of drink, mind, not another drop. You should be grateful that God hasn't punished you worse, mortal sin on your soul and you not in a fit condition to receive absolution. I never heard the like!" He paused for breath, his eyes lit with anger.

"And is that all you have to tell me?" she said sadly.

"What do you mean — I . . ."

But she had picked up her bag and was preparing to leave.

"Now, just a minute. I want you to come back and see me. You'll do that now?"

But she went out in the hall and it was very awkward in front of the Protestant taxi driver.

"You'll take this lady back to her hotel," he said to the man. "And I'd be obliged if you'd make sure she's staying there before you leave her. If not, well, bring her back here and we'll try to find out more about her."

"All right, sir."

She had opened the front door. Father Quigley

hurried forward and caught her by the arm. "Now, Miss Hearne, remember what I told you. Come back and see me when you're feeling better. Tomorrow. Just give me a ring and I'll arrange to see you."

But she paid no attention. Too far gone in drink, Father Quigley judged. He nodded to the taxi driver and the man took her arm and walked her to the presbytery gates. She got into the taxi, leaving Father Quigley standing at the presbytery door, troubled, sensing his failure. A terrible thing, drink. Or the change of life, it might be. A bit young for that. Hearne? I wonder who would know her. At the Plaza Hotel, doesn't live there at all. Or she might be from out of town. But then, why pick on me? She might. He thought of his fire and the *Tablet*. But he did not close the door. He waited.

The taxi driver, who had not yet been paid, carefully placed Miss Hearne in the back seat of his car and started the engine. But as the car moved away, it passed the gates of the church. Miss Hearne rapped on the glass panel behind his head. "Stop!"

"But the Reverend said to take you back to the hotel, mum."

"Stop. I want to go into the church for a minute."

He stopped. These bloody Papishes, you never knew what they were up to. "It's a long time on the meter," he warned.

"You'll be paid. Just wait here."

She left her bag on the seat and got out of the car. Faltering, her red hat awry on her head, she walked through the gates and into the quiet darkness of the vestibule.

He didn't understand, he could only say the silly, ordinary things you would expect him to say. Words, all he had was words. Supposing he knew that there was nothing in the tabernacle — ah then, what could he say? And perhaps he did know, he was so angry at me asking, he ran outside into the hall once to compose himself. Was he afraid? Afraid, because he knew?

She passed the Holy Water font. What use? Only water, dirty water in a cold marble bowl. She entered the church.

It was the quiet time. The church was empty except for two aged housewives who toiled around the side aisles, offering up prayers before the pictured agonies of the Stations of the Cross. And one old man in the front bench, sitting as quiet as a piece of furniture, his rosary lax in his hand. Old people. Old people with nothing left to do but pray.

Over the main altar, the sanctury lamp glowed red. In dark side alters, candles guttered before painted statues. Our Lady, Saint Joseph, Saint Patrick. Sightless saints.

Slowly she walked up the centre aisle.

O God, I have sinned against You, why have You not punished me? I have renounced You, do

You hear me, I have abandoned You. Because, O Father, You have abandoned me. I needed You, Father, and You turned me away. I prayed to You, Father, and You did not answer. All men turned from me. And You, Father? You too.

The painted Mary smiled from the side alter; blue robed, with white virginal tunic and delicate painted hands uplifted in intercession. O Mary Mother, why did you not intercede for me? Why do you smile now? There is nothing to smile for.

O Sacred Heart, why did You ask this suffering? The reason, tell me, I will bear it. But a reason, not the reasons Your priest has given. They are no reasons for this terrible thing.

The red sanctuary lamp swung gently as a draught of cold air blew across the altar. The wind ruffled the little white curtain that screened the tabernacle door. It was very quiet. Only her own footsteps she could hear.

And now? What will become of me, am I to grow old in a room, year by year, until they take me to a poor-house? Am I to be a forgotten old woman, mumbling in a corner in a house run by nuns? What is to become of me, O Lord, alone in this city, with only drink, hateful drink that dulls me, disgraces me, lonely drink that leaves me more lonely, more despised? Why this cross? Give me another, great pain, great illness, anything, but let there be someone, someone to share it. Why do You torture me, alone and silent behind Your little door? Why?

"I hate You," she said, her voice loud and shrill in the silence of the church. And she waited. Now, surely now, in His anointed, consecrated place, a thunderbolt, striking down, white and terrible from the vaulted roof. And leave a shrivelled nothing on the ground.

She bent her head for the blow. But the only sound was a banging door as a priest entered the church. No sign. The red sanctuary lamp swung from side to side.

No one.

Only bread.

But if He still waited, if He stayed His hand?

She walked towards the altar, quickly now, her dark eyes on the little white curtain. One way. One way above all. Let it end now, let it end for ever. Let Him strike, terrible in His wrath, a God of Judgment, crumbling the defiler of His temple.

She reached the Communion rail and fumbled with the catch of the gate. She bent over it, her whole body trembling uncontrollably as it suddenly swung free. Open. Her path only six steps up to the altar, up to the golden door.

O God. O Father. Now.

She did not see the two women start up in fear from their prayers. She did not see the agitation of the old man in the front bench as she slowly climbed the steps. She did not see Father Quigley run down the centre aisle.

She went forward, her head up, her dark eyes wild, waiting the thunderbolt.

Now.

She reached the altar platform and drew the little curtain aside. The small door filled her whole eye, golden, mysterious, terrifying.

Behind it?

Or wafers of bread?

Trembling, she put her trembling hands on the door, scrabbled to find the lock. But the door was rough, encrusted with a motif of crucifixes.

In the darkness of the nave, someone shouted.

Now! Now! She tore at the door. Now, the thunderbolt. But the door would not open. Small, golden, Holy of Holies, it remained shut against her trembling weeping onslaught.

"Open. Let me in!" she screamed.

"In!" the church screamed back. "In!"

But the door rejected her. It would not open. Blood ran from her nails. The altar cloth slid sideways along the marble of the altar table. Candlesticks crashed on the steps.

"*You!*" she screamed. And red light filled her eyes, golden doors merged, fell away in crumbling segments. He came out, terrible, breathing fire, His face hollow-cheeked, His eyes devouring her. His Mother ran up the altar steps, her painted face still sadly smiling, lifted her as she lay broken on the steps. Saint Joseph knelt gravely on her right.

And He, His fingers uplifted in blessing, bent over her, His bleeding heart red against His white tunic. Lifted her in His arms and His face was close to hers.

"Why did you do this?" He said.

But she could not see His face. It went warm and sick and blurred and the red lamps burned again, filling all of her eyes, carrying her off to darkness, all darkness, all forgetting.

"Why did she do it?" one of the kneeling housewives asked Father Quigley.

And he looked down at the bloodstained hands, the bruised face and straggling hair of the woman in his arms. He looked, and then he looked at the locked tabernacle.

"God knows," he said.

# CHAPTER
# NINETEEN

Gerry Dickey, driver, employed by Hanlon's Car
Service, Our Own Limousines: Funerals,
Weddings, Special Outings, tied the two old-
fashioned trunks on his luggage rack. Then he
brought the Humber around to the side entrance
of the hospital.

After a few minutes, a nurse held the door open
and the lady who had hired the car came out. She
had another lady with her, and the lady had on a
red raincoat with a tear in it. The sick lady walked
very slow and she had dark-brown rings around
her eyes and a kind of tremble to her whole body
when you were close to her. There was a young
girl came out after them, a tall bit of stuff with
black hair and a good figure. Gerry Dickey got out
and opened the back door of the car while the two
ladies and the girl got in. Then he started the
Humber up.

"And where to now, please?" he said.

"Earnscliffe Home," the lady that hired him

said.

"Earnscliffe?" the sick woman said. "O Moira dear, I couldn't go there. I couldn't."

"Now, don't worry, Judy, it's all arranged. We have a private room for you and you need convalescent care until you get back on your feet."

"But I wouldn't be happy there," the sick one said. "Besides, I can't afford a private room."

"Never mind about that. Owen and I will take care of it. Just you think about getting well, that's the main thing."

"But I don't want to stay there."

"You won't have to stay more than a month or two. And after that, Una will help you find a nice room somewhere, won't you, Una?"

"Of course. And you'll be up and about in no time."

I wouldn't like to bet a quid on that, Gerry Dickey thought, looking at the sick one through his rear view mirror.

"O, but Moira, I'd be ashamed to . . ."

The good-looking one leaned forward at this point and closed the glass panel which screened Gerry Dickey off from his fares. Did she see me looking, I wonder? No, not likely.

"What about Number Ten?" asked Night Sister.

"O, she's all right," said Eileen Herlihy, who was going off duty.

Nora Nelligan, who was replacing her, took a chocolate out of the box left by a patient's brother that morning. "What's the matter with that one, anyway?"

"She had an accident. Nervous breakdown or something. Nothing wrong with her that the pledge wouldn't cure."

Nora Nelligan put on her white cap. "Who's looking after her?"

"She's Dr Bowe's patient. Do you know him? A GP?"

Nora Nelligan saw Dr Bowe's bald head and bulging waistcoat. Married and a family. I have no luck at all. Sure, I get all the old doctors. "O him," she said.

"Hurry up now, girls," said Night Sister. "Number Fourteen needs her enema."

"Good afternoon, Father," Sister Mary Paul said. "Father Quigley, is it?"

"That's right."

"O, from Saint Finbar's. Of course, I should have known. And who would you be wanting to see, Father?"

"You have a Miss Hearne here?"

"O, indeed we have. She's in number ten. I'll take you there, Father."

Together they went out of the reception office and along to the lift.

"And how is she getting along?"

"Well enough, Father, all things considered. She'll be out of here in a few weeks. But you know, Father — is she one of your parishioners, by the way?"

He nodded.

"She's very depressed," Sister Mary Paul said. "She wanders a bit, the poor soul. For instance, she's always telling the nurses that God won't listen to her. A bit off her head at times. I don't think she means it, though. Many's the time I've gone in and seen her lying there praying."

"Has she asked to see a priest?"

"No, Father, she hasn't. But I'm sure she'll be glad to see you, Father."

"U'm," said Father Quigley.

The priest, tall, black clad, took off his black over-coat and his white silk scarf. He laid the scarf on his black hat. He sat down on the hard chair and put his black boots together, side by side. His long spatulate fingers clasped his bony, black-clothed knees as he leaned forward and looked at the woman in the bed.

"And how are you feeling now, Miss Hearne?"

The woman stared vacantly at the foot of her bed. With her right hand she held the grey woollen dressing-gown tight around her throat. "I'm all right, Father, thank you."

And you're happier now, aren't you, Miss Hearne? You've — ah — you've put all those black thoughts behind you, haven't you?"

Her eyes wandered to the ceiling. "Yes," she said.

"Good. I'm very glad to hear that. I've offered

up special prayers at Mass for that intention. Ah, yes, it's a wonderful thing, prayer. Think now of the comfort it is to know God is watching over you at a time like this. And you're in good hands, the nuns are very kind, is that not so?"

"Yes," She was still looking at the ceiling.

"That's right. And you know, Miss Hearne, when we feel lonely and out of sorts, it's a great consolation to remember that we all belong to one great family. The Holy Family. Ah, many's the time I think of those who don't believe in God, how lonely they must be, no friends around them, deliberately turning away from God's mercy. Yes, it's good to know God is always with us, is that not so?"

"Yes, Father."

"Yes, I often think of the unbeliever, the poor blind devil without a friend in this world or the next. Yes, a lonely man, he who turns away from the sight of God. When a prayer, one word of repentance might save him. When the church militant would rise up to aid and guide him. Ah, yes, one little prayer. Little do we know the power of prayer. I'm sure you're making a special effort to pray hard in these days of rest and repose. Yes, I'm sure you are. Have you been to confession yet?"

She closed her eyes. "There's a priest comes to hear confessions here," she said. "Twice a week."

He coughed uncomfortably. "I see. Well, if I were you, I'd make an effort to go as soon as you

**311**

feel up to it. I'd be very glad to hear your confession now, if you like."

She did not answer.

He coughed again. "Sister tells me you're making great progress," he said. "Maybe she'll let you up to go to Mass this Sunday. They have a lovely little chapel here, have you seen it?"

"No, Father."

"O, yes, a lovely little chapel, one of the nicest in the country. Beautiful stained-glass windows, a labour of love it was for the artist who did them. I knew him, De Lancey was his name."

She put a trembling hand on the coverlet. "I'm sorry I fainted in the church," she said.

Fainted! Well, I suppose that's one way of putting it. That Mrs O'Neill said she doesn't remember any of it. Just as well. I suppose she's tired, the poor soul. "O, it happens all the time," he said. "If I had a pound for everyone who fainted in Saint Finbar's, I could put in a new organ."

Her trembling hand retreated from the counterpane, hid itself under the blankets.

"Well, I mustn't tire you now, Miss Hearne. I just wanted to make sure that all those black thoughts have gone. And they have, haven't they, thanks be to God?"

"Yes Father."

"Good. And now you won't forget to pray hard, will you, Miss Hearne? Don't forget now. Well, I must say goodbye, I have to run. I'll try to come back and see you before you leave here."

"Thank you, Father." Warning: he warned. Obey. And I am alone. Like those unbelievers, no friends I would have. No help. O, no, not that, why must I suffer this? Help me, help me pray.

Sister Mary Paul stood up behind her desk, her beads rustling, her starched head-dress slightly awry as she turned her head to greet the doctor. "And how are you today, Dr Bowe?"

"Can't complain. You wanted to see me, Sister?"

"Yes, Doctor. You've been to see Miss Hearne?"

Dr Bowe adjusted his muffler around his neck. "Yes, she's much better than the last time I examined her. Nothing really wrong now, just undernourishment. And she's a bit depressed."

"O, we noticed that. She's on special diet. Do you want that continued?"

Dr Bowe felt his chin. "She needs building up," he said. "Wasn't eating the proper food."

"Well, we'll feed her up, don't you worry. When do you think she'll be ready for discharge? You know, Doctor, I have a feeling she'd be happier in a place of her own. She doesn't take to the life here. She hasn't talked with any of the other patients since she came."

"Friends are paying for the room, is that right?"

"O, yes, Doctor. Professor O'Neill. There's been no financial problem."

Dr Bowe stared absentmindedly at the small hairy mole on Sister Mary Paul's temple. Cancer, that? She should have it looked at. "I was their family doctor years ago," he said. "She's had a very hard life, spent years looking after a bedridden aunt. The aunt was a bit senile, she should have been committed really, but Miss Hearne wouldn't hear of it."

"You don't think there's anything hereditary there?"

No, no, nothing of the sort. Still, in view of the family history, and the fact that she's got no relatives to go to, I'd like to keep her here a while."

"Well, don't worry, Doctor, we'll keep her cheerful. And she'll stay here until I hear from you. Will you tell Professor O'Neill, by the way?"

"I'll give him a ring."

"Much better. But she still needs cheering up."

These words were spoken in a whisper by Sister Mary Annunciata who showed Moira O'Neill into number ten. As soon as she had delivered herself of this opinion, the nun threw the door wide open and sailed in ahead of Mrs O'Neill on a wave of hospital cheeriness.

"Well, now, Miss Hearne, and what do you think I've got for you? A visitor. Mrs O'Neill has come to see you."

She sucked herself backwards then on the same wave and closed the door, all cheeriness and smiles.

Mrs O'Neill wondered whether she should offer a kiss, or not. But the poor thing hardly seemed to see her. She sat down and put a little box of cakes on the bedside table. "I brought you these in case you feel a little peckish around tea-time."

"Thank you, Moira. It's very good of you."

"And how do you feel, Judy? I hear you're doing splendidly."

"O, I'm much better, much better, thanks. Thanks for sending the children up to see me."

"But they *wanted* to come." That was the wrong thing to say, Mrs O'Neill chided herself. "You'll never lack visitors while the O'Neills are around," she amended. "There's so many of us."

The woman in the bed sighed. "Did you have any luck finding a room?" she said

"Not yet, Judy. As a matter of fact, Dr Bowe phoned up Owen last night and said he thought you should stay here for another couple of weeks at least. So that you'd be fit as a fiddle when you came out."

"But I'm all right. There's nothing the matter with me. I've put on an awful lot of weight."

"That's fine, Judy. I hear Father Quigley made a special visit to see you. An awfully nice man, I talked with him when he took you to the hospital that day."

"Yes, he was here."

"Owen's coming to see you on Sunday. He'd have come today, but you know, he's terribly busy with classes and exams just now."

The sick woman nodded. "I'm getting up on Sunday," she said.

"See? You'll be on your feet in no time. O, you'll put all this behind you in a month or two."

"Moira?" the sick woman's hands found the sides of the bed. She levered herself free of the blankets and sat up.

"Yes, Judy. Can I get you anything?"

"No, no, you've been very good. Very kind — Moira — I'm sorry."

"You've said that before, Judy. We've been through all that before. No need to worry about it, it's forgotten. You weren't yourself. You were ill."

The sick woman sighed and leaned back on the pillows.

"Why, I can't wait to have you over again. Sunday doesn't seem the same without you. I can't tell you how much we're all looking forward to seeing you at home again."

The sick woman closed her eyes.

"And not only Sundays," Mrs O'Neill said hurriedly. "Why, any time you feel the need of a little company, you only have to drop in."

"You've been very kind. Very kind. You and Owen. I don't know how to repay you."

"Well, don't try then. You have lots of good friends, Judy. Don't forget that."

Friends. O, how did I deceive myself all these years? A friend is hurt when you are hateful. No one is Christ. Friends are human, they resent. You don't resent, Moira. No, you pity me, you

316

urge me to come again. Come and we will be nice. We will feel sorry for you. No, I have your charity. I lost friendship for it. You are paid. You are rid of me.

"Thank you, Moira," she said.

# CHAPTER
# TWENTY

She sat at the bare white dressing-table and saw her face in the mirror. Old, she thought, if I met myself now, I would say: that is an old woman.

"Good morning, Miss Hearne." Through the mirror-glass Nurse Nora Nelligan advanced, rosy red and starchy white, waving a thermometer like a conductor's baton. "So today's the great day Up and around, eh?"

"Yes."

Nurse Nora Nelligan pointed the thermometer, slipped it in her patient's mouth. "There now." Took hold of a wrist and consulted her wrist-watch. "After this, I'm going to take you down to the chapel. I want you to get a good seat before the crowd gets in. Sister's given you permission to go to Mass, did she tell you?"

With the thermometer in her mouth, she could not reply. She shook her head. Sunday. Of course. But how can I tell her? I don't want to, no, never again to look at that door. How can I say that, how?

Her pulse is up, I suppose it's the excitement, Nurse Nelligan noted. But she said nothing: never tell a patient. She picked the thermometer out of the sick woman's mouth, shook it, and put it in a jar of antiseptic. "Well, are we ready for the big journey?"

"Nurse, maybe — maybe it's too soon. Maybe I shouldn't . . ."

"O, nonsense, you'll be quite all right. We'll take good care of you. Just take my arm now and we'll walk slowly."

Her face if I say I won't. O, why didn't I think of it, why didn't I say I was too sick when they came this morning?

"Here we are," Nurse Nelligan said. "It wasn't such a big trip, now was it?"

The chapel was already half filled with patients. Nurse Nelligan, seeing that she did not make the Sign of the Cross, dabbed her own fingers back into the Holy Water and put some on her patient's brow. "There you are."

Very slowly the sick woman touched forehead, breast, points of shoulders, breast.

"That's it," Nurse Nelligan said. "Now, I'm going to put you here, in this back seat, in case you feel faint. But don't worry. I'll be over there, with the other nurses, and I'll keep an eye on you. If you get up to leave, I'll come out and take you back to your room."

The patients were noisy. Old women and young women, all wearing the same grey dressing-gowns as she herself. Scuffling feet in carpet slippers or incongruous street shoes. Whispering and coughing. She looked along the rows of faces but there was no sign of Edie Marrinan. Too ill to move. I should have asked about her. Or she could be here somewhere. We all look the same.

In their high stalls on either side of the sanctuary, nuns knelt, hands joined in prayer, faces screened by their head-dresses. Prayed.

Believe. They believe. United: there is comfort in being a nun. One of many. They watch the altar. What would they say, holy nuns, if I told them I went up there, I struck at that golden door? In God's house I defied God. And nothing happened. I am here.

The whispering died. A priest, his vestments green for hope, came out of the sacristy, peering cautiously over his veiled chalice. An altar boy followed. The Mass began.

She did not kneel. She saw the priest genuflect, the sole of his shoe showing beneath the white skirt of the alb. Before her, row upon row of bent heads moved at variance, like ears of corn in a cross breeze.

The priest mumbled Latin. Strong and clear came the nuns' response. All rose for the Gospel. She did not rise.

The sacrifice continued. The altar boy picked up the little bell and rang it. All heads bowed. She felt alone and uncomfortable among those bowed heads. The priest elevated the Host for the congregation to adore. Small white circle of bread rising above his head, then sinking down again. The little bell rang. Heads raised. About her, noise and coughing.

The bell rang again. Heads bowed. Silence. The chalice, containing wine, was raised and lowered. The bell.

She was feeling tired. Why, the Mass was very long. If you did not pray, if you did not take part, then it was very, very long. If you did not believe, then how many things would seem different. Everything: lives, hopes, devotions, thoughts. If you do not believe, you are alone. But I was of Ireland, among my people, a member of my faith. Now I have no — and if no faith, then no people. No, no, I have not given up. I cannot. For if I give up this, then I must give up all the rest. There is no right or wrong in this. I do not feel, I do not know. Why should I suffer this?

O, Lord, I do not believe, help my unbelief. O, You — are You — ?

The Mass was over. The priest went to the foot of the alter and knelt.

"*De profundis clamavi ad te, Dominum!*" he cried.

The nuns joined in, reciting the prayer. Other prayers. And I have cried out. I am alone. Without prayer.

". . . thrust into hell, Satan and with him all the

other wicked spirits who wander through the world seeking the ruin of souls. Amen."

The patients began to move out of the pews.

"Are you all right, Miss Hearne?"

"Miss Hearne. Are you feeling ill?"

She shook her head. "No, I'm all right."

"I'll help you back to your room then," said Nurse Nelligan. She dabbed the Holy Water on her patient's brow. The sick woman made the Sign of the Cross.

"That's our chaplain that said Mass," Nurse Nelligan said. "Father Donnelly. He fairly races through it, doesn't he?"

"I thought it long."

"That's because you're tired. Back to bed for you. That's enough for one day."

In bed, in the white stripped room, her mind flickered back, seizing the moments, the faces, the conversations of the weeks that had passed. The priest, when he came and talked: he warned. Sister Mary Annunciata trying to cheer me up, what could I have said? Atheist, she would have cried, and run off to pray for me. No, I am no atheist. I do not believe, O Lord, help my unbelief.

What will become of me?

She lay alone a long time. The Angelus bell tolled. An angel of the Lord declared — pour forth we beseech Thee — Help me, do not leave me!

The Angelus bell was silent. There was no noise

in the room. No noise anywhere. In this place: white, stripped, still.

Trembling, she sat up, found the cord beside her bed and pressed the buzzer. Waited.

Sister Mary Annunciata put her head around the door. "Yes, Miss Hearne?"

"Sister, will I be here much longer? Are they going to discharge me soon?"

"As soon as you're well."

"And when will that be?"

"O, I don't know. Two or three weeks perhaps."

"Sister, I wonder would you do something for me?"

"Yes, Miss Hearne."

"In my trunk over there, there are a couple of pictures. It's very bare in here. If I'm going to stay a while, I'd like to have them up."

Sister came inside and closed the door. She was smiling. "There," she said triumphantly. "You see? Life isn't so bad after all. I knew you'd cheer up, yes, I knew it. Now, where is this trunk?"

"In the closet. The keys are in my bag."

Sister Mary Annunciata wrestled the trunk out of the closet and unlocked it.

"Under the tray, Sister."

Sister Mary Annunciata unwrapped tissue paper. "O, is that your mother?"

"No, my aunt. Could you put her up on the dressing-table where I can see her?"

"There we are. And another picture, you said?"

"Yes. That one."

"O, how nice! The Sacred Heart. Where would you like it?"

"Would it be possible, over the bed?"

"Well, we don't like to mark the walls. But I can put it here, beside your aunt's picture. There. You'll be able to look at it now."

"Thank you."

Sister Mary Annunciata smiled. "Yes, you're heaps better, thanks be to God. And do you know something? There's chicken for lunch. It'll be along in a little while."

Alone again, she looked at the opened closet. Her shoes were there. Long pointed shoes with the little buttons on them, winking up at her. Little shoe-eyes, always there.

She smiled. The familiar things. How often I've thought that.

And on the dressing-table, her aunt in sepia tones. Aunt D'Arcy's picture. More real now than aunt herself. For she is gone. It is here. It is part of me.

And You. Were You ever? Is this picture the only You?

It is here and You are gone. I is You. No matter what You are, it still is part of me.

She closed her eyes. Funny about those two. When they're with me, watching over me, a new place becomes home.

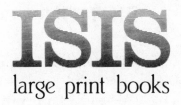

# ISIS

large print books

We hope that you have enjoyed this book and will want to read more.

We list some other titles on the next few pages. All our books may be purchased from ISIS at either of the addresses below.

If you are not already a customer, or on our mailing list, please write and ask to be put on the mailing list for regular information about new ISIS titles.

We would also be pleased to receive your suggestions for titles that you would like us to publish in large print. We will look into any suggestions that you send to us.

Happy reading.

**ISIS, 55 St Thomas' Street, Oxford OX1 1JG, ENGLAND, tel (0865) 250333**

**ISIS, ABC – CLIO, 2040 Alameda Padre Serra, PO Box 4397, Santa Barbara, CA 93140 – 4397, USA**

# FICTION

| | |
|---|---|
| Douglas Adams | **The Hitch Hiker's Guide to the Galaxy** |
| Harold Adams | **When Rich Men Die** |
| Kingsley Amis | **One Fat Englishman** |
| Jack Barnao | **Hammerlocke** |
| Stan Barstow | **Joby** |
| Simon Brett | **A Box of Tricks** |
| Simon Brett | **A Nice Class of Corpse** |
| Vera Brittain | **Account Rendered** |
| Vera Brittain | **Born 1925** |
| John Buchan | **Huntingtower** |
| Anthony Burgess | **The Pianoplayers** |
| J L Carr | **A Month in the Country** |
| Truman Capote | **Breakfast at Tiffany's** |
| Angela Carter | **Fireworks** |
| Susan Cheever | **Doctors and Women** |
| Colette | **Gigi** and **The Cat** |
| Joseph Conrad | **The Secret Agent** |
| Margaret Drabble | **The Waterfall** |
| William Faulkner | **The Sound and the Fury** |
| Timothy Findley | **Famous Last Words** |
| Paul Gallico | **Thomasina** |
| John Gardner | **Icebreaker** |
| John Gardner | **No Deals Mr Bond** |
| Leon Garfield | **Shakespeare Stories** |

# FICTION

| | |
|---|---|
| Stella Gibbons | **Cold Comfort Farm** |
| Nadine Gordimer | **A Sport of Nature** |
| Graham Greene | **The Tenth Man** |
| Doris Grumbach | **The Magician's Girl** |
| Giovanni Guareschi | **Dom Camillo and the Devil** |
| Jeremiah Healy | **The Staked Goat** |
| Patricia Highsmith | **The Talented Mr Ripley** |
| Anthony Hope | **The Prisoner of Zenda** |
| Geoffrey Household | **Watcher in the Shadows** |
| Elspeth Huxley | **The African Poison Murders** |
| Christopher Isherwood | **Goodbye to Berlin** |
| M R James | **A Warning to the Curious** |
| Haynes Johnson & Howard Simons | **The Landing** |
| H R F Keating | **The Body in the Billiard Room** |
| H R F Keating | **Under a Monsoon Cloud** |
| Margaret Kennedy | **The Constant Nymph** |
| Rudyard Kipling | **The Light that Failed** |
| Gaston Leroux | **The Phantom of the Opera** |
| Doris Lessing | **The Grass is Singing** |
| Doris Lessing | **The Fifth Child** |
| Jack London | **The Call of the Wild** |
| Peter Lovesey | **Rough Cider** |
| Peter Lovesey | **Bertie and the Tinman** |
| Bernard Malamud | **The Fixer** |

# FICTION

| | |
|---|---|
| David Malouf | Harland's Half Acre |
| W Somerset Maugham | The Moon and Sixpence |
| A E Maxwell | Gatsby's Vineyard |
| Carson McCullers | The Heart is a Lonely Hunter |
| Ralph McInerny | Cause and Effect |
| Brian Moore | The Colour of Blood |
| Katherine Moore | Moving House |
| Edna O'Brien | Girls in their Married Bliss |
| Edna O'Brien | The Lonely Girl |
| Edna O'Brien | A Pagan Place |
| Jerry Oster | Nowhere Man |
| Alan Paton | Cry, The Beloved Country |
| Anthony Powell | The Fisher King |
| Mary Renault | The King Must Die |
| Mary Renault | The Bull from the Sea |
| Mary Shelley | Frankenstein |
| Alan Sillitoe | Out of the Whirlpool |
| Muriel Spark | The Girls of Slender Means |
| John Steinbeck | Cannery Row |
| Patrick Süskind | Perfume |
| Alice Walker | Meridian |
| Rebecca West | Sunflower |
| Tenessee Williams | The Roman Spring of Mrs Stone |
| Dornford Yates | Blood Royal |
| Dornford Yates | She Fell among Thieves |

# THRILLERS, CRIME AND ADVENTURE

| | |
|---|---|
| Simon Brett | **A Nice Class of Corpse** |
| John Buchan | **Huntingtower** |
| Joseph Conrad | **The Secret Agent** |
| Peter Dickinson | **Perfect Gallows** |
| John Gardner | **Icebreaker** |
| John Gardner | **No Deals Mr Bond** |
| Patricia Highsmith | **The Talented Mr Ripley** |
| Elspeth Huxley | **Murder on Safari** |
| M R James | **A Warning to the Curious** |
| H R F Keating | **The Body in the Billiard Room** |
| H R F Keating | **Under a Monsoon Cloud** |
| Peter Lovesey | **Rough Cider** |
| Peter Lovesey | **Bertie and the Tinman** |
| A E Maxwell | **Gatsby's Vineyard** |
| Ralph McInerny | **Cause and Effect** |
| Brian Moore | **The Colour of Blood** |
| Mary Shelley | **Frankenstein** |
| Patrick Süskind | **Perfume** |
| Dornford Yates | **Blood Royal** |
| Dornford Yates | **She Fell among Thieves** |

# SHORT STORIES

**Echoes of Laughter**

| | |
|---|---|
| Angela Carter | **Fireworks** |
| Roald Dahl | **Roald Dahl's Book of Ghost Stories** |
| Leon Garfield | **Shakespeare Stories** |
| Thomas Hardy | **Wessex Tales** |
| M R James | **A Warning to the Curious** |
| Barry Pain | **The Eliza Stories** |
| Saki | **Beasts and Superbeasts** |
| E OE Somerville & Martin Ross | **Further Experiences of an Irish RM, Volume 2** |
| E OE Somerville & Martin Ross | **In Mr Knox's Country: An Irish RM, Volume 3** |

# POETRY AND DRAMA

| | |
|---|---|
| Lord Birkenhead (Editor) | **John Betjeman's Early Poems** |
| Joan Duce | **I Remember, I Remember...** |
| Joan Duce | **Remember, If you will...** |
| Robert Louis Stevenson | **A Child's Garden of Verses** |
| Leon Garfield | **Shakespeare Stories** |
| Dan Sutherland | **Six Miniatures** |